PRAISE FOR *THE CREST*

The Crest is a well-researched page-turner set in Prussia, Germany in 1917. It follows the career of an idealistic, patriotic young man, Gerhard, as he leaves home to fight for Kaiser Wilhelm and the Fatherland. The story that unfolds is rich in historical detail and suspense. It was a pleasure to read Jerena Tobiasen's novel both for its vivid imagery, vibrant prose and well developed characters.

~ **Roberta Rich,**
author of *The Midwife of Venice*, *The Harem Midwife*, and *A Trial in Venice*

We find in *The Crest* by Jerena Tobiasen a well written novel spanning the many years of that troubled era that included the 20th century's two great world wars. It touches you deeply in its illustrations of the hardships soldiers endured in their innocent belief that they were serving their countries and the families who were waiting for their return.

In communities away from the killing fields, life moves on and people work together: celebrating different occasions, getting married, having children. Yet at the same time they anxiously fear for their future as warmongering leaders fight among themselves over territory and resources, sacrificing misled civilians caught in the middle.

Jerena skillfully crafts representations of two such different settings to perfection: the painful and visceral realities of war, and beautiful portrayals of love, life and nurturing. Let's all encourage the latter for all of Earth.

Well done and worth the read.

~ **Nasreen Pejvack,**
author of *Amity, Paradise of the Downcasts*
and *Waiting.*

The Crest is an exceptionally well-written and detailed book. It follows the life of a German family through World War I and World War II-- not something you read every day. The details are exquisite. I imagine that the author did a fair amount of research to get them right. If you like war stories with a human angle or sprawling family sagas, you will love this first book in the Lange family story.

~ **Malcolm van Delst,**
author of *Do the Wrong Thing*

ALSO BY JERENA TOBIASEN

THE PROPHECY SAGA
The Crest
The Destiny

❖

THE
EMERALD
THE PROPHECY BOOK II

JERENA TOBIASEN

The Emerald
Copyright © 2019 by Jerena Tobiasen

This is a work of fiction. The plot and the
characters are a product of the author's
imagination, and any similarity in names
is a coincidence only. While real places and
establishments have been used to create an illusion
of authenticity, they are used fictitiously. Facts have
been altered for the purpose of the story.

Cover Design: Ana Chabrand,
Chabrand Design House
www.anachabrand.com

Author Photo: Robert M. Douglas,
Copyright © 2018

Interior Formatting: Iryna Spica, Spica Book Design
www.spicabookdesign.com

ISBNs:
978-1-77374-035-5 (Print)
978-1-77374-036-2 (E-book)

This book is
for
Robert McKellar Douglas

ACKNOWLEDGEMENTS

While the seed of my saga began with the kidnapping of a friend's son some thirty years ago, this story is my own. Along the way, I have been inspired by others and wish to acknowledge their contributions, including:

- My parents, from whom I learned the art of storytelling.
- Henry Fast, who edited my use of the German language.
- Captain Alex Smith, who read my sea story and provided recommendations to enhance it.
- Brie Wells, Gaelle Planchenault and Julie Griffiths, who read the rough work and helped me keep the faith.
- Ben Coles of Cascadia Author Services, who read my manuscripts and gave me hope, and his gang of talent,

who helped turn my manuscripts into novels.

- And last, but certainly not least, my wonderful husband, Robert McKellar Douglas, an artist with vision. He not only encouraged me while I wrote, but helped me with research, travelled with me, listened as I bounced ideas around, read my scenes when requested, and provided feedback when I needed it; he is the one who inspired me to keep writing better. "Good photographs are images of the exceptional," he says. "A great painting highlights the universal." I sincerely hope that my readers feel *The Prophecy* delivers an exceptional image that highlights the universal.

CHAPTER ONE

Nicolai Kota led the caravan along the outskirts of Liegnitz toward a small lake where the city hosted its annual fall festival. Sycamore leaves were fading from summer greens to the yellow and orange of early death. He reined in the horse to halt his *vardo* and raised his arm to stop the other wagons trailed behind.

"I'll head into Liegnitz from here," he said. He kissed his wife's creamy cheek, noting how the sun glinted off the emerald dangling above her breast, suspended on a heavy gold chain. He handed the reins to her and hopped down. "Lead the caravan into the grove. Assume that we'll be assigned the same location as other years."

"All right," Rosalee said, tucking an errant curl of dark hair under her kerchief. "We should be circled by the time you catch up."

"Give me a few minutes to saddle Bang," Nicolai said, walking to the rear of the vardo. Rosalee set the brake, prepared to wait.

Nicolai beckoned the driver of the next wagon to join him. Hanzi, the band's *kris*, set the brake of his vardo and dismounted gingerly. He limped along the side of his horse toward Nicolai, obviously aching from the hours of inactivity.

As kris, Hanzi was responsible for overseeing the laws and values of justice for the *vista*, the name given to a community of nomads. He had become kris the same year that Nicolai's father was elected *voivode*, more than twenty years ago. Hanzi leaned on his walking stick, his gait encumbered with arthritis. He stopped and stretched, running his gnarled hand along Bang's flank, straightening the saddle blanket as he did so.

"Rosalee will lead the vista into the old grove," Nicolai said. "I'd appreciate it if you could keep an eye on everyone. Some of the young fellows have been a bit rambunctious lately."

"I will, Chief," Hanzi said. "Do you want anyone to accompany you?"

"No need," Nicolai answered.

Hanzi tipped his hat and returned to his own vardo.

"Papa, can I go with you?" Punita asked.

Startled out of his thoughts, but not surprised to hear the question, Nicolai turned from Hanzi's departure to see his nine-year old daughter nuzzling the horse's muzzle.

"I can't imagine you'd allow otherwise," he said, grunting as he hefted the saddle in place. "Make yourself useful, my love. Get the bridle. Watch your fingers with the bit. You know he likes to nip."

"Yes, Papa," Punita said, skipping to the back of the wagon where the bridle was stored.

A moment later, Rosalee appeared at his side. "You're taking the imp, I hear."

"Yes. Can you manage alone until we get back?" he asked, tightening the cinch.

3

"I'm sure some of the other girls will help," Rosalee said, watching her daughter coerce the bit into a resisting mouth.

Nicolai walked around his prize racehorse checking the tack before mounting. When he was seated, Punita passed the reins up to him and waited for his hand. He reached down, and she clasped both hands around his wrist. As he lifted, Punita used her legs to scramble behind him, onto the horse's rump.

"Hold tight to the saddle, Punita. He's going to prance."

"I'm ready, Papa."

Nicolai settled in the saddle and touched his heels to the barrel of the horse. As predicted, Bang began dancing sideways before lunging forward.

"We'll be along in a while," Nicolai said to Rosalee, reining Bang in a circle. "I plan to visit with Alexi Puchinski once I have our business licence and confirmation that the usual grove is appropriate."

Nicholai gave Bang a nudge with his heels, and the horse leapt forward eagerly.

✤

Rosalee watched the horse canter toward town, raising her hand in farewell. When the horse and riders disappeared into the small forest ahead, she returned to the front of the vardo. Perched on the bench, she released the brake and snapped the reins. The horse leaned into its task, and the other wagons rolled in line behind hers. When she was certain all of them were in motion, she clicked to her horse and its pace quickened. As one, the caravan snaked toward the grove.

She led the caravan to a grove situated on the edge of the lake near the fair grounds. As she entered the grove, she guided the horse to the right of the clearing. The others followed. She continued until her horse closed in on the last wagon, completing a circle of privacy and protection.

Those who were driving wagons that would be used during the fair formed a semi-circle outside the grove along the side that edged the fair grounds. Some wagons carried goods that would be emptied, so they could be set up to create a stage. Ornate wagons would be used for telling fortunes, reading futures, and selling potions.

The Kota family had two vardos: the twelve-foot high *ledge*, which was used for day-to-day living, and the *kite*, a modified Reading wagon that Nicolai had had built for Rosalee soon after they married, from which Rosalee conducted her business. Built in the town of Reading, the kite was ornate on the outside, but simple on the inside. The berths and cooking facilities had been replaced with a table and chairs for guests who came to have their fortunes told.

Rosalee set the brake, climbed down from the bench and began unhitching the horse. Before long, one of the men arrived to lead the animal to a holding pen for grooming and grazing. Thanking him, she set about organizing the space around her ledge for family use during the time of the fair.

Three young girls—friends of Punita— ran up, offering to help collect wood and build a fire. Accepting their help, she left them and walked through the camp to ensure that everyone was satisfied with the locations of their respective vardos.

Soon the smell of campfire smoke wafted through the enclosure. A current of voices rose as folks bustled to and fro, organizing the glade that they would call home for the next few days.

Rosalee paused as she approached the fifth wagon. A group of boys—not yet men—had gathered away from the vardos. They lounged against trees and teased one another.

"Excuse me, gentlemen," she said, looking at them sternly, "When you have finished your break, would you mind filling the water barrels? I think you'll find that most of them are empty, and we'll need fresh water to prepare the meals."

As she spoke, they straightened themselves and walked toward her.

"We'll start on that straight away," the oldest, a boy of seventeen, acknowledged.

"Thank you, Helwig," she said, continuing on her tour. Approaching the next vardo, she noticed three other boys lingering behind it. They moved into the vardo's shadow when they saw her. *These are the boys who concern my husband. I'll ask Hanzi to keep an eye on them until Nicolai returns.*

"Samson! Where are you?" a woman's voice bellowed from within the wheeled home.

"Your father will be back soon," she warned them. "You and your brothers best get busy."

CHAPTER TWO

The ride into Liegnitz was as uneventful as any ride on the back of Bang could be. Many of the vista folk thought he was possessed by the devil himself and suited his name, but Punita knew that her father preferred to say that the creature was simply high-spirited.

The horse pranced and tossed his head while the vardos were still in sight, but once the coolness of the forest surrounded them, Bang settled and walked quietly along the worn animal path. The path was too narrow for his dancing, and the trees and shrubs restricted any attempt to defy saddle and riders.

Small birds twittered, filling the forest silence. Unseen creatures scurried along the forest floor, causing vaporous rustling sounds as they disturbed the decaying carpet of twigs and leaves.

Punita knew better than to chatter while riding Bang. She had experienced his nasty temperament on more than one occasion and understood very well why her father used the Roma word for devil to name him. Instead, she closed her eyes and let the forest sink into her soul, inhaling the forest fragrances of green life and rotting death.

"Papa, how long is the ride into Liegnitz?" she asked, keeping her voice low and speaking directly to her father's ear.

"Not long," he whispered in Punita's direction.

"Have I been to Liegnitz before?"

"Once. When you were but three years old."

"Is it a big city?"

"No. But it is not a village. It has several churches, some with twin spires. A train station. Hotels. Even some fine restaurants."

"Do the people like us?"

"No more and no less than other towns. But, we have friends here."

Bang stepped lively from the trees into the mid-day sunlight. It was unusually warm and bright for autumn. Punita, who had been leaning against her father's back, sat straighter. She drew her worn straw hat onto her head as Nicolai reflexively tipped the brim of his fedora lower.

They rode the remaining distance in silence as they moved away from the forest and closer to the roadway. Bang's ears pricked forward in anticipation. The twin spires of the town churches appeared ahead of them. Nicolai eased his hold on the reins, and Bang broke into a canter.

"Not far to go now," Nicolai said, updating his daughter. "Hang on to the saddle. You don't want to land in the road."

While her father worked to hold Bang's enthusiasm in check, Punita tightened her hold on the leather saddle and gripped Bang's hind quarters with her heels.

The forest scents dissipated as they neared the town. Punita's nose twitched at the aroma of frying onions and roasting meats.

Her stomach growled, and she smacked the flat of her hand against her belly, hoping that Bang would not react to the sudden gurgling. She need not have fussed. Back-firing automobiles, passing horse-drawn wagons, and bellowing beasts drowned out the sounds of her belly.

Most town folk carried on with their business, ignoring the chestnut horse and its two riders. Occasionally, however, Nicolai heard comments directed to him about the quality of the stallion, or words exchanged between equestrian admirers. He thanked those who spoke to him directly with a tip of his hat and abstained from any private exchanges.

Nicolai enjoyed the rhythmic placement of Bang's hooves, rocking the riders from side to side, leather creaking with the weight shift. He also enjoyed time alone with his daughter. The horse pranced on, snorting and tossing his head.

"Bang is so clever," Punita whispered. "He knows when he's the centre of attention."

12

When they arrived at the sandstone building called the New Town Hall, Nicolai held out his left arm to his daughter. She grasped his wrist with both hands and he lowered her until her unshod feet caused a plume in the dry dust of the roadway.

"Watch your toes," he warned when Bang shied sideways.

Punita jumped to grab the halter and held it fast. Bang started to jerk his head in opposition to her weight, but Nicolai's flat hand on his neck and crooning words stilled him. Nicolai dismounted and passed the reins to Punita.

"Lead him out of the sun and see if you can find him some water in that direction—I think there's a small pond, if I remember correctly," he pointed the way. "I may be a bit of time, so pay attention to your safety."

As she walked away, Nicolai added, "If you find water, clean yourself up too."

"Yes, Papa," Punita answered, leading the horse toward the pond.

Nicolai walked smartly toward the

13

arched entrance of the New Town Hall, anxious to get his business out of the way. He placed his hand on the heavy oak door, admiring the ornate carvings of hunters and stags with the twin spires of the churches in the background, and pushed it open.

Entering the cool corridor, he removed his fedora and bashed it against his jacket and trousers, trying to shake off some of the road dust. He rubbed the toe of each boot behind the alternate leg in an attempt to polish them and waited while his eyes adjusted to the darkness.

When he could see clearly again, he proceeded along to the licence office, passing several doors—some open, some not. In one office, he heard a quiet exchange between a man and a woman. His own footsteps echoed along the corridor, a clomp-clomp of leather meeting tile, punctuating the constant tap-tap of someone using a typewriter. He followed that sound to the end of the corridor where a door gaped, then passed through the opening.

"Hello. Excuse me," he said, addressing a buxom blonde in a tweed business suit sitting at a desk overloaded with papers and cards. A tall counter separated pedestrians from office workers. The woman raised her eyes from her work and squinted at him.

"What is it?" she asked appraising him.

"I've come to acquire a licence for the 1928 Fall Fair. My group will provide entertainment."

"Yes, of course. I thought I recognized you," she responded, rising from behind the desk and taking a form from the top of a filing cabinet. "You were here several years ago. Yes?"

"We were," he confirmed, bobbing his head. "We have travelled far and wide since then. And now we are here again."

"Shall I help you fill in the form, or can you read?" the clerk asked in a matter-of-fact way.

"Thank you for your offer. I can do it." He took the form and she handed him a pen, pushing the bottle of murky ink toward him.

✦

Form completed, and money paid, the clerk handed him the licence.

"Thank you," he said. "I hope to see you at the fair. Perhaps you'll enjoy the entertainment, or have your fortune told?"

"Oh, yes! My family is quite looking forward to it," she said. "I've been thinking about having a reading of the tarot cards."

"Very good!" he encouraged. Then, taking the licence she offered, he bid her good day, gave her a charming smile, and sauntered back along the corridor toward the carved oak doors.

CHAPTER THREE

Outside once again, Nicolai tucked the licence into the inner pocket of his jacket and strolled in the direction of the park, looking for Punita and his temperamental horse.

He found Punita sitting on a gnarly root under an aged sycamore tree. She jumped to her feet when she saw him approach. Bang, grazing a few feet away, raised his head and nickered his own greeting.

"Did you find water?"

"Yes Papa." She pointed to her right. "The water in this pond is fresh. I asked a man who said he's the gardener here."

The pond was large, with a small island in the middle and a water fountain placed for accent that ensured the water circulated on a regular basis. Pink and white cabbage flowers edged the pond. Lily pads and water grasses vied for places along the water edges.

"Bang thought the flowers would be a nice treat, so I had to bring him away before he ate them all."

"I see he's been grazing here as well," Nicolai nodded toward a patch of shortened grass. "That should keep him happy for a while. But let's get him away, shall we? You're sitting under a sycamore tree and these are its seeds."

He bent to retrieve a dried seedpod. Punita leaned in with curiosity.

"In the spring," he said, "these seeds can make a horse very sick. At this time of year, even though they're old and dried, there's still a risk. We don't want to take any risks with Bang. Do we, fella?"

He scrubbed Bang's neck with his knuckle, and Bang snorted in response.

"No Papa." Punita appeared concerned, but Nicolai's spontaneous sideways hug reassured her, and she brightened.

Taking the reins in one hand and his daughter's hand in the other, he led them along the side of the street, away from the park and the New Town Hall.

18

"Where are we going now?" Punita asked, skipping beside him.

"You've heard me talk of Alexi Puchinski." Punita nodded. "He lives here in Liegnitz and I thought we might visit him. I'm glad to see you washed yourself."

He stopped and used his hat again to brush the dust from the rags she called clothes.

"We should have allowed time for you to put on a better dress," he said. "You look like a beggar. Oh! And you actually have feet under all that dirt. I thought you were wearing shoes!"

"Papa! You know I hate wearing shoes."

She wiggled her toes, then skipped along beside him again, causing more dust plumes. Small clouds swirled about her feet, coating her freshly washed feet and calves with a new coat of powdered dust. Nicolai rolled his eyes.

"Keeping you clean and tidy is an impossible feat," he admonished. "One day, Punita, you will take pride in your appearance."

19

"If you say so, Papa," she responded, dismissing his concern.

Their destination was only a few blocks from the park and their conversation filled the distance.

"Ah! Here we are." Nicolai said, stopping mid-block to assess the five-storey hotel at the end of the street.

"Where are we, Papa?"

"See that magnificent building at the end of the road, just opposite the train station? The pale-coloured one with all of the windows?" Punita followed his pointing finger and nodded. "Can you read the words across the top?"

"Yes. It says *das Grand Hotel etabliert 1850*," Punita recited.

"Which means ...?"

"It means that the Grand Hotel was established in 1850." Punita said, inflating her chest with pride in her observation.

"So," she puzzled, "... the name of the hotel is Grand Hotel. The Hotel is grand to look at and it also has that name!"

20

"Well done, daughter," Nicolai praised her. "And that hotel is owned by *Herr* Puchinski."

"Oh," she said contemplating her father's words. "But, didn't you say Herr Puchinski is one of our people?"

"He is, in a fashion." Nicolai took her hand as they approached the imposing structure.

"His mother was born into our vista, but she married a man whose family built the hotel and has operated it for a very long time."

"Is he our cousin, Papa?"

"Yes, he is. A distant cousin, but we're of an age, he and I. Herr Puchinski is a very trustworthy and respectable man."

"Look, Papa," Punita's neck bent as she gazed upward, pointing. "Look at that round window ... way at the top! What's that for? Do you think the room is round too?"

"I have no idea," Nicolai responded. "You'll have to ask Herr Puchinski."

He led Punita along the side of the hotel, into a work yard behind it.

"What are these buildings?" she asked.

As Nicolai pointed to each building, he told her.

"That one is for laundry. That is a bake house. That is the gardener's shed, and that … is a barn. We will leave Bang in the barn, out of the sun and harm's way."

At that moment, a young groomsman exited the barn and Nicolai summoned him. Following a brief introduction and explanation, the groomsman took Bang's halter to lead him to the stable. Nicolai flipped a coin to the boy, thanking him and warning him to be wary of the devious creature.

Father and daughter stopped at the rear entrance of the hotel, which was less imposing than the front, and once more Nicolai removed his hat and used it to beat off some of the dust that had accumulated during their walk. He re-pleated the peak of his fedora and ran his fingers through his hair to tame it. Then he looked at his daughter to ensure that she had followed suit. She had not. He shook his head in hopelessness.

Punita stood, mouth agape, in the middle of the entrance staring down a long, dimly lit and carpeted corridor.

"Papa, look at these walls!" she whispered, running her hand along the dark carved wood and tracing her finger over the textured pattern in the wallpaper. "They're beau-ti-ful!"

"Come along," he said, snatching her wayward hand and tugging her into the cool hallway.

"Why so many doors?" Punita whispered again. "There're four doors, Papa!"

Nicolai did not respond. He was listening.

The first three doors, two on the left just inside the entrance and a third further along, were closed. The fourth door, which was opposite the third, was slightly ajar. A wedge of light cast from the room illuminated the brilliant jewel colours of the carpet and reflected the warmth of the polished wood.

23

Voices filtered through the crack in the fourth door. Nicolai, with an ear cocked, walked toward the sound, the fall of their footsteps muted by the carpet. The volume of the voices grew until he and Punita stood outside the open door. Punita reached past her father and gently pushed the door open to see inside. The creak of a door hinge announced their arrival.

"Is that Herr Puchinski?" Punita asked in a clear voice. "He looks like you, Papa. Sort of."

Inside, a young woman had been talking with an older gentleman in a fitted grey suit. They turned abruptly toward the creaking door.

"Nicolai!" Herr Puchinski rushed toward Nicolai, extending a hand of welcome. "What a pleasure to see you, cousin."

The young woman returned to her desk and rolled a clean sheet of paper into her typewriter. The sound of tapping keys filled the room. Punita stared in amazement.

24

"And this small thing?" Alexi Puchinski asked with affection. "Can this be Punita? The little imp who loves horses?"

Punita's head snapped toward the neatly dressed man, her eyes large and mouth glued shut.

Alexi invited them into his office and asked the young woman to arrange for refreshments. She left the office, closing the door behind her.

⚜

As the men sat and spoke of wind and weather, Punita wandered about their cousin's office, admiring the blood red of the leather chairs, the backs of which were pinned with buttons covered in the same leather, making cross-marks at the indentations. The chairs were trimmed with a shiny black wood.

The floor was made from planks of deep red wood streaked with black veins. Under Herr Puchinski's desk and the armchairs stretched a woven blue rug patterned with reds and greens and purples. It was almost as festive as some of her dance costumes and was the only thing in the room that spoke of her cousin's heritage.

Most of the walls were covered in shelves, each filled with books and ledgers, except for one alcove. Punita ran her fingers lightly over a shelf of books, feeling the ridges of the leather bindings and golden words embossed on the spines. The room had a unique smell all of its own, a blend of leather, wood, wool, and aromas from the nearby kitchen.

A soft rap sounded from the hall-side of the door. Herr Puchinski stood from behind his desk as if to respond, but it opened seemingly of its own accord.

"Pardon, sir," another young woman said, pressing the door ajar and wheeling in a cart laden with an array of food and drink.

"From the kitchen, sir," she said. She poured tea with milk and sugar for the men, and handed a frosted glass filled with something thick and frothy to Punita.

Punita's belly gurgled at the sight of it.

"Thank you," she said, remembering her manners. She took the cold glass and sniffed. She did not recognize the smell, but it looked similar to a drink her mother made with yogurt. She took a tiny sip that left a white bubbly moustache over her upper lip. She licked it away, her eyes wide with pleasure and slurped a little more. Her hand snapped to her belly with embarrassment when another growl followed. The men, who had been watching her reaction to the beverage, chuckled and resumed their conversation.

"Is the drink tasty, miss?" the server asked.

Punita nodded.

"Yes, my mama makes something like this. But this is ... sweeter ... and cold!"

"That will do, Inge, thank you," Herr Puchinski said dismissing the server.

Inge left the room, and their host invited Nicolai and Punita to help themselves to the slices of bread, cheese, meats, and assorted squares of cake. Punita had never tasted such wonderful delights and sampled everything. The adults waited, appearing amused that she enjoyed the food, then picked at the remainder.

"Herr Puchinski," Punita said suddenly, pointing toward the alcove that she had noticed earlier. "Who's that?"

The men stopped talking and turned to Punita.

"Do you mean the man in the painting," her cousin asked, "or the horse?"

The space within the alcove was filled with a painting of a stately gentleman in an unfitted black suit and a high white collar. He had a long grey-streaked beard that reached to his belt. With pride, he stood next to an unsaddled chestnut stallion.

"The horse looks like Bang, but this is very old, isn't it?"

"For someone so young, your German is very clear," he said, turning to Nicolai. "Is she fluent?"

"Yes, the entire vista has made an effort to learn German," Nicolai answered. "Some

28

speak better than others. Some speak Polish or Russian better than others. Some speak all languages, or bits of them.

"We speak the language of our people when we are travelling. It's easier and keeps our business private. But when we stop to participate in fairs, we find it more prudent if we're able to speak the host language with some degree of intelligence. More respect, you understand."

"Very clever," Herr Puchinski acknowledged. "But Punita is so young."

"And I can speak the other languages too. Papa taught me," Punita added, inflating her chest with pride. "I can even read and write in German. Not so much the other languages."

"Indeed!" Herr Puchinski said, seemingly impressed.

"Yes, and you should hear Papa when he talks," she laughed. "He sounds just like the people he's talking with. He imitates them, but not in a mean way. It seems as though he's lived in the place his whole life." She shrugged. "He just sounds like them."

"Ah, I see," Herr Puchinski said. "I think you're suggesting that your papa has a talent for grasping accents and dialects."

"Yes!" she agreed. The room filled with silence, Herr Puchinski appearing to contemplate his guests' language skills.

"Who's that?" Punita asked again, returning their attention to the alcove.

"That," Herr Puchinski answered, "is a painting of my great-grandfather and his prize race horse."

He put his hand on Punita's shoulder and guided her to another spot.

"Stand here and you can admire it better."

He stood behind her and gazed upon the old painting.

"My family has bred many generations of race horses, but that is the horse that made my family wealthy. In 1868, at the fall fair, my great-grandfather offered to purchase a horse that had won every race that year. It didn't matter that the race was short, or long. It didn't matter that he ran every race with little rest in between. My great-grand-father knew a magnificent horse when he saw one and was prepared to pay well for it. Alas, the owner wouldn't sell."

"The owner was my great-grandfather," Nicolai added, joining them at their view-ing point. "He did, however, offer to sell a two-year-old that he had been training."

"My great-grandfather finally accepted the offer," Herr Puchinski said, "when he realized he could not convince your great-grandfather to part with his winning stallion. In the end, he paid a dear price for the two-year-old. And he was proud to say he never regretted it."

"That young horse was already well-trained, I can tell you," he continued, his eyes drifting back to the painting. "My great-grandfather was more than pleased. He continued the training, and that horse went on to win many races and some very large purses."

Punita stepped forward, gazing at the painting with new admiration.

"In fact," he chuckled, "great-grandfather won such a vast amount of money, that he decided to invest it in two things."

Punita turned to peer over her shoulder. "What two things?"

"First, he built this hotel when there was no other hotel in Liegnitz, and he made it the very best. He wanted its patrons not only to come to enjoy all it had to offer, but also to have them return again. And they did. And they continue to do so," he said proudly.

"Second, he put that stallion out to stud when he was too old to run. We've enjoyed generations of winners from that fellow." He nodded toward the horse in the painting.

"Is he related to Bang, Papa?"

"He is indeed. As our cousin has enjoyed many generations of the offspring of the great King Rom, so have our people. Bang is one of his descendants too."

"How wonderful!" Punita said, clapping her hands together.

At that moment, another knock on the door announced the return of the young server to remove the dishes. Herr Puchinski bent his knees, bringing his face to Punita's eye level. Punita took a step backward, mindful of her soiled skirt and her cousin's fine suit.

"Would you like a tour of the hotel, while your father and I discuss a little business?" he asked.

"Oh, yes!" she answered with joy. "Will someone come with me? I'm not afraid to go by myself. I just wouldn't want to miss anything."

"I have just the guide for you," Alexi replied.

As Inge wheeled the trolley out the door, Herr Puchinski asked her to escort Punita to the kitchen, giving her instructions to locate his son Stefan. Stefan was to take Punita on a tour of the hotel. Punita looked at her father, who nodded agreement even as his eyes warned her to behave.

Inge pushed the trolley of soiled dishes and Punita followed, down the hallway and into the kitchen.

CHAPTER FOUR

Punita was instructed to sit on a tall stool in the corner of the kitchen while Inge went in search of Stefan.

"Now, don't touch anything," Inge said, eyeing Punita's dirty clothes. "You don't want to get dirt on anything, especially the food."

Punita sat on the stool, enthralled with the activities in the kitchen. Chef, under-cooks, pot scrubbers, and dishwashers, everyone dressed in white, and constantly moving and chatting. Shiny copper pots and utensils hung on hooks dangling from the ceiling. Bundles of drying herbs, onions, and garlic hung from another series of hooks. Baskets of fresh vegetables and fruit sat ready for preparation. One man disappeared into a cold room and reappeared with slabs of meat and several chicken carcasses. They were all quick and efficient, focussed on the business at hand. She closed her eyes and tried to distinguish the variety of aromas. *Lamb stew, roasted chicken, shredded carrots...*

"Hello."

Punita's eyes popped open, startled to see a young boy standing in front of her, his height obstructing her view of the kitchen.

"Hello," she replied shyly.

"I'm Stefan," he added.

Contrary to her natural disposition, Punita did not move. She openly stared at the boy standing before her. He was handsome, about twelve years old, with black hair that curled around his ears and collar. She wanted to reach out and move the mop that threatened to cover his dark eyes.

"Stefan Puchinski," he stated, smiling at her, "Your tour guide."

He held out his hand and she finally moved, placing her hand in his for support as she hopped off the stool.

"Let's go this way," he said, still holding her hand. "I know my way around every corner of the hotel."

35

He snatched two sugared cookies off a trolley that had been rolled in from the bake house and smiled sweetly in response to the baker's stern glower. Ushering Punita out of the kitchen, he led her back along the corridor to the first door at the rear entrance of the hotel. Opening the door, he started up a flight of stairs and invited her to follow, handing her one of the pilfered cookies.

They hiked up four flights of stairs, where Stefan ushered Punita into the private suite that he and his father called home. From there, he led her through the remainder of the hotel, showing her all of its nooks and hidey-holes. Afterward, they wandered through the gardens and the outbuildings, and she introduced him to Bang.

When they returned to the back entrance of the hotel, Stefan paused near the kitchen. He waved at the pastry chef, a broad smile consuming his face from lips to eyes.

"May we snitch a piece of cake, please?"

"Of course, Master Stefan. Would you like plates?"

36

"No, thanks," Stefan said, "We can wrap them in napkins."

The chef handed them white linen napkins and settled a piece of iced chocolate cake onto each one.

"Mind you return the napkins," he said.

"We will," Stefan assured him. With a sparkle in his eye he turned to Punita. "Come on. This way!"

He led her back toward the first door at the rear entrance of the hotel, and up the flight of stairs. This time, they continued to climb until the stairs ended on the last of the landings.

The door leading off the landing was small, almost half of what a normal door might be. With his free hand, Stefan turned the knob and ducked into a musty-smelling attic stuffed with old furniture and fixtures, some draped in large cloths for protection against dust and damage.

"This is the top of the hotel," he coughed.

Swirls of dust motes billowed around them, dancing in the rays of light pushing through dirty windows. Stefan waved his free arm trying to clear the motes from his face and sneezed.

"Believe it or not," Stefan said, rubbing his eyes, "this is my favourite place in the entire hotel. Follow me, but mind where you step."

Punita followed, gingerly stepping in Stefan's foot prints, waving floating motes and spider webs from her pathway. She felt her body shudder but was too slow to contain the explosive sneeze that followed.

"Sorry about the mess," Stefan said, wiping his nose on the hem of his sleeve.

"Are you afraid?"

"No. What's so special about this place?" she asked, bending forward to use the hem of her skirt to wipe her face.

"Here. Hold my cake for a minute and I'll show you," he said. "I need two hands for the next bit."

Punita took his cake and he turned toward a circular window built into the centre of the outside wall.

"The one I saw from the street," she muttered, "and the room isn't round after all!"

"Pardon?" Stefan asked, distracted from his task.

"Nothing," she replied.

The window was at least as high as Bang's ear tips and veined to hold the glass in small pieces. Stefan lifted a stool that stood in shadow at the side of the window, set it near the window's centre, and climbed onto it.

"Stefan. Be careful," she hissed.

"No need to whisper," he said. "No one can hear us up here."

She watched him reach high to the top of the window and heard a grating sound. He was a black shadow in the brightness of the window. She watched his silhouette step carefully off the stool and replace it. Returning to the centre of the window, he leaned down and she heard the grating sound again.

"What are you doing?"

"Releasing the latches that hold the window in place." The silhouette traced his finger from one side of the window to the other.

"See this black band?"

"Uh-huh."

"Watch!"

Stefan stepped to the left of the window, raised his right hand and gently applied a steady pressure to a window pane above the centre black band. Slowly, the top of the window leaned forward, out of its casing and over the roof, while the bottom half leaned into the attic.

When he could grasp the lower part of the window, he coaxed it until more of the lower half rose inside the attic, creating an opening wide enough for them to pass through.

"Come on," he said again, lowering himself to slide through the opening at the bottom of the window. When his second foot disappeared, she stepped forward.

"Hurry up!" he said, sticking his head back into the room, startling her.

He extended his hand to help her. Mistaking his intention, she plopped his cake into his open hand. He chuckled at her response.

"You'll want to step carefully out here," he said. "The sudden bright light can put you off balance."

He transferred the cake to his free hand and reached in again.

"Take my hand," he urged.

Punita put her hand in Stefan's, noting how soft and warm it was. His fingers closed firmly around hers and tugged her through the gaping window, out into dazzling sunlight.

From the street, the peak of the roof had looked pointed. From the top of the hotel, Punita realized that only the facade was peaked. Her feet were on a flat platform that was as wide as a man's foot is long. Stefan continued to hold her hand, guiding her slowly forward along the platform.

"We can sit here," he said, lowering himself to the platform, his legs dangling down one side of the roof.

The sun was warm on their backs as they nibbled at the cake. Punita was mesmerized by the view.

"Now I know how a bird must feel!"

"I'm glad you like it," Stefan said. "I thought you might."

"Do you come up here often?" she asked.

"When I first found it, I did, but in the past few years I've only had time to come once or twice a year. Between school studies and helping around the hotel, I have little time to spare."

They sat quietly for a few minutes, enjoying the view and each other's company.

"Punita," he asked, almost formal. "Will you tell me about our people?"

"Don't you know?" she asked.

"Not really," he said. "Papa grew up here in the town, and so have I. We go to the fairs, but I only know what I see. I want to know what it's like to live in a caravan."

"Oh. Well ..." She wondered where to begin, then started with an explanation of who they were and the structure of the camp.

"We live simply and have few possessions. Everything we own must be easily packed up and moved. Family is the most

42

important thing, then the horses, then our wagons. We live together in a vista."

"A vista?"

"Yes, that's what we call our caravan. Our group of families. In some way, we are all related. If the vista gets too large, some folks might leave to form a new vista, or they might join a different or smaller vista. Usually, when a woman marries, she moves to her husband's vista." She paused, letting Stefan absorb her words.

"I'm never getting married!" she declared as an aside, then continued.

"Papa is the voivode—the chief—of the vista. And Mama is the *phuri dai*. She is the senior woman and looks after the welfare of the other women and children. She also looks after ways to earn money and organizes the women when work needs to be done."

"Voivode and phuri dai," Stefan repeated trying to pronounce the words as easily as Punita had.

"Uh-huh." She giggled at the words tripped awkwardly over his lips and

43

continued. "Among all of the vistas, our vista is one of the biggest and most important. Mama is from a very important vista too. People thought it was a very good arrangement when mama and papa decided to marry. My parents are very smart—even if I'm the one to say so—and when my grandfather died, the vista thought it was best that Papa be elected as voivode to take his place. So, we have two generations of men as voivode. When the last phuri dai died, Mama was elected to replace her."

Punita clapped her hands with anticipation.

"One day, I hope to be phuri dai of the vista too," she mused, then sadness overtook her countenance. "But that would mean that Mama would have to die. Perhaps I don't need to be phuri dai."

She sighed deeply before continuing.

"It is very lucky indeed when a vista has a clever voivode and a clever phuri dai, and they are married to one another." She swung her legs below her, watching people scurry in the street.

"Impressive," Stefan said, nodding his head.

"Papa is very good with numbers and manages the vista's money. He taught me how to do numbers too. He also plans the route we take each year. And remembers the vista's history."

"You should do well in school then, if you've inherited their talents," Stefan said, encouraging her to continue.

She blushed at his compliment.

Honking in the square below distracted them and they watched as a truck and a horse-drawn cart negotiated their way around pedestrian traffic that had gathered in the square five stories beneath them.

"How does the vista earn money?" Stefan asked.

"We usually earn good money at fairs, Papa says. People pay for our entertainment, of course," she said.

"The men trade some of the livestock they've bred and trained. Papa says there's always money to be made racing and selling

45

horses too." She hesitated, searching for the right words. "You know, it's curious. If people see us in the street, they will cross to walk on the other side. They think we're dirty, or not equal. Yet, outside of the town, those same people will come to us. Asking for information about the animals. What to feed them. How to breed them. What to do when an animal is sick."

She stopped and looked at Stefan.

"They wait for our smithies to shoe their horses. Or ask what wares we have to sell or trade. Sometimes I just don't understand people," she said, huffing.

"Your father is asking after you, Master Stefan." The sound of an adult voice startled Punita and she looked around to see Inge peering through the opening in the bottom of the window. "You'd better come in. You're scaring the people on the street."

The children looked down in the street, realizing only then that the folks gathered in the square below were looking up at them.

"How did you find us?" Stefan asked.

"The baker told me that he saw you disappear up the back stairs. And some of the folks in the square came in to the registration desk expressing concern that the two children on the roof might fall."

Giggling, the children cheekily waved to the folks in the square and clambered in through the window.

"Here. Let me help you lock this window," Inge said, reaching up to fasten the top latch while Stefan locked the lower one.

Window locked, they followed Inge out of the attic and down the back stairs to Herr Puchinski's office.

"And give me those napkins. I'll return them to the kitchen before someone misses them."

⚜

"Did you enjoy the tour?" Alexi asked Punita when the children entered his office.

"It was wonderful, Herr Puchinski," Punita answered. "I never could have imagined so many secret spots in a building like this."

47

Bashful, she looked through lowered lashes to see Stefan standing by his father.

"Can we not think of another way for you to address me? Herr Puchinski is so formal, and, after all, we are family."

"What about Cousin Alexi, or simply Cousin?" Nicolai suggested.

Punita blushed and agreed.

"Perhaps you'll show Stefan around the fair tomorrow," Cousin Alexi said. "Introduce him to the vista."

"I would like that very much," she blurted in response, "that is, if he wants too."

"That would be great fun," Stefan agreed.

The men shook hands and Nicolai and Punita took their leave. Stefan accompanied them to the barn and admired Bang, agreeing that he too bore a strong likeness to King Rom.

Nicolai thanked the groomsman for his good care of Bang, reseated the saddle and mounted.

Punita grabbed her father's wrist and jumped. He swung her behind him and cautioned her to hold on tight, then he gave the horse a nudge and they set off. Bobbing up and down on the rump of the horse, Punita turned around and waved her straw hat in farewell. Stefan stood next to the barn door, waving back.

As soon as they were clear of the town, Nicolai gave Bang his head and he trotted toward the forest.

"Clever fella," Nicolai said, giving the horse a firm pat on his withers, "you always remember your path. Hang on to your hat, Punita. He's going to run!"

CHAPTER FIVE

Bang had slowed to a ginger walk by the time they entered the grove where the vardos were circled. Nicolai spied Rosalee talking to folks nearby. He swung his leg over the stallion's withers and slid to the ground. Reaching for Punita, he noticed Samson loitering behind his family's wagon.

"You there! Samson!" Nicolai hailed. "If you're not otherwise occupied, will you take Bang to the horse paddock?"

Samson, a tall, gangly boy of fifteen with a freckled complexion and light brown hair that hung straight to his collar, approached with reluctance. Bang shied sideways and started prancing, his ears pressed close to the crown of his head. Samson jumped back.

"Are you afraid of the horse, boy?" Nicolai asked.

"No. No, sir." Samson hesitated, slipping his hat from his head in deference.

Nicolai held out the reins to him, but he did not readily reach for them.

"He doesn't like me though," Samson said just as Bang lowered his head, teeth bared. "He always tries to nip me."

"Here now. We'll have none of that!" Nicolai jerked the halter, so the bit turned Bang's head. "No biting!"

Bang bobbed his head and flicked his ears, growling in response. Nicolai held the reins out for Samson once again. The boy hesitated at first, then took them.

"Brush him down and see that he gets food and water."

Samson acknowledged the instructions and led the horse away to the paddock, holding the halter firm and at arm's length to ensure a safe distance from gnashing teeth. Bang followed with a menacing prance, sidling when space permitted.

"Don't you think that's a bit risky?" Rosalee asked, walking up behind Nicolai.

Together, they watched Samson lead the spirited horse toward the temporary coral.

51

"I do. At the same time, though, the boy needs to understand discipline. He's old enough to know how to handle the horses, but he bullies the others into doing his work. Then, he laughs at them when the horses are unruly."

"Punita, dear, did you enjoy the ride?" Rosalee changed the subject, seeing Punita approach.

"Yes, Mama. I had a wonderful time. It was all so magical."

"Well. I'd like to hear about this magic. But first, I think you need to clean yourself up and prepare for dinner. You can tell me everything while we eat."

Punita skipped off toward their ledge, and Rosalee linked her arm in her husband's leading him out of the wagon ring.

"I'm concerned, husband, about Samson and his siblings. If something isn't done to change their attitude, they will be standing before the kris."

"I know. That's why I sent him off with Bang. I would rather one of the other boys groomed him, but I want a word with Samson. I'm going to follow him now and will see you at dinner."

Nicolai watched his wife depart in search of their daughter, her skirt swishing in time with her gait. Then, he headed toward the horse paddock.

Samson led Bang to the make-shift paddock, tied the reins to the fence, and went off in search of another boy to groom him. When Nicolai reached the paddock, the fifteen-year-old was standing with his arms folded across his chest, delivering instructions to Helwig. Nicolai paused behind a sycamore tree and watched.

"The voivode sent you to tell me to groom Bang?" Helwig asked Samson in disbelief.

Two years older than Samson and a full hand taller, Helwig peered down at Samson. Helwig's tanned biceps bulged as he held the horse steady and ran his hand first along Bang's neck and then his legs. Helwig kept his hair tied at his nape when he worked with the horses, but wisps of golden brown strands had escaped their binding and lifted with the breeze.

Although Helwig appeared twice the size of Samson, Samson did not hesitate to bully him into the work.

"Yes, of course he did. Why do you ask?"

"The voivode is very particular about who handles Bang."

Helwig removed the saddle, setting it on a bale of hay. Before he could take further action, Nicolai stepped from behind the tree.

"What's this, Samson?" he barked. "Helwig, what are you doing?"

Helwig shuffled a safe distance from Bang and responded.

"Grooming the horse, Chief, as you've asked."

Nicolai's arm shot out, clamping on the collar of Samson's shirt before the young man could escape.

"Not so fast, boy," he said, glaring at Samson. "I gave you very specific

54

instructions for grooming this animal, none of which involved Helwig."

"You may go," he said to Helwig.

Helwig acknowledged his chief's instructions and disappeared into the trees. When he was out of sight, Nicolai released Samson's collar, jerking the boy to stand between him and Bang. The air around them crackled with tension.

"When I give you instructions," Nicolai growled, "I expect them to be obeyed."

Bang lowered his head and lunged toward Samson, but the tethered reins held firm, and his gnashing teeth failed to connect. Samson jumped clear, screeching.

"Groom the horse," Nicolai commanded, taking a seat on the bale of hay. "I'll supervise."

"Yes, sir." Samson hung his head and set about his task.

Nicolai watched the boy groom, feed, and water the horse. A few times, he corrected Samson's technique, but overall he was impressed with Samson's skill.

Samson released Bang into the paddock and locked the gate. Bang appeared to revel in the release by kicking up his hooves and jumping stilt-legged into the air.

"Bring the saddle," Nicolai instructed.

Samson hefted the saddle and other gear into his arms and followed. Nicolai slowed his gait to allow Samson to walk abreast of him.

"You did a fine job."

Samson's head snapped up. His face indicated surprise at the compliment.

"Thank you, Chief," he answered, his voice sounding full of shame and uncertainty.

"Samson, I don't understand why you avoid the work, when you do it so well. Are you just lazy?"

"No, Chief," was all the boy said, although Nicolai gave him ample time to say more.

When they reached the voivode's ledge, Nicolai directed him in the deposit of the saddle and gear.

"I don't want to see or hear of you bullying others again to do the work that is

56

assigned to you." Nicolai placed a firm hand on Samson's shoulder, forcing the boy to look up at him. "If I do, there will be consequences. Do you understand?"

Samson nodded and ducked his chin, as if trying to hide his shame.

"Off with you then and pull your weight."

Samson departed, heading in the general direction of his mother's home.

The following day, the vista worked together to set up the area of the fair that had been assigned as their entertainment alley. They assembled tents for displays and games, a stage for theatrical performances, and strategically placed the kites for readings.

When all was organized, the players set up the props and practised their parts. The musicians found the locations that would complement their performances and practised as well.

The fortune tellers rolled their kites into the designated spaces and staged them for private entrance. Many fairgoers enjoyed the readings as a form of additional entertainment. Others heard their predictions as solemn truth and preferred not to be seen coming and going.

The Reading kites were typically the most decorated of the wagons, often painted red and trimmed with gold and white and green. The rails were intricately carved to reflect the life of the nomad, nature scenes, and other events that were important to the particular reader.

In the camp, those whose work was done in the entertainment alley shook out their costumes and made them ready for opening day.

A racetrack had been constructed years before at the far end of the fairgrounds, opposite the entry gate. Throughout the day, riders and grooms took racehorses to the track for exercise, warming them up and readying them for races the next day.

The nomads were not the only ones exercising their horses. Other competitors had arrived during the days leading up to the fair. They too were training their horses and taking the opportunity to assess the racing competition.

Near the racetrack, some of the men set up a lean-to with a paddock and smithy gear. While the vista camped, those who supervised the care of the horses inspected each one for health and soundness. They also welcomed local farmers and other fairgoers who had questions about animal husbandry, needed smithy work, or had an interest in trading livestock.

At the end of the day, the travellers found their way back to the camp for their evening meals and final rehearsals.

Nicolai sauntered past the ledge, waving to Rosalee. "I'm going to check on Bang and wash up."

"Fine, dinner will be ready when you are," Rosalee responded.

Nicolai followed the path to the paddock, lost in his thoughts of the races to be held tomorrow. He paused, hearing rapid footsteps on the path ahead of him.

Something's amiss. As he stood listening, Punita flew into his arms, startling him.

"Whoa! What's the hurry?" He caught her arms to steady her.

Breathing heavily from her run, Punita gasped for air.

"Papa, you must come quick. It's Bang!"

She turned and ran back along the path, leading the way. Nicolai jogged to keep pace with the small shadow guiding him.

As they neared the paddock, Nicolai could hear Bang screaming and the other horses protesting.

"What the—!"

In the twilight, it was difficult to see through the chaos of milling horses, but they parted as he approached, settling with his presence. It was then that Nicolai heard the whoosh of air prior to each of Bang's screams. Bang seemed to writhe in fear, his bulging eyes glistening in the fading light, drawing Nicolai's focus.

"Punita, run and find Hanzi and the kris council," Nicolai whispered, hunching down to Punita's level. "Tell them to come immediately, and quietly."

Punita ran.

Within minutes, members of the kris council arrived, the first in time to witness the torture being inflicted by Samson. He had Bang tethered tightly to a post in the centre of the paddock. The stallion's movement was restricted to stamping his hooves and stepping sideways.

Using long branches of a thorn bush, Samson continuously raised his arms and beat the animal from withers to hindquarters, not caring where the blows landed. Nicolai could no longer wait for the remainder of the council or the kris to arrive.

"Stop! Immediately!" he bellowed.

Startled, Samson dropped the branches and turned to run in the opposite direction. He ran directly into the arms of one of the first council members to arrive at the scene.

While council members secured Samson, Nicolai wrapped his arms around Bang's neck whispering to calm the agitated creature. Bang ceased dancing, relaxing to Nicolai's comforting words.

Council members arriving later shone their torches into the paddock, providing light for Nicolai's inspection. He ran his hands along the horse's body, examining the damage. Blood streaked his coat and covered Nicolai's hands.

"What is going on?" Hanzi demanded in a loud whisper, trying not to disturb the anxious herd further.

The kris hobbled into the centre of the paddock with the aid of one of the council members. Nicolai was too distressed to answer and left it to one of the first witnesses to state the details.

Samson stood off to the side, each of his arms securely pinned by his captors. He struggled to free himself, but the men held him firm. Samson hung his head.

"Where is his father?" Hanzi asked, turning toward the gathering of men.

Punita had perched on a paddock rail, and watched the chaos transform into order.

"Here, Kris Hanzi," Samson's father answered from the shadows.

"Your son has done evil work here this evening. Take him away. We will hold council and decide his punishment."

The man seized his son from the two men who had held him and dragged him from the paddock. Samson writhed, trying to break free of his father's grip.

A council member stooped to retrieve the bloodied thorn branches.

"Hold on to those," Hanzi instructed. "Nicolai, will the horse heal?"

"Yes, Hanzi. What I won't know until daylight is whether he will race tomorrow."

Nicolai's arm snaked around the horse's neck again and he stroked the shoulder.

"I'll do what I can to mend him tonight and see the results in the morning."

"I hope he can run," blurted the council member holding the bloody branches. "He always wins a sizable purse."

"We're done here for now." Hanzi announced.

"We'll hold a council fire after the evening meal. Someone make sure that Samson and his father are present."

⚜

The kris council meeting did not last long. Sufficient of the council members had witnessed the beating, or at least the consequences. They all agreed that final judgment would be withheld until the extent of the damage inflicted on the horse could be determined. In the meantime, Samson was restricted to his family's vardo. He was banned from the horse paddock, the horses, and the fair.

Samson started to protest when he heard that he had been banished from the fair, but his father's swift hand slapped Samson's face and silenced the protest before he could form his words.

"Shut up!" his father bellowed. "You've done enough damage for one day. And now others must do your work as well as their own."

Samson struggled to break his father's grip, but his father's fingers dug deep into the flesh of his upper arm and held him fast. When he resisted, his father yanked on Samson's arm and dragged him away forcefully. The council had ordered Samson's father to supervise the boy until further instructions were provided. Samson's parents were prohibited from attending the fair in order to ensure he obeyed the council edict.

With Samson and his father removed, Hanzi called the meeting to an end and invited the evening rehearsals to begin.

The following morning, people rose early, fuelled by excitement of the fair. Nicolai arrived at the horse paddock as daylight broke to the chirping of small birds that lived in the trees enclosing the grove. He braced his tongue on the roof of his mouth and released a shrill whistle. Bang's whinny answered, and the horse trotted to the fence, looking for his master.

In the early light, streaks of dried blood stood out against his chestnut coat. Bang stilled as Nicolai slid his hand over the lash marks, taking care not to aggravate the horse's injuries. Bang's flank shuddered, and he nickered when Nicolai's hand touched a large welt.

"How is he this morning, Papa?" Punita asked, appearing at her father's side.

Nicolai jumped. He had been so absorbed in the inspection that he had not heard his daughter approach.

"He's well enough, considering the damage that Samson might have done had you not alerted us." Nicolai gave his daughter a reassuring smile to hide his own concern. "But he'll not run today. The cinch would have to sit on this welt, and the pain would be too much."

Nicolai led Bang to the edge of the lake and Punita helped him clean the wounds more thoroughly. They applied a pungent herbal ointment to facilitate the healing and left him in the paddock with those horses that would not be needed for the day. The men assigned to handle livestock would take turns guarding the paddock to ensure no further harm was done.

Together, father and daughter walked back to the ledge where they joined Rosalee for their morning meal and prepared for their day in entertainment alley.

CHAPTER SIX

The alley thrummed with activity and entertainment: musicians, singers, actors, and readers. Aromas of all sorts filled the air: roasting meats—rabbit, chicken, sausage—as well as quick breads and warm apples.

Farm wagons pulled up to the gate to deposit excited children and adults who would wander the length of the alley, hopefully leaving their coins behind.

Rosalee stood at the foot of her kite. She had washed the dust off it earlier in the day. The red and gold paint was shiny and inviting. Hers sat further along the alley, resulting in less business, and for her, less business was better. Her responsibilities as phuri dai often called her away from the kite, resulting in smaller earnings. At the end of the day, it mattered not. Money collected by the vista during the fair would be deposited into one moneybox and shared among all.

Rosalee watched the fairgoers wander along the alley, stopping to inspect the goods for sale, listening to the entertainers, or buying food or drink. A young woman with chestnut-coloured hair caught her eye. She held the hand of a little girl whose hair was straw blonde.

Trailing behind, her two young boys pointed out spectacles that provoked their curiosity. Contrary to the little girl, the boys had hair of blue black. Rosalee would not have thought the children natural to the woman with the chestnut hair, until they approached her. It was only then that she saw the family likeness.

"Here we are," the woman announced to the children, bringing them to a stop at Rosalee's kite.

"Hello," she said, greeting Rosalee with a broad smile and bright eyes. "We're the Lange family and some of us have come for a reading."

"And who will have a reading?" Rosalee asked, returning the smile.

"My son Paul and I will, please," Paul's mother answered. "I'm Emma, by the way. Paul, you go first. When it's my turn, you can watch your sister and brother."

"Yes, *Mutti*," the older boy answered, the pink of his cheeks deepening.

"I am Rosalee, Master Paul," she said, beckoning the strapping boy to follow her up the stairs.

"Mutti, see how pretty the lady's dress is!" exclaimed Gerda. "So many colours. And listen, to the tinkle of the shiny circles. They sound like little bells when she walks."

Emma bent low to hug her daughter.

"Why, yes, you're correct! They make a lovely sound, don't they?"

Gerda nodded her head and hid behind her mother's legs, peering at the woman in the bright costume.

Still pink-faced, Paul followed Rosalee up the steps and into the Reading wagon. As Rosalee closed the door, she directed Paul to a chair in front of which stood a table. She walked around the table and sat opposite him.

"Is that incense I smell?" Paul asked.

"It is," Rosalee confirmed. "Do you like it?"

"Yes," Paul answered. "It makes everything in here feel mystical."

Another pink blush appeared above his collar.

Darkness had closed in around them when Rosalee had closed the door. She was quick with matches, and soon candlelight filled the cabin.

The table was covered with a red and white checked cloth. In the centre sat a crystal ball mounted on a golden base carved with two-headed snakes and crows, their eyes gleaming with semi-precious stones. To Rosalee's right at the corner of the table sat a bulging square of black cloth. She lifted the crystal ball and its base and placed them on the table to her left, covering it with the black fabric. Retrieving the stack of tarot cards that now lay exposed to her right,

Rosalee shuffled them and, as she shuffled, she regarded Paul. He visibly relaxed his hands and rested them on his knees.

His eyes were clearly drawn to the large emerald resting above her breast. It hung from a heavy gold chain that dangled from her neck. She knew how it reflected the candle light, and that her slow movements made it appear as if a fire burnt within. The boy appeared to realize how low his gaze had dropped. He coughed, and promptly returned his focus to Rosalee's face. She smiled warmly.

"Have you any concerns today, young sir? Any questions for the cards?"

When Paul failed to answer, Rosalee placed some of the tarot cards on the table and began the reading. Sometimes she exposed a card, sometimes she dealt a few, carefully placing them with the others she had spread between them on the checked cloth. She invited him to ask questions and, when he did, she asked him to choose more cards. She then arranged his choices on the table and revealed the answers.

"I see you come from a powerful lineage," Rosalee remarked at one point. "You will be an inspiring leader and a hero to your people one day, but before you are called a hero, you will see much danger, much death and horror. You must take great care, or you yourself will die."

He sat unmoving, eyes fixed on the cards.

"Shall we ask the crystal ball if there is more in store for you?" she said cheerily, trying to pull his attention back.

Rosalee swiftly folded the cards and returned them to the corner of her table, covering them again with the black cloth. She grasped the crystal ball and its pedestal and moved them to their original position.

She caressed the globe before her, peering at images that danced through wisps of time. Shadows took on momentary shapes, then evaporated on fleeting tendrils of foggy thoughts.

"If you survive," she continued, "you will marry your one true love."

She looked at Paul, peering into his charcoal eyes.

"Marrying one's true love is something rare. You must treasure the privilege," she told him.

She sat quietly for several moments, focussing on the crystal ball. Paul's eyes wandered over the interior of the kite, apparently contemplating Rosalee's predictions.

Rosalee leaned toward the globe and brushed her fingers over the familiar eyes staring back at her. She reached for the deck of tarot cards, gave them a quick shuffle, and placed three on the table.

"Curious," she mused aloud, "eyes like melted dark chocolate."

"Pardon me?" Paul asked, leaning toward her. "I don't understand."

"Do you know anyone with eyes the colour of melted dark chocolate?" Rosalee asked sharply, suddenly reluctant to say more.

"Aside from you, no," he answered. "Will I?"

"That is not for me to say," she said abruptly.

She returned her gaze to the crystal ball, placing her palm over it, and sighed deeply.

"The reading is over for today, young master. The crystal has gone silent."

"But, what about those brown eyes?" he insisted.

"I can only say that they will play a significant role in the future of your family. What that role might be, I cannot say. But you must take care!"

Rosalee rose from her chair and indicated Paul's way to the door. As he rose, he set his payment on the table. She opened the door for him, allowing bright daylight to fill the doorway. He descended the stairs, hailing his mother as he did so. Rosalee watched him go, disturbed by the visions revealed to her. Deep in her soul, she felt an ominous pull. *If the orb is correct, that boy's future and mine are already somehow connected. I must investigate further when I have time.*

⚜

Punita loved dancing most of all, and she was excited to perform later in the morning wearing a new blouse and skirt that her mother had sewn for her. As she wandered through the stalls of goods, she noticed a petite woman leave her mother's kite and shepherd her children deeper into the fair. Her mother descended the stairs and stood next to a large wheel, frowning.

"Mama, why are you frowning?" Punita asked, sidling up to her mother.

"It's nothing, my love," Rosalee replied, caressing her daughter's cheek.

Punita felt her mother's eyes lingering on her face for a long moment, those brown eyes that were dark and depthless. People often remarked that Punita had her mother's eyes, the same colour of melted dark chocolate.

"You perform soon," her mother said. "You should get back to the ledge and change into your costume."

Before Punita could skip out of sight, Rosalee welcomed her next guest.

CHAPTER SEVEN

Nicolai sauntered through entertainment alley, speaking to his folks operating the stalls and collecting any excess amounts of cash to reduce the risk of theft. At the gate to the fair he turned and regarded the length of their entertainment alley. The colours, sounds, and aromas of a fall fair always exhilarated him. *Fall fairs are special*, he thought, *and given the throng of people and the bustle of business here today, the vista's income from the fair will be more than satisfactory. It will see us easily through the winter.*

The voivode made his way to the caravan, where he planned to deposit the cash in the safe that he kept in his ledge, then check on Bang. Rosalee had asked him to check on Punita too, expressing concern that their daughter was slow to return, and she would have to perform soon.

The clearing was quiet. Only a few of the elders remained in the camp. They were either smoking and chatting near a fire or napping. Three guards had been stationed around the ring to ensure that fairgoers did not enter the private section inadvertently.

"What, the—" Nicolai muttered as he approached his own ledge.

Rosalee and Punita kept a tidy camp. Although the discrepancies were small, Nicolai saw that some things were out of order. A barrel laid on its side. A stool with a broken leg leaned against it. The door was ajar.

"Punita?" he called. "Are you in the wagon?"

As he reached his hand toward the door's handle, it flew open, banging his hand aside. Samson and Punita filled the doorway. Samson's left arm wrapped around Punita's neck. He had stuffed a rag in her mouth and his hand held it fast. Punita clawed at his arm, trying to make him release his hold. Samson jerked his knee upward, catching her in the small of her back, knocking them off balance.

Punita's wide eyes conveyed her fear. Tears trickled from the corners of her eyes. She panted heavily through the rag and Samson's fingers.

"Aw-aw!" she cried out. Nicolai heard her plea clearly. "Papa!"

Then he saw the knife, its sharp blade reflecting the light that filtered through the doorway. Samson pressed the point into the tender flesh just behind the right of Punita's jaw. A bead of crimson blood glistened. Bruising was beginning to show high on her cheekbone and around her right eye.

"Samson, what is the meaning of this?" Nicolai demanded in a booming voice, hoping that others would hear him and take action.

He set the cash box on the ground at his feet, freeing his hands.

"Stop! I'll hurt her," Samson warned, looking nervous as he swayed from foot to foot.

Nicolai hesitated, contemplating his next move.

"What is it you want, Samson?"

Nicolai slowly placed his foot on the bottom step.

"Stop!" Samson cast his eyes to the cash box. "I want the money."

"Why?" Nicolai asked to buy time while he calculated his next move.

"I need to get away from here."

"Why?" Nicolai asked again. He watched Punita collect herself and focus on him.

"No one likes me," Samson blurted. "My father beats me, and my mother does nothing to stop him."

"I'm disturbed to hear that, Samson." Nicolai said, lowering his voice, sensing others nearby. He switched to the calming voice he usually applied to the horses. "Why did you never report the beatings to council? We could have intervened."

"He told me," Samson seemed to choke on his words. "He told me that he would kill my mother if I said a word to anyone."

80

Nicolai saw Samson's elbow drop, easing the pressure he kept on the knife. He looked to Punita, held her eyes for a moment, then lunged forward grabbing Samson by his ankles and yanking him out of the doorway and down the stairs. Off balance, Samson's arms shot in the air, releasing Punita. The young girl scrambled deeper into her wheeled home, sobbing.

As he fell, the back of Samson's head struck the top step before he slid on his back to land at Nicolai's feet. Nicolai watched the boy struggle to clear his head and stooped to snatch the moneybox out of his reach.

"Punita!" he yelled. "Punita, are you safe?"

Punita stepped into the doorway, shaking. Hiccupping between sobs. The rag that had gagged her was clasped in her left hand.

"I'm all right, Papa."

"Put this inside," he handed the moneybox to her.

"Voivode," a voice came from behind

him, "We'll take it from here. You look
after your daughter."

Nicolai stepped away from Samson, still
crumpled at his feet, and let others take him
away. As they did so, Hanzi approached.

"I've been watching that boy," Hanzi
said. "Trouble he is."

At that moment, Punita returned to the
doorway, Nicolai reached up and she fell
into his arms, wrapping her legs around
his waist and her arms around his neck. He
hugged her to him and let her sob.

"Lately, I've suspected that something
was amiss in that vardo," Hanzi said,
pointing toward the wagon where Samson
lived. "When I saw Samson loitering near
your ledge earlier—where he had no business being—I went to get help. I wasn't
fast enough, and I'm sorry for that, Punita,
dear." Hanzi ran his gnarled hand gently
over Punita's hair.

"His parents will have some explaining
to do," the old man continued. "They're
supposed to be monitoring him. Such a

shame that a family should come to this."
Worry wrinkled the brow of Hanzi's weathered face as he turned to walk away.

"Kris," Nicolai stopped him. "He said
his father beats him. We need to investigate
before we hold a council meeting."

"As you say." Hanzi nodded and hobbled off.

"Punita, come inside. I'll look at your
wounds. Then you can rest."

"But Papa! I need to change for the per-
formance," she protested.

"Not today," he said in his horse-calm-
ing voice.

Nicolai set his foot on the bottom stair
for a second time, bracing the door open
with his back. From the corner of his eye,
he saw Rosalee flying through the camp,
her colourful scarf of blues and greens and
shining disks billowing behind.

"Nicolai! Punita! What's happened?"
she panted, leaning against the vardo.
"Hanzi sent one of the guards to tell me to
come home quickly."

As her heavy breathing subsided, she looked up at Punita and saw the welts forming around her daughter's right eye and along the jaw bone. Her breath caught in her throat.

"Punita! What's happened to you?"

She reached her hand toward her daughter's face and gently traced her finger over the darkening skin.

"Come inside, Rosalee." Nicolai carried Punita up the stairs. "We have some injuries that need tending."

✤

In the wagon, Punita sat on her father's lap trying to stifle her sobs while her mother cleaned her face and applied herbed ointment around her eye and over the knife prick. When Rosalee concluded her ministrations, Nicolai asked Punita to stand and raise her blouse, so they could inspect her back where Samson had kneed her.

"It's not so bad," Rosalee observed. "It looks like Samson missed the spine and caught the muscle. Hold your blouse out of

84

the way, dear. I'll rub some ointment into the bruising, so it heals quickly."

"Punita was squirming at that point," Nicolai recalled. "It's a good thing. The consequences could have been a lot worse."

"I'll just make a calming tea," Rosalee said, taking the kettle from the table and descending the stairs.

"It will take a few minutes to cook the water over the fire, but I think we could all use a cup."

While Rosalee made the tea, Nicolai continued to hold Punita on his lap and rocked her until she relaxed into light slumber. A short time later, Rosalee returned with the tea and poured out three cups.

"I have something for the two of you to consider," Nicolai began, his voice waking Punita. "We've talked about it before. About sending Punita off to school. It is with a heavy heart that I suggest ... it's time."

"No, Papa!" Punita sat rigid in her father's arms.

"I agree," Rosalee said, interrupting Punita's protest. "Punita, you are almost ten. It's time. And we are in a perfect place to arrange it."

"We are, indeed," Nicolai brightened, guiding Punita to sit on her own.

Rosalee handed her a steamy cup of tea, while Nicolai stored the moneybox in the vista safe.

"Punita, one of our options was to have you attend school in Liegnitz. You would live with Cousin Alexi and his son."

Nicolai let Punita absorb the offer and watched her brighten.

"Liegnitz is a very pretty town," she said, "and I like Stefan. He's a nice boy."

"You'd have to wear shoes, Punita," Rosalee said, and the three laughed knowingly.

Punita looked at each of her parents and nodded. "I will do it. I will wear the shoes!"

⁂

Hanzi sent two men to retrieve Samson's father, who was eventually located at the racetrack. Members of the kris council interviewed first Samson, then his father. They also sought out folks from neighbouring wagons and Samson's mother.

Samson's mother was discovered in her vardo with a black eye, a swollen nose, and injuries to her ribs. Her younger children were huddled together in fear. After some insistence from Hanzi, Samson raised his shirt to reveal fresh welts and bruising on his back, around his ribs and kidneys. The other boys had similar bruising, but the injuries were older and partially healed. Pressed further, Samson's mother assured the council that her husband had yet to harm their three small girls.

A council meeting was held early the following morning before the second day of the fair began. Once the kris council had considered all of the evidence, a decision was made to evict Samson's father from the vista, with an order that he never contact any member of the vista again. He was given half an hour to collect his personal items and leave the camp.

"I protest! You can't order me to leave!" he bellowed.

"The kris council has spoken," Hanzi said, glaring at him. "You will carry out the order, or you will be assisted. Make your choice ..."

Samson's father stomped off in the direction of his vardo, his fisted hands pumping with anger.

"I hope you all burn in hell!" he yelled.

Two members of the council followed him to ensure that the order was carried out.

Samson's mother was invited to remain with the vista where the members would help her with the raising of her seven children, including her eldest child, Samson. She accepted the offer.

Samson was also given a choice—remain with his mother or leave the vista. If he chose to stay with his mother, he was to assume responsibility for his family. He would be banned from any contact with the racehorses until he could prove that he was capable of handling the responsibilities related to their care, and for the following year he would only participate in fairs if his involvement was necessary; not for amusement.

Samson decided to stay. He accepted the council's edict.

At the same time, a petition was put before the council to reconsider a marriage that had been arranged for the following month. The girl's father questioned whether the match with Samson was still suitable.

After some discussion, the council agreed that the marriage would be delayed one year to allow the girl's family an opportunity to witness a change of character, with the girl's family given the option to break the marriage contract any time within that year. Since the incident was Samson's first offence and the girl's family understood the root of his behaviour, the arrangement was acceptable to her family.

CHAPTER EIGHT

The day after the fair ended, the vista rested for the morning. By midday, some had begun packing their vardos in preparation for travel, while others dismantled entertainment alley.

Nicolai and Punita left Rosalee to organize their home and the kite, while they headed to the paddock to check on Bang. They bathed his wounds and applied the fresh herbed ointment that Rosalee had concocted. Their eyes watered, and their tongues tingled in response to the tangy mixture of cayenne and mint.

"He won't be ready for a saddle for several weeks yet," Nicolai said with disappointment.

"At least the flies won't bother him in the meantime," Punita said, giggling.

"You're right about that, girl." He wiped the ointment from his hand with a rag.

"Let's go wash this stuff off our hands or none of the other horses will come near us."

He gathered up the medical aids and set them outside the paddock, then led her to the lake.

"We'll need two horses this morning. One will have to carry your things."

"Yes, Papa."

"You can ride alone, or with me. As you wish," Nicolai said, baiting his daughter.

He knew that Punita loved riding the spirited horses he selected for himself, and that she also loved to ride alone. Her response was quicker than he expected.

"I'll ride with you, Papa. If I'm to be away from you for a long time, I'll be close to you today."

They selected two bay horses for their ride into town and returned to the vardo to organize the things that Punita would take with her. While Punita considered what possessions would be needed, Nicolai told her of his discussion with Cousin Alexi. He spoke of the arrangements to be made for her schooling, and of her board with their cousins at the hotel.

As Rosalee contemplated her daughter's requirements for the next several years, she realized that Punita had no clothes that would be appropriate for life in a town and attending school and said as much to Nicolai. Nicolai agreed and obtained an allotment from the vista's coffers.

"I'll give this to Alexi," he said. "He will see to it that Punita has everything needed."

Rosalee helped Punita bathe, then she brushed her daughter's hair and braided it, threading a fern green ribbon throughout the twists. Punita wore a new white blouse and full green skirt, sewn by her mother and embroidered with brightly coloured threads stitched into flowers and butterflies. Nicolai polished her brown leather sandals.

"What will you take with you?" Nicolai asked.

"Nothing," Punita said, "except the gold bracelet that you made for me, Papa. I think I will leave the rest here."

Her eyes wandered about the wagon before resting on her father.

"Until I come home again."

"Including the new costume that I made for you?" Rosalee asked.

"Uh-huh. I don't think there will be a time to wear it in the city," Punita said, clearly already missing her mother.

"Then you must take this," Rosalee said, lifting her own hair and reaching behind to release the clasp of the golden necklace that always hung from her neck. The weight of the large emerald dangling from the chain dropped away from her.

"My mother gave me this the day she died. As every mother before her has done. It is yours now," she said, fastening it below Punita's braid.

"No Mama!" Punita shrieked. "You're not dying! You mustn't remove it!"

"Punita, it is the *chakra* of my heart. Never remove this and you will know that you are always with me."

Punita searched her mother's face, her eyes filling with tears. She threw her arms around Rosalee's neck and sobbed.

"I will always cherish it, Mama. And all of our wonderful memories. I will miss you and Papa so much."

She reached for Nicolai and hugged him fiercely.

Nicolai placed a hand on either side of Punita's face as if to memorize the beautiful features of his only child.

"It will be six years before we see you again," he said. Tears filled his eyes. He kissed her forehead and turned her away.

"Say good-bye to your mother," he said a little too briskly.

"Let's see how you look," Rosalee said, turning Punita in a circle at the foot of the stairs.

Appearing satisfied, Rosalee pulled her into a tight embrace. As her husband had done, she embraced Punita's face.

"A thousand kisses, until we see you again," she said and kissed every inch of her daughter's face, causing giggles from both. Rosalee removed a finely stitched shawl from her shoulders and wrapped it around Punita.

"You'll need this too. It'll be chilly in the forest."

"But Mama, this is your best," Punita protested.

"It's yours now," Rosalee said fastening it in place before hugging Punita tightly. "The green matches your skirt."

"I will cherish it too, Mama!"

"Punita, you are taking so little with you. We don't need the second horse," Nicolai said, spying Helwig across the camp and beckoning to him.

Helwig jogged toward them.

"Helwig, be a good fellow, and return this horse to the paddock, will you?"

"Yes, sir." Helwig reached for the reins, then glanced at Punita. "We'll miss you, Punita. I suppose you'll be a woman the next time I see you."

Punita straightened.

"Yes, and you'll be married and a papa no doubt!" she replied. "Farewell, Helwig."

"Farewell," he answered leading the horse away to the paddock.

Nicolai mounted the saddled horse and reached his arm down to his daughter.

"Good-bye, Mama."

Punita hugged Rosalee one last time, then wrapped her hands around her father's wrist and jumped. He swung her up behind him and touched his heels to the barrel of the horse.

"I'll be back in time for dinner," he assured Rosalee, then guided the horse out of the camp.

"A thousand kisses, Mama!" Punita said waving frantically.

"A thousand kisses, my sweet," Rosalee said waving back, visibly struggling to keep her emotions in check.

Folks along the way stopped what they were doing and waved good-bye to Punita as well, wishing her best fortune in her schooling.

✤

Rosalee tried to shake her sense of sadness by turning her attention to packing and readying the ledge for the impending departure.

Her mind wandered until it settled on the day her six-year old daughter had asked her why all of the other families had so many children "and you have only me?"

Rosalee had knelt beside Punita and hugged her.

"For a very good reason," she had answered. "You were so perfect when you were born, and we loved you so much that we couldn't imagine a need for more children."

She had hugged her daughter again hiding the single tear that trickled down her cheek. Each day, she mourned the loss of the seven lives that she had not carried to full-term. Punita had been conceived in the early days of their marriage. Her pregnancy was healthy and normal, but when it came time to deliver Punita, she had encountered difficulty.

Her labour had been long and tiring, and finally it was Nicolai who had turned

Punita, enabling the delivery. From that day, he had teased Rosalee—always in private and only in love—that she was the smallest mare he had ever assisted.

Subsequent pregnancies had ended in miscarriage. Fearing that further miscarriages could be fatal, Rosalee and Nicolai had accepted that they would never have another child. They had been blessed with Punita, and they were grateful.

Rosalee remembered how Punita had been a happy child who brought joy to the vista. She was clever and quick. As soon as her daughter began walking, she had insisted on being with Nicolai when he worked the horses. On her second birthday, Nicolai had sat her upon a small horse and walked it around the paddock. She had squealed with glee. Nicolai had recognized her passion for being amongst the horses and taught her how to feed and groom them. Eventually, he taught her how to train them, and how to assist with the delivery of the foals.

Punita had proven that she had a head for business too. Nicolai had taught her about the treasury and how to manage the money. She loved to hear his stories of the vista history and the routes they travelled, and often recited them.

She also understood the responsibilities of the phuri dai, and studied Rosalee's supervision of, and work with, the women and children of the vista.

Punita was a child full of zeal, and no matter how much time she spent learning her responsibilities to the vista and to her parents, she ensured her chores were completed by the end of each day. She had told her parents many times that her evenings were meant for dancing and singing, not chores or other distractions.

Punita had played with the other children, as required by vista rules, but always preferred to pass her time with her parents.

Rosalee collapsed into a chair and raised her apron to her eyes. Education was important, but that did not mean she was happy to see her daughter leave. She cried until the tears stopped, then she washed her face and began the dinner preparation.

☩

Nicolai and Punita rode directly to the Grand Hotel and sought out Cousin Alexi, who expressed his delight in welcoming Punita into his family.

"You'll be just like a daughter to me," he said.

The men discussed the cycle of the vista and Alexi acknowledged that it would be six years before it returned to Liegnitz.

"It will be a long time, Punita, but we can write to each other," Nicolai assured her. "You know how to reach us. If you need anything before then, you let me know. I'll come as quick as I can."

"Yes, Papa," she said, tears trickling from under her thick lashes.

"It's easy to make plans," Nicolai said, "but sometimes one has to be brave to carry them out. Be brave my little warrior."

He knelt to embrace her one last time.

"Remember always that we love you."

"I love you too, Papa," she sobbed, throwing herself into her father's arms.

Tears soaked the frayed collar of his old blue shirt.

By the time Stefan arrived at the door of his father's office, dressed smartly in his school uniform, Nicolai was leaving. When Alexi explained the arrangement, Stefan expressed pleasure to hear that he would have a new companion.

"A little sister," he teased.

Punita stood with Alexi and Stefan on the front step of the hotel where they waved good-bye to Nicolai. Nicolai flipped the reins and clicked to the bay. In response, the horse quickened its step and trotted down the street.

"A thousand kisses, Papa!" Punita shouted after him, vigorously waving with both hands.

When Nicolai was out of sight, Alexi put his hand on Punita's shoulder. The soft fabric of his grey suit caressed her cheek.

"Come along then. We have some shopping to do. You'll need clothes to begin with, to say nothing of books and supplies for school."

❖

Alexi and Punita spent the remainder of the afternoon visiting shops that sold the items she would need for school and life in Liegnitz, including clothing and warm outerwear to see her through the winter, proper shoes and boots. Alexi felt her enthusiasm for shopping diminish when they entered the cobbler's shop.

"Come, my dear," Alexi coaxed. "You must be fitted. You will not survive a winter in Liegnitz without boots."

Punita's brow creased with reluctance, but she did as her cousin asked. *How will I ever learn to wear the shoes and boots? My feet need freedom!*

After shopping and dinner in the hotel restaurant at a table always reserved for them, Alexi left Stefan and Punita in their suite to occupy themselves while he returned to his office to work for a few hours. Punita immediately set to work hanging her new clothes and organizing the room that had been designated as her bedroom. She was amazed to have been given a room that was hers alone.

When her work was done, Stefan suggested a walk through the town, so she could get her bearings. Before dinner she changed into a new woollen skirt and knitted sweater, hose and sturdy brown shoes. She freed her hair from the tidy braid and brushed it until it shone. To keep her warm in the cool of the evening, she took a woollen jacket that matched the brown of her skirt and the red cloche hat that Alexi had insisted she buy. From under the hat, her dark mane fell in wavy cascades to her waist.

"Let's go," Stefan said, leading the way down the back stairs.

He had changed from his school uniform before dinner. For the evening, he wore casual slacks and a white cotton shirt, with a red knit pull-over vest and navy woollen jacket. He tugged a wool cap over his slicked-back hair. Out on the street, they walked side by side.

"I looked for you yesterday," he said when they were a distance from the hotel. "I couldn't see you anywhere. Does it have something to do with your black eye?"

Punita's fingers touched her bruised eye gingerly. She hung her head, wondering whether she should tell him. In the end, she decided to be honest. She told him about Samson and the punishment directed by the kris council.

"Kris council?" he asked.

She explained the authority of the kris and the council he oversaw.

"A vista is a remarkable society. Isn't it?" he said. "It's very similar to a town. It just operates on wheels."

"Yes. It is," she responded, happy that he understood and appreciated their people. "Perhaps tomorrow I will tell you about the children, and how wonderful it is to grow up...on wheels."

"All right," Stefan said. "For now, let's complete the tour of Liegnitz."

Then he guided her toward the New Town Hall and the park where she had watered Bang a few days before.

CHAPTER NINE

A lexi spoke with the administrator of the nearby school where Punita would attend. They agreed that she would not commence her studies until the new year. In the meantime, Punita was to sit a series of exams to determine the level in which she would begin. Any deficiencies would be remedied by studies conducted by Alexi and Stefan until her formal schooling began.

Stefan was a student of Knight Academy, an elite school for boys. He excelled in his studies and was confident that he could tutor Punita under his father's supervision. Once dinner and Stefan's studies were complete, Stefan reviewed lessons with Punita. During the day, Punita continued her studies under the supervision of Cousin Alexi.

To their delight, father and son found Punita's desire to learn heartening. She absorbed all that they taught like a sponge absorbing every drop of moisture in her path. The study routine was effective and by Christmas the administrator deemed her ready to commence classes in January.

⚜

Stefan was freed from his studies for the days between Christmas and New Year's Day.

"You will particularly enjoy Silvester," Stefan told her as Christmas excitement in the city began to escalate the week before the holidays. "New Year celebrations are very different from Christmas ones. We'll have dancing and fireworks and all sorts of fun!"

They shared stories of their Christmas traditions and realized that many were similar, but others were different.

"I suppose that's because the vista is always travelling," Stefan said. "I think some of our traditions would be difficult if we were moving about all the time."

"Tell me about your Silvester," Punita encouraged. "Ours wasn't much different from every other evening, except that anyone able to keep their eyes open that long stayed up until midnight, and, if anyone had alcohol, it was shared amongst the adults."

Stefan entertained her with his description of the gathering of people in their best dress for a late party, the fine and elaborate dinner hosted by the hotel, dancing, and the amazing fireworks that were released at midnight in the front courtyard of the hotel.

"Even if people are unable to attend the dinner and the ball, they can gather around the court yard to watch the fireworks," he said. "I prefer to watch them from the roof."

"Oh! How wonderful!" Punita exclaimed, eyes bright with delight. "Will we do that this year?"

"Of course! If you like."

"Stefan," she began her question with hesitation, "will you tell me how you discovered the window to the roof."

"What? Oh."

He appeared surprised by her question. He lowered his eyes to his hands, as if remembering.

"It was the year my mother died. She'd only been gone a month. Everyone was so excited about Silvester evening and the new year. They were laughing and dancing. Having fun."

He swallowed hard and swiped a tear from his cheek.

"What's Silvester?" Punita asked.

"Oh!" Her interruption caught him off guard. "Another way of saying New Year's Eve," he said. "I'm sorry if I confused you."

"You didn't." She smiled at him. "I just learned something new, and that's a good thing, Papa says." She nodded her head, encouraging him to continue.

"My mother always made Silvester special for me. She was gone and, I thought then, no one cared. I found the music and loud voices overwhelming. I had to escape." He raised his eyes to meet hers. "I don't really know how I got there. I just ran up the stairs. I intended to go to our suite but, well, I was crying so hard I missed the landing."

He blushed.

"I'd never seen the little door before, and it was enough of a distraction that I had to open it. The window was huge. I could hear the noise below and was drawn to the flashing lights. I rubbed the dirt from a pane and looked out. I was amazed at what I saw from up there. I thought: this must be what it looks like from heaven."

Once again, Stefan swiped a tear from his eye, as he swallowed audibly.

"I was too small then to open the window. Besides, it was too dark, and I didn't know it had latches. But I returned to the attic whenever I could," he said with more confidence. "The window fascinated me. Eventually, I figured out the latches and, by the next Silvester, I had figured out how to get out on the roof."

"I'm sorry about your mother, Stefan."

"No need. She died long ago. She was very ill, and now she's not." He forced a smile as if to look brave. "I think of her every Silvester. Up there on the roof, I feel closer to her."

110

✠

In January, Punita began her studies.

At the end of each day, she returned to the suite at the top of the hotel where she lived with Alexi and Stefan. The suite was well appointed with three large bedrooms, a sitting room, and dining room. Each bedroom had a bathroom included, similar to the rooms let to hotel guests. Alexi's room was larger, designed for him and his wife.

"My parents installed the two smaller bedrooms hoping that I'd one day have a sibling," Stephan had told her when she first toured the suite. "Papa and I decided that you should have the second room. It's the mirror image of mine. Our clothes closets are built into the same wall."

"I love it!" Punita had exclaimed, running her fingers over the rich red wood of the dresser. "The little desk is tucked into the corner under the window in such a way that I will have plenty of light for studying and writing letters to my parents! See how the daylight that fills the room bounces off the large mirror. It makes the room so bright."

"Even on the dreariest of winter days," Stefan had agreed. "I have the same in my room."

Although Punita carried an emptiness within her that only her parents could fill, she revelled in the room that was hers and found comfort in it. It was a pretty room, decorated in cream and rose and green. The bedcover and pillows were trimmed in pink frills and the cover itself had large pink roses on a cream background. Two small armchairs were covered in a fabric striped with cream, green, and rose, as were the draperies. Rag rugs in shades of green covered the parquet floor. Because the suite was tended by hotel staff on a regular basis, her room was always clean and smelled of wood polish. She embraced its orderliness, and found the smell of the wood polish calming.

"This room is perfect!" she told Stefan on many occasions. "I feel cozy in here."

Other than the large mirror, the walls in

her room were bare. Alexi had told her to cover the walls as she wished, but she had not bothered. She focussed on her studies. Her father had often stressed the importance of a good education, and she was determined to make him proud.

As soon as her schoolwork was complete, Punita would curl into one of her armchairs, wrapping herself in her mother's shawl when it was chilly. She enjoyed the quiet time alone and read until Stefan arrived from school. She travelled the world through novels of adventure and admired the descriptive emotions in books of poetry. One of her favourite stories was *"Little Women"* by Louisa May Alcott; a story of a family of daughters whose father had gone off to war, and their escapades during his absence. She tried to imagine life in such a large family, then her thoughts wandered to her vista family and ended with thoughts of her parents. She clasped the emerald that hung from her neck and sent loving thoughts from her heart to the two she loved most in the world.

At the end of his day, Stefan would knock
on her door and stick his head in before he
sat down to his own studies. He would sit
in the chair opposite her and tell her tales of
the Academy or guide her in some aspect of
her studies with which she struggled.

Each evening, Punita and Stefan would
descend to the hotel's restaurant and have
a meal with Alexi. On weekends, she and
Stefan worked around the hotel, learning
the business that one day he would inherit.
In time, she felt as though she were part of
a family again, that she had two families.

Usually, they ate their evening meals in
the hotel restaurant, at the table reserved
for them. Their breakfasts and midday
meals were sent up from the kitchen and
they ate in their suite. On occasion, an intimate evening meal might be served in their
suite, especially when Stefan and Punita
where studying for exams.

Regardless, there was always a bowl of
fresh fruit on the sideboard for snacking.
Punita took advantage of the fruit late in

the afternoon, relishing the tang of citrus or the sweet of dense flesh. The hotel received seasonal fruits from all over Europe and Asia—oranges from Spain, mangoes from India, figs from Afghanistan. Their exotic fragrance mingled with the homey smell of wood polish.

Punita soon settled into the comfortable rhythm of her new surroundings. Days blended into weeks which soon became months and years, and, although she was aware of the passage of time, she often wondered how six years of her life had passed so quickly and so happily. In that time, she had become familiar with every nook and hidey-hole, celebrated every Silvester on the roof with Stefan, flourished in her studies, and matured in body and mind.

In the year of her fifteenth birthday, Cousin Alexi reminded Punita that the vista would be returning to Liegnitz for the fall festival. She struggled to keep her focus on her studies, so excited was she to show her parents her scholarly accomplishments and to share her experiences during her stay at the hotel.

Punita knew that she would not return to school in the fall. Instead, she awaited the arrival of the vista and would depart with her parents at the end of the fair. A small corner of her heart broke, as she accepted that she would have to say good-bye to Alexi and Stefan.

         ✦

"What's troubling you?" Stefan asked, plopping into the chair opposite her, interrupting her day dreaming, the latest book of poetry open on her lap.

"What do you mean?" she asked.

"You have been sulking for weeks now," he said. "Usually, you flit about like a butterfly, impossible to snag in a net, happy and laughing. Lately, all you do is sit in here and read. Or pretend to read."

Stefan glanced at the book on her lap.

Punita closed the book, folded her hands over it, and scowled at him.

"I'm not sulking," she said. "I'm sad. Grieving even."

"Grieving! Why? Has someone died?"

"No, you silly," she said, amazed at his ignorance. "For someone as educated as you are, you're not very observant."

He looked at her, puzzled.

"What is the date?" she asked.

"Why, it's Friday, June 1st, 1934! You know that."

"Yes, I do," she said, as if speaking to a five-year-old. "And that means that I will complete my studies at the end of the month, and that the fall fair is only months away. And you will complete your studies at the Academy at the end of the month and be off to university."

Her fine-boned hand rose to her breast and fingered the emerald that hung from the gold chain—her mother's heart. The smooth surface of the gem comforted her.

Stefan inhaled but she stopped his words before he could speak.

"I'm leaving, Stefan."

117

A single tear escaped and slid down the side of her nose. Stefan slid off his chair and onto his knees. He took her small hands in his. On his knees, he was as tall as she was seated on the chair. He looked into her dewy eyes.

"Your eyes remind me of dark chocolate," he said. "Melted chocolate, actually. They're always so glossy and bright!"

Punita grinned bashfully and eyed him from beneath her great fans of dark lashes.

"Six years have passed too quickly," he said, sitting on his heels. "You and I, we have grown together in so many ways." He paused. "You're wrong, you know. I do understand your grief."

Punita hung her head. Another tear slid past her nose and splashed onto the book cover.

"It breaks my heart to think of life without you. And your father, of course."

She looked into his dark eyes. She wanted to brush the shock of black hair that threatened to cover them, but he held her hands fast.

"You are so small, my dear Punita. Like a little bird sitting still on a branch," he whispered. "Sometimes I worry that you will break."

His index finger caressed the outline of the fragile bones in her face.

Stefan rose to his knees again, cupping her face in his hands. His thumb intercepted another tear as it escaped wet lashes, and he leaned toward her, kissing her lips chastely. A second kiss followed, and she felt the soft fullness of his lips take possession of hers, gentle and loving. A sob escaped her lips, and Stefan kissed her yet again.

"I'm sorry! I shouldn't have done that," he said, hastily withdrawing, a pink flush creeping over his shirt collar.

Punita's hands covered his, holding them still against her cheeks. Their eyes locked for a moment, before she lowered her hands gracefully to her lap and hung her head. A dark curtain of tresses fell between them.

Stefan lowered himself to his heels again and reclaimed her hands. The wristlet of

love knots made by Punita's father grazed
the knuckles of his right hand.

"I don't want you to go," he said. "I need
you to stay."

His sincerity pierced her heart.

Rising again, he took her in his arms and
held her to him.

"I will speak with Papa and see if we
have any options," he said, his lips caressing her ear.

CHAPTER TEN

That evening, a woman joined them for dinner. Cousin Alexi introduced her as a long-time friend. Stefan appeared to know her too. Her name was Mathilde Svensen. Punita had never met anyone like her and could not stop herself from observing every fine thing about the stranger.

She had seen beautiful female guests in the hotel on many occasions, but Mathilde was different. Punita was at a loss to explain that difference, except perhaps to say that she had a presence.

Mathilde's short, white blonde hair clung to her skull like a cap of fine down. Small curls kissed her temples and ears. Her skin was fair and flawless, as though she were made of porcelain. Her eyes may have been the blue of ice, but her heart was as warm as sunshine. Her ruby red smile was wide and genuine, and framed small perfect white teeth.

Punita would have guessed Mathilde's age to be between thirty and forty years, but she had no way to be certain without asking, which she would not do.

Not much taller than Punita, Mathilde carried herself with grace and dignity, and seemed to reflect an inner confidence. Punita was in awe of her.

Punita and Stefan were already seated at their usual table when Mathilde appeared, floating into the dining room on Alexi's arm. She wore a floor length gown of pale blue silk that rippled as she walked, catching light and shadow like water rippling over stones in a brook.

She wore cream-coloured leather gloves so finely made that they fit like a second skin, caressing her forearms up to her elbows. The neckline of her dress was wide and open, not unlike the neck of the blouses worn by the vista women. One small strand of creamy pearls encircled the base of her slender neck. Feathers coloured the same blue as her dress capped her shoulders and fluttered as she removed her gloves. Her dainty, heeled slippers were made of the same leather as her gloves and were only glimpsed when she gathered the hem of her dress out of the way of the chair legs. A hint of lavender encircled her.

Mathilde enchanted the three of them throughout their meal, entertaining them with stories of her youth in the north. Her voice was musical and welcoming.

Each time Mathilde looked at Punita, Punita felt as though she could sit at the woman's feet and listen to her stories forever. Stefan appeared to be just as mesmerized. Each time Mathilde looked at him, his ears turned pink and he fidgeted. Her eyes reflected amusement at his discomfort, but she never laughed at him.

Mathilde's opinion of Alexi was reflected in her eyes and voice when her attention was directed at him—tender and intimate.

After the meal, they bid each other good evening. Stefan and Punita returned to their suite, and Alexi escorted Mathilde into the lounge for a cocktail.

"Gosh! Isn't she amazing!" Stefan and Punita blurted together as Stefan closed the door to the suite.

They stopped and looked at each other, eyes wide, then burst into laughter.

"Yes," she said.

"Amazing," he said, again. "Can you tell by her accent that she comes from Norway?"

"No," she responded softly, her eyes seeking his. "But, it's so beautiful that I will hear it in my dreams." They were standing near enough that she sensed his hand reach for her cheek.

"Good night," he said, leaning toward her.

She closed her eyes as he neared, then opened them abruptly when he kissed her chastely on the forehead.

"Good night." Punita's quiet voice betrayed her disappointment. She hung her head as she turned toward her bedroom. Stefan heard her disappointment and grabbed her arm, turning her to him again.

124

"I love you," he said, cupping her face and placing a gentle kiss on her quivering lips. He walked her to her bedroom, ushered her inside, and closed the door.

Moments later, Punita stood in front of her mirror, brushing loose her bound hair. In the next room, she heard the voices of Alexi and Stefan, then a door closed. She turned out the lamp and crawled into her bed. She did not fall asleep readily. Her mind raced, imagining herself as elegant as Mathilde and loved by Stefan.

The months remaining to the fall fair passed in a flurry of activity. Punita and Stefan each graduated with honours, he from the Academy and she from the last level of school she would ever attend. They worked in the hotel throughout the summer, but found time for picnics and adventures, rides in the country, and evenings on the roof.

"I will treasure all of these memories when I leave," Punita told Stefan one evening in late August, while they sat on the roof.

His legs straddled the roof peak and she sat between them, held secure by his welcoming arms. He nuzzled and kissed her neck with a feather-light brush that caused an eruption of goose bumps on her arms, and an awakening deep inside.

She had noticed a change in him during the past months. He was more confident and expressive. He had lost the shyness of the boy she had lived with for six years, while she remained bashful and uncertain.

❖

Late in September, Alexi suggested that they take the afternoon off.

"Go for a ride," he said. "Enjoy your time together. The fair will be here soon enough."

Dressed in equestrian attire, they took two of the horses that Alexi kept for guests and rode out of town with a picnic basket fastened to Stefan's saddle.

"Where shall we go?" he asked.

"Let's go this way," she suggested, pointing to a lane running off to their right. "This dirt road will be kinder on the horses' hooves."

They guided their mounts in the direction she had indicated. The air was fresh after rain the previous evening. The warmth of the day had not yet dried the dampness that overlay the dust on the road. The horses plodded past the fields, side by side.

"Look at that odd post." Punita indicated some time later. "Such a bright colour compared to the nature around it. It's almost golden."

"Indeed," Stefan answered. "I know the boy who lives there. Paul. Paul Lange is his name. I'm told it is one of the colours used in the regimental uniform worn by his father and grandfather."

"They've lived here a long time then?"

"Yes, his family has lived in the area almost as long as we have."

They rode past the gatepost, further into the farmland until they found a cozy place for a picnic, under an old sycamore tree near a burbling stream.

Stefan shook out a blanket and spread it between two gnarly roots. Punita set out

127

the food that had been packed in a reed basket provided by the hotel kitchen. She passed a glass of lemonade to Stefan, feeling a thrill when their fingers brushed. They ate in silence, allowing the singing of small birds to serenade them, the lower notes provided by the scurrying of creatures in the grass at the edge of the stream.

As they packed the remnants of the meal into the basket, Stefan took her hand and raised it to his lips. His mouth lingered over her knuckles. Punita felt his eyes searching her face as if he had something to say. Her pulse quickened. She felt a faint throb where his finger rested at her wrist.

"Would you like to stop and visit with your friend Paul?" she asked, attempting to divert the intimate moment.

"No," he said, releasing her hand. He stood then and brushed his trousers as if he were covered in leaves. "I checked the drive as we rode past. The vehicles are gone. He's likely away. I'll see him another time."

❖

When they arrived back at the hotel, a stable hand greeted them at the barn and reached for the reins of both horses.

"I'll groom the horses," he said. "You go along. Herr Puchinski has been asking for the two of you."

They looked at one another, shrugged, then raced into the hotel.

Stefan knocked on the closed door of his father's office and opened it on hearing his father's response. Punita followed behind, her vision momentarily blocked by Stefan's bulk. Then he moved.

"Papa!" she screamed, running into Nicolai's arms.

"Mama!" she turned and embraced Rosalee, kissing her cheek.

Beaming, she placed a hand on one arm of each parent.

"I can't believe you're finally here!"

Nicolai placed his hands on her shoulders and turned her to face him directly.

"Alexi, who is this young woman?" he said grinning. "I left my imp of a girl with you, and now you tell me that this is she? You jest! You sold my daughter and now try to give me an imposter."

Rosalee's laughter filled the room like the ringing of small bells.

"Mind you," Nicolai continued. "She is very beautiful. Perhaps I will keep this one instead. She could bring a fine bride price."

"Papa!" Punita said, laughing.

He winked at his wife.

"What do you think, Rosalee? Should we keep this imposter?"

Punita stamped her foot for attention, a smile of affection lighting her face.

"It's me. Your daughter Punita. How can you not know? Every stallion knows its filly!"

With that comment, they all burst into laughter.

"Perhaps we'd recognize you better if you weren't covered in dust," her mother said in a gentler voice. "I see some things haven't changed."

"Indeed," Alexi said. "Why don't you two scoot upstairs and wash? I have invited

Nicolai and Rosalee to stay here, in the hotel. Come down when you're ready, and we'll go in to dinner."

Stefan and Punita raced up the stairs to do as they were bid.

Dinner was a happy occasion full of catch-up stories. Nicolai and Rosalee told of the six-year adventure that the caravan had followed, the many fairs and constantly changing landscapes. With sadness, they reported that Hanzi would likely not survive the coming winter. His health was failing. But, they added, Helwig had been shadowing him for several years and folks felt that he would make a fine kris in the future. Samson had caused no further trouble following his father's departure. He had married the girl to whom he had been betrothed and they had three small children, with another on the way.

They also talked of the success of the hotel business, Stefan's graduation and intentions of higher learning. And Punita described life in the city for her parents—what it was like to live through the seasons and not try to outrun the winters, how different people interacted and, of course, her schooling. She treasured her time in school, she told them. And to Alexi and Stefan she expressed her sincere appreciation for all that they had done for her.

"I will never forget either of you," she said, tears flooding her eyes. She used her starched white napkin to staunch the flow before it began.

Punita's parents complimented Alexi and Stefan for the fine job they had done taming their wild daughter and ensuring that she received adequate schooling.

"Adequate!" Alexi choked on a mouthful of food. "My dear cousins, you can be very proud of your daughter. She was always at the top of her class.

Punita felt a rush of blood pinking her cheeks, and lowered her eyes, embarrassed at the attention.

CHAPTER ELEVEN

T he next morning, at the end of breakfast, Alexi invited the Kota family to join
Stefan and him in his office, where they could
continue their conversations over coffee.

They gathered around a coffee table in
the centre of arm chairs and a settee. Punita
sat snuggled between her parents. Inge
appeared with a tray of coffee and small
cakes and closed the door as she departed.
The aroma of fresh coffee filled the room.

Alexi caught Nicolai's eye and nodded.
Stefan and Punita reacted to the exchange
by turning toward Nicolai. He looked down
at his daughter and took her hand.

"Punita, my daughter," he began. "You
are the product of the love of our marriage—your Mama and me—and we want
you always to be as happy as we have been
these many years."

"I am, Pa—"

"Shhh!" he stopped her words with a calloused finger to her lips.

"Yes, yes. We know you are happy. And we know that you have missed us as much as we have missed you. These things you have told us. But, you must listen to what I say to you now."

He turned in the settee, to better see her face.

Reflecting on conversations that he and Rosalee had had with Alexi the afternoon before, he told his daughter that he had received an offer of marriage from a suitable young man and that he was inclined to accept it. Nicolai saw the pain in her eyes when she looked toward Stefan, but Stefan's eyes were focussed on his hands neatly folded in his lap.

"But Pa—"

"Shhh!" Nicolai stopped her again.

"Your mother and I have discussed this. And we agree that it is a good match."

He held his finger to her lips to stifle her returning protest.

"If you truly do not approve of the match," Nicolai said, looking to his wife and back to Punita, "your mother and I will accept your refusal. I have said as much in response to the offer."

Punita ceased her protest but continued to squirm.

"Now, Punita, you know your happiness and safety are of primary importance to your mother and me, and considering the unrest in the world today, it is most urgent that we see you safe and settled. No one knows where tomorrow will find us. However, we believe that it would be wise to arrange the match now but delay the wedding for another year. In any event, the groom has other obligations and will not be available for another year."

Punita pulled her hands free from Nicolai's and jumped to her feet.

"Papa! I cannot—" She stamped her foot.

"Punita, hear what your father has to say," Rosalee said, her words firm.

"Punita," her father began again.

She rolled her eyes but held her tongue.

"Will you marry Stefan?"

Nicolai saw Punita's face form a negative response. It disappeared as she covered her mouth with her hands to stifle it.

She swivelled to face Stefan and Alexi, who were grinning broadly.

"Uuugh!" Punita stamped her foot again, smiling with them all. Then she hooted with joy and twirled on the spot. "Yes. A million times!"

They all rose from their seats and embraced each other as family in the truest sense.

Their celebration was interrupted briefly when Inge wheeled in a cart carrying a bottle of champagne icing in a bucket, and fluted crystal glasses. Alexi poured out the effervescent wine and handed a glass to each of them.

"To a long and fruitful life full of happiness and many children," he toasted.

They raised their glasses in salute and sipped.

"Wait!" Punita stopped them. "What other obligations?"

She looked at Stefan as she delivered the question.

"I'm sorry," he said. "I haven't had a chance to tell you. I've only received word this morning. I am required to serve one year in the youth military. Father and I agree that you would be better off with your parents for the year, while I'm away."

Punita plopped onto the settee.

"I feel like a great sailing ship at sea on heavy swells," she said. "The wind has filled my sails and carries me off course!"

Once again, they all laughed, taking turns to assure her that the year would pass quickly, and all would be well.

Alexi cleared his throat to get everyone's attention.

"Nicolai, I know you and Rosalee need to get back to camp and that you have things to arrange for the fair. You are most welcome to spend your evenings in the hotel, but please feel free to go, if your time is needed elsewhere."

Rosalee and Nicolai took their leave

before midday, feeling the responsibility to be in the camp at such a critical time. Punita was to remain in the hotel until the day of the fair. On that morning, Alexi and Stefan would accompany her, with bags packed. She would provide the tour that Stefan had missed six years prior, then remain in camp to help pack up the next day.

CHAPTER TWELVE

That evening, when they went down for dinner, Alexi escorted Mathilde into the dining room, resplendent in shades of lavender.

"Mathilde!" Punita exclaimed, "I'm so happy to see you again."

At the end of another enjoyable meal together, Mathilde winked at the gentlemen and invited Punita to join her in her room for a night cap.

"Oh, I don't know if I could drink another drop! But I would welcome the conversation." She looked at Alexi and Stefan, smiled sweetly. "It seems I am always surrounded by men!"

The women left the men in the foyer and made their way along the corridor past the reception desk and Alexi's office.

Mathilde stopped at the second last door, next to the one that led up the back stairwell. She inserted a key and turned the knob.

"Come in." She beckoned to Punita and disappeared into the room.

"This is your room?" Punita asked, amazed to have lived in the hotel for six years without knowing. "I always presumed it to be a cleaners' closet."

Mathilde chuckled and removed her gloves, tossing them on a nearby sideboard. They landed next to a tray of crystal glasses and a decanter half filled with a golden red liquid.

"Yes," she answered, "but I'm not here all the time. I travel, and ..."

A light rap sounded at the door before it partially opened.

"Pardon, Madame. May I bring you anything?"

"Not for me, thank you, but will you please bring the young lady a raspberry *lassi*?"

"As you say." The door closed again.

During the moment of distraction, Punita gazed about the room, which was very different from Cousin Alexi's suite upstairs. She had never been in one of the hotel rooms and wondered whether other rooms were like this.

On one long wall was a large canopied bed that would sleep three large men shoulder to shoulder. Although it was built with rosewood, every accessory, including the linen and bed cover, was an ivory colour. A chandelier hung in the centre of the room, and smaller ones hung on the wall on either side of the bed. Prisms of light danced on the pale rose walls.

"Now then. Why don't you have a seat over here," Mathilde said, indicating toward an armchair covered in the same striped fabric as the chairs in Punita's room.

The other chairs, including a strange one she had never seen before, were all similarly covered.

"What is that?" Punita asked pointing to the odd piece of furniture on which Mathilde was about to recline.

141

"This, my dear, is called *une chaise longue*. One of my favourite pastimes is to put my feet up on this long chair and read."

"How lovely," Punita marvelled. "I enjoy reading too."

Their conversation was interrupted by a second rap at the door. The server entered and placed a glass of a thick pink refreshment on the small table next to Punita's chair. Without asking, the girl poured a glass of bourbon from the decanter and handed it to Mathilde. Mathilde thanked the girl for her service and the door closed behind her once again.

"Have you tried the *lassi*?" Mathilde indicated to the beverage near Punita. "I think you will find it refreshing after our meal. It's made with yogurt."

"I have had a lassi before," Punita responded, reaching for the glass, "but never a pink one."

She sipped the drink.

"Mmm. This is wonderful! I haven't had a lassi since the day I came here, and I never thought to ask for another. Mmm." Punita sighed in delight, taking another sip. "And I heard you ask for raspberry?"

Mathilde nodded.

"A lassi is tart to begin with," she said. "I find raspberries complement it. At this time of year, raspberries are not always available, but I had heard that some arrived earlier today."

"I will have to tell Mama about the raspberries," Punita noted. "For our people, it is a recipe that has been handed down from mother to daughter for generations. But only plain." Punita took a few more sips. "Thank you for a lovely memory."

A lull of time passed between them as they enjoyed their refreshments.

"What do you know of me?" Mathilde asked.

"Oh!" Punita was not expecting her question. "I know only those things that you have shared during our meals together. And, what I observe."

"And what have you observed?"

"You are the most beautiful and graceful woman I have ever met or seen for that matter. You tell wonderful stories—you could keep my people entertained for hours!" She hesitated. "And, you appear to have won the heart of Cousin Alexi. I think, sometimes, that even Stefan has an affection for you." She glanced down at her drink. "As have I," she whispered sheepishly.

"Thank you, my dear. I am fond of all of you as well. It warms the heart to have acceptance and affection."

Mathilde set her glass on the arm of the chaise and stretched her legs before her, flexing toes encased in the sheerest stockings Punita had ever seen.

Clasping her hands in her lap, Mathilde continued.

"I am delighted to hear of your intended marriage to Stefan. I think it is a good match, and you will have a wonderful life together. I have invited you to join me this evening, because I have a wedding gift for you. We never know what our future will bring, and so I'd like to give it to you now. If I may."

Punita looked about the elegant room and saw no wrapped gift. Mathilde made no effort to rise in order to retrieve one.

"I asked you what you know about me. And from your answer, I surmise that you have no idea of my business."

"I do not."

"Hmm. Well, let's just say that I have certain skills that men find pleasing. They seek me out for more than just my storytelling."

She cleared her throat, searching for gentle words.

"I don't spend time with just any man, however. I am particular about the company I keep."

"Oh," said Punita, not knowing what to say or how to respond. "I'm afraid I still don't understand. Unless you're talking about sex. I know about sex."

"Yes and no. Sex may be involved, but there are other, possibly more pleasing, aspects to consider."

Mathilde went on to describe the art of pleasing a man, one of the most important tools of which was listening, which enhanced the art of conversation.

When Mathilde had shared her thoughts with Punita, she left Punita to reflect on them further and excused herself into the adjacent bathroom. A moment later, Punita heard water running and Mathilde appeared at the door.

"Come," she said, inviting Punita to follow her.

Punita tipped the glass back to allow the last drops of her raspberry bliss to trickle onto her tongue, then set the glass on the small table and followed Matilde into the bathroom.

Punita could not have imagined a grander room for bathing.

In the centre of the room was a great white bath tub with golden clawed feet and a golden faucet. The room also held another chaise, with a white furred rug under it. The sinks, towels, flowers in a vase, fabric on the chaise, and curtains on the windows were all a snowy white, stunningly complementing the polished rosewood cabinetry. The sink faucets were golden too.

The only other obvious colour in the room was the powder blue of the walls and matching silk ribbons used to tie the curtains back. An elegant chandelier abounding in crystal and tiny lights hung over the tub, and wall sconces hung on either side of sparkly mirrors mounted on the wall above each of two sinks.

Steam rose from the tub as it filled with hot water. Something frothy and fragrant floated on the top.

"Scented oil," Mathilde told her.

Mathilde gracefully reclined on a nearby chair and instructed Punita to remove her garments, and step into the tub.

Punita tentatively did as she was told and followed Mathilde's instructions for exfoliating and bathing. Satisfied with Punita's efforts, Mathilde rose from the chaise longue and shook out a fluffy white towel.

Punita stepped out of the tub and Mathilde wrapped her in it, gently rubbing her body until the water was absorbed.

"What a fetching necklace you have," Mathilde noted. "Is that an emerald?"

Punita raised her right hand to finger the medallion.

"Yes. My mother gave it to me when I left the vista to come here. The emerald represents the green heart chakra of generations of women in my family," Punita told her.

As an afterthought, she raised her left hand to reveal the gold bracelet of love knots.

"My father made this for me when I was eight, to remind me that he would always love me."

"You have two wonderful treasures," Mathilde commented while she motioned Punita toward a stool that stood in front of one of the mirrors.

"Sit, please." She removed the pins from Punita's hair and brushed it until the dark tresses shone in the twinkling lights. Finally, she removed the towel and asked Punita to complete a turn, so she could assess their progress.

She dabbed a light scent behind each of Punita's ears and on the inside of her wrists.

"Lavender?" Punita asked.

Mathilde smiled in acknowledgement, then lightly drew a line in Punita's budding cleavage, using the stopper from the scent bottle. Turning Punita, she drew another line with the stopper, from the top of her spine to the dimples at the bottom.

"Turn once more for me," she asked. As Punita turned, Mathilde expressed her observations.

"You have lovely hair, full of shine. The sun has streaked it with delightful golden highlights. Hair and cleanliness are important tools for a young woman. You are fifteen, you said?"

Punita nodded.

"Your figure is developing nicely. During the next few years, your body will be most desirable. Stefan will not be able to keep his

149

hands off you," she concluded, her pleasure expressed in her smile.

"Thank you," Punita said, more than just her cheeks turning pink.

"Almost done," said Mathilde walking toward a rosewood cupboard that stretched from floor to ceiling. "We just need to wrap the gift."

From the cupboard, she took a flowing gown of satin cream, with a shaped corset trimmed in pale pink ribbons. She draped it over Punita's head, letting its folds flutter to the floor, lifted her hair free and tied the ribbons. She held out a gossamer robe and Punita slipped her arms into it. Mathilde tied a pink bow to close the robe, and once more reached into the cupboard.

"Try these. They should fit," she said, setting on the floor a pair of pink slippers with feathery toes and glass heels.

Punita stood admiring the fineness of the fabrics that draped her, while Mathilde walked around Punita appraising the result of her ministrations.

"Follow me, and take care you don't trip with those slippers," Mathilde said, her hand on a door next to the cupboard.

The door opened into a narrow stair-well. Punita followed her up two short flights of stairs and stopped behind her on a small landing. Mathilde rapped on the door and opened it, inviting Punita to precede her into another room.

CHAPTER THIRTEEN

With the last of her teachings, Mathilde told Punita that the rooms below were for her private use, and that, if she entertained, it was always in the room in which they stood.

"My motto is 'Always allow yourself a means of escape'. I entertain here. The rooms below are for me alone."

Punita surveyed the room, a lovely extension of Mathilde's own, with similar furnishings.

"Enjoy my gift," Mathilde said with a wink, a kind smile glowing on her face.

Then she closed the door behind her and retreated down the stairs.

Punita wondered about the gift as she wandered about the room admiring the femininity. Another rap sounded, on a different door.

"Come in," Punita said cautiously.

The door opened, and Stefan stood in the doorway.

"May I come in?" he asked, his voice sounding reticent.

"Of course," Punita said, tugging at the robe to better cover herself. "Stefan, I don't understand."

Stefan closed the door behind him, stepping further into the room. She realized that he too was dressed differently. Instead of street clothes, he wore lounging trousers and a matching robe made of burgundy silk.

"You look so handsome," she said, uncomfortable with the newness of their intimacy. "That colour complements your skin."

Thanking her for the observation, Stefan stepped closer and took her hands in his.

"Our parents have arranged our marriage to occur in one year but, because that time is so far off and the politics of the land are so unsettled, they have arranged for us to have one night together before we part. Mathilde volunteered to help."

"I see." Punita was still trying to absorb Stefan's explanation. "But who is Mathilde?"

"Mathilde is a woman who entertains men. Not just any men, mind. She has few clients, and they pay well. My father is one. She is also available to enlighten certain young men, training them in the art of love and loving. Her training was my father's gift to me for my eighteenth birthday."

"Oh!" Punita slowly began to understand.

"It is not her practice to teach young women. Her time with you, and this night. They are gifts from Mathilde."

Punita looked up into Stefan's eyes, warmed by his expression. He took her hand and led her to the settee. On the table in front of the settee sat a decanter of sweet liqueur and two small glasses. He poured two glasses and passed one to her, inviting her to sip as he did. She felt a fire descend from her lips to her belly, and involuntary contractions of muscles below. Stefan set his glass on the table and took her hand.

154

"Will you show me what you've learned this evening?" he asked, his voice husky with desire.

"Yes," Punita said demurely. "Will you show me what you've learned?"

She looked at him through her long black lashes, trying to remember what to do next.

In answer, he leaned forward and kissed her tentatively. Her lips parted, and she leaned into him, waiting for him to react. Feeling her response, Stefan took Punita in his arms and together they forgot about the world for one adventurous and fulfilling night.

With the energy of youth and the lessons of Mathilde, Stefan and Punita shared the wedding gift many times, until they reached a point of exhaustion and slept entwined as one, bound by their love for one another.

⚜

"I'm going to take a bath," Punita announced late the following morning.

Light was filtering through the window, promising a crisp day ahead. She scrambled off the rumpled bed, tugging the sheet to cover the small red stain that marked the end of her innocence, and padded naked and tousled into the bathroom.

"I'm starving, "Stefan said, watching her awkward gait and smiling. "I'll order food."

He knew she would have some tenderness and bruising, thanks to Mathilde's detailed enlightenment. He telephoned down to the kitchen and placed an order for breakfast, scratching his whiskers as he spoke. Then he rose from the bed and knocked on the bathroom door.

"May I come in?"

"Uh-huh," Punita answered.

She had bundled her hair atop her head, which now rested against the back of a tub identical to the one in Mathilde's bathroom. Steam from the bath escaped through foamy bubbles that blanketed her.

"This is so nice. I could stay here all day," she said with her eyes closed. "The warmth is seeping into my very soul."

"I've ordered some food," he said, "and thought I'd shave. But ..."

Her eyes shot open as he stepped into her womb of comfort and knelt between her legs.

"Stefan!" she screeched playfully before he stifled her squeal with his lips once again.

Waves of water rocked them together and overflowed the tub as once more they became one.

A while later, she padded out of the bathroom, her hair wrapped in a towel, snuggled into a heavy cotton hotel robe. Stefan stood naked before the mirror, shaving and humming something tuneless.

A soft rap sounded at the door.

"Come in!" he bellowed, as Punita ran into the bathroom and hid behind the door.

"Just leave the food," he bellowed again, without interrupting the razor's stroke. "We'll serve ourselves, thanks!"

When she heard the hall door close again, Punita padded out of the bathroom and dished scrambled eggs, fried sliced tomatoes, and tiny sausages onto a plate. By the time Stefan had finished shaving and was settled on the sofa next to her, Punita had already consumed half of her meal.

"Who knew that making love could leave a person feeling so hungry!" she exclaimed in amazement, before biting into a piece of buttered French bread topped with a slice of white cheese.

"Not me," he said, observing the healthy portion of food he had selected for himself.

"Stefan!" she exclaimed. "At least put your robe on! You'll catch a chill."

He laughed but took the time to locate and don a robe nonetheless.

"What can you tell me about the vista that you haven't already shared?" he asked, as they ate their meal.

"Hmm. I suppose, considering you'll finally see it tomorrow, two things might be interesting to you." She chewed and swallowed a bit of egg before continuing. "I never did tell you about the games that children learn, nor about our family talent."

Her smile was enticing. He set his fork down and rose toward her.

"No!" she squealed, curling away from him. "Sit and eat, or I won't tell you."

Finished with her food, she left the sofa and poured coffee for each of them. When she returned, she sat cross-legged, feeling snug in the hotel robe, and enjoying the aroma wafting from her cup.

"Which do you want first?"

"Well, since I have already experienced your lovely talents," he said, grinning at Punita's feigned look of offence, "perhaps I should hear about the games."

"All right." She settled herself, pressing her fingers to her swollen lips to ensure they were up to the task. "This will be a bit of a story."

Punita began.

"Although nomads are often looked upon as suspect by those who lead more stationary lives, they are renowned for their ability to entertain. From an early age, they are taught to sing and dance and, if they

159

show an interest, they are taught to play instruments, usually tambourine, violin, and guitar, or to act and perform short theatrical plays.

"For a child, life as a nomad is exciting and fun. Adults teach them many games to keep them safe, out of trouble, and as a means of education. Not all of them are fortunate to go to school for formal education. They have to be sent away for that—into a city or town, to live with friends or relatives. From the games, they learn to run, to hide, and to be decisive.

"We call our favourite game simply the Game. The Game remains in play whether the caravan is moving or encamped. Each morning, the children gather around the voivode, who holds up the token he has chosen for the day. Then he hands it to the child who won the Game the previous day, repeating to the other children that their duty is to track the token, endeavour to take it from the holder, and keep it till the end of the day. Whoever holds the token at the end of the evening meal is declared the winner when it is handed back to the voivode.

"If they are encamped, the children are expected to do their chores and keep the game in play. It is vital that they be proficient at the Game. If a threat arises, they should have their wits and training to keep them safe. *Practice makes perfect*, the children are often reminded.

"Before they start singing in the evening, the voivode calls forth the last child to hold up the game token of that day. Everyone cheers, of course, and that child is rewarded for their successful day by being appointed as the one to begin the Game the next day. No one can win the Game twice in a row," Punita said, concluding her description of the Game.

"Amazing!" Stefan said, enthralled with her description. "It sounds challenging. Do you think I could learn the Game?"

"It is indeed, and no you can't," Punita answered. "They would never show an outsider—and you are an outsider to them, regardless of the blood connection."

161

Stefan dropped his chin, feeling dejected.

"Perhaps they will teach you once you've earned their trust," Punita said, as if trying to cheer him. "In the meantime, watch the children tomorrow and see if you can spot the ones in the Game."

"I will," he said, brightening. "Now tell me about the singing. You said 'before they start singing', the winner of the Game is announced."

"Ah, yes!" Punita straightened, and began another lengthy explanation, this time about the musicality of her people.

"At the end of most days, everyone assembles around their cooking fires for a hot meal and, once the meal is cleared, the entertainment begins. While they clear away the meal, the women warm up their voices, humming and yodelling, practicing as a chorus, or rehearsing words for a new song.

"The men bring their musical instruments, and lovingly open the tattered boxes that have been handed down from father to

162

son. Slowly, the women and children join them around the community fire.

"The singing begins with favourite songs, and everyone sings together. The performers exercise their vocal cords, and the children learn the words and music of traditional songs. Many of the ballads tell the tales and history of the nomads. Aside from being favoured songs, the words are meant to help everyone remember who they are and where they've come from.

"As evenings progress, individual talents became more evident. The actors might rehearse a new play. Singers and musicians wander around the community fire, serenading the gathering. Sometimes they wander alone; sometimes together in a small group, taking turns at performing.

"The best of the musicians add a flourish to their music, by applying a special technique that is exclusive to nomads. The technique is called *vibrato* and adds half tones—called semitones—in between notes. Vibrato, a fast variation in pitch, produces a

163

stronger, richer tone to the music. The style of music is unique and takes years to perfect. It can make the music quite lively and bring energy to the gathering." Punita's eyes sparkled as she recalled the excitement she felt during those evenings.

"How remarkable," Stefan said when Punita sat back, folding her hands in her lap. "I look forward to seeing—and hearing—the performances tomorrow. For now, let's dress and do something fun together."

"All right, but," she hesitated, "I left my clothes down stairs. I can't go walking about the hotel in this," she said, fingering the gossamer fabric she had worn the night before.

"I wonder," Stefan said, opening the door to the stairwell leading down to Mathilde's room.

"Ha!" He bent down and retrieved a pile of neatly folded clothing and two pairs of shoes. "God bless Mathilde!"

CHAPTER FOURTEEN

O n their way out, they passed Alexi's office.

"Stefan!" he called to them.

Stefan and Punita entered his office and approached the red wood desk where he sat, paper work strewn across the green ink blotter. He placed a fountain pen carefully to the side of the blotter.

"Punita, were you able to complete your packing yesterday?" He spoke to them as if their night together had never happened.

"Yes. I have just a few more things to add to the case."

Alexi retrieved his billfold from the pocket of his jacket hanging behind the office door.

"Here," he said, handing a wad of bills to Stefan. "Take Punita shopping and buy what she'll need for travelling."

Stefan slid the wad of bills into his bill-fold, stowed the billfold in his jacket pocket and took Punita's hand.

"Thanks, Father. See you later."

They walked through Liegnitz hand in hand, wandering in and out of shops, purchasing a few extra items that might prepare Punita for the next months and year on the road. By midafternoon, exhaustion began to creep into their bones and their pace slowed.

"Let's go back to the hotel. I could use a cup of tea. And a nap," Punita smiled sweetly, looking up at Stefan through her thick lashes.

"Gosh, I was hoping for something more … spirited," he said, teasing her. He stifled a yawn before reaching his arm around her shoulders.

"You're mad! I can hardly walk!" She pushed him, and he playfully staggered a few steps away from her.

✢

In the lounge of the hotel, they sat next to each other on a settee and ordered tea and savoury cakes.

"Shall I tell you about our family talent?" she asked, a defiant spark in her eyes. "And no, it is not what you think."

"I'm all ears," he said, adding a lump of sugar to his tea.

She told him that, in addition to learning the Game, every young woman was expected to learn other skills that could be employed as entertainment, such as music or acting.

"The women in my family are renowned for their art of fortune telling—reading crystal balls and palms, interpreting tarot cards, observing human nature, and of making potions for ailments and for love. And, they each had their own unique vardo for conducting their business.

"The Reading wagons become part of entertainment alley whenever the vista participates in a fair, but they can also be pulled off to the side of a trail and opened for business while the remainder of the caravan passes on. Stopping during a migration is helpful. People don't always have coin for

167

payment. Sometimes they pay with a basket or bunch of vegetables, a cured meat, a brace of rabbits, a small fowl or a chicken, occasionally a basket of eggs."

"You know," Stefan said, as she finished her explanation, "Father and I are very fortunate. We want for nothing. If we are tired, we sleep in our bed. If we're hungry, we eat. And our business comes to us. It's not so easy when you travel, is it?" he asked.

"No," she answered. "Sometimes, we might go days without meat, but we always share so everyone has food in their belly."

"Well," he said, taking her hands in his and raising them to his lips. "At the end of the next year, you will never have to worry again. Nor will your parents, should they ever choose to give up their wheels."

His eyes twinkled with love.

"In the meantime," he said, sitting straighter, "do you think I might have my fortune read tomorrow? I'd like confirmation that I will be the happiest man in the world for the rest of my life."

168

✦

Punita directed Cousin Alexi to a grassy space under a nearby tree, where he could park his van, then guided him and Stefan to her family's ledge. They spotted Nicolai conversing with several men and she led them to the group. Nicolai offered introductions, then separated from the men to walk his guests to his own vardo where Rosalee awaited. She was dressed in her costume, ornate in colour and trimmed in jewels and golden disks.

"Mama, how beautiful!" Punita said, turning her mother about. "A new costume. It's so dazzling!"

Rosalee blushed at the compliment.

"I worked on it over the summer and this is the first occasion I've had to wear it."

"Punita, why don't you escort Stefan through the camp?" Nicolai suggested.

"I'd like that very much, sir."

"Then, let's go!" Punita exclaimed, taking Stefan's arm and leading him off.

169

✥

Stefan and Punita walked hand in hand, comfortable with their new-found intimacy. They stood out amongst the caravan folk who, at first glance, thought them to be misguided fairgoers. On second look, they recognized Punita and greeted her and her betrothed with sincere welcome.

Punita introduced Stefan to Samson and his wife, marvelling at the three children produced in the time she had been away, and congratulated them on the one yet-to-be-born. Quietly, Samson assured Punita that his children would never know the terror he and his siblings had suffered at the hands of his father.

If no one stopped them, Punita and Stefan continued to wander through the camp and, as they walked, she reminded him of the stories she had shared during the past six years, thus providing a context that would help him understand. She took him to the horse paddock where they encountered Helwig and heard of his marriage and young family.

"And I understand that you have been learning the responsibilities of the kris from Hanzi," Punita said.

"Hanzi has been very generous with his time and knowledge," Helwig responded. "His contribution to the vista has been as invaluable as those of your parents. I for one will miss working with him."

"Why? What has happened?" Punita asked.

"He told me just this morning that he will be stepping down the next time we set up camp," Helwig replied. "I suppose there'll be an election before the fair starts."

"I hope you plan to put your name forward," Punita said encouragingly. "I think you'd be a very just kris!"

Helwig ducked his head, muttering his thanks at her compliment.

Talk shifted then to the horses. When Punita called out to Bang, he trotted over to the fence, whinnying and tossing his head.

"Ha!" she said, grabbing his halter and

hugging his muzzle. "I thought you'd forget me, old man."

Bang tossed his head, grunting.

"You might be six years older," she said to him, "but you haven't changed your attitude. Although, horse, stud life seems to suit you."

She laughed when Bang nodded his head and pawed the dirt in response. Her comment had a double edge, and, still smiling, she peered at Stefan covertly to see if he caught her meaning. He stroked her back in acknowledgement.

When Stefan extended his knuckles to greet the stallion, Bang lunged. Startled, he snatched his hand out of reach of gnashing teeth.

"I warned you the first time you met him," Punita said laughing. "Bang can be a nasty creature."

From the paddock, the young couple meandered toward entertainment alley. Stefan was familiar with the alley, having gone to the fair each year with his father.

On the heels of Punita's tour, however, he viewed the alley and the entertainers with more appreciation.

✤

"Ah, here we are," Punita said, stopping outside an ornately decorated wagon with the words 'Learn your future. Hear your fortune.' painted on the sides.

Punita's aunt stood at the foot of the steps waiting for her next patron. She winked at Punita.

"Tell your fortune sir?" she beckoned.

Stefan hesitated, and turned to Punita with a questioning look. She shrugged indicating that it was his decision.

"How much?" he asked.

"Well," she said slyly, "we usually charge the handsome ones a bit more. But, today I am feeling generous. You're a friend of Punita's, I see."

"We're to be married next year," he said with enthusiasm.

Punita stood silent, letting her aunt tease him.

"Then, you must let me tell your fortune without cost," she crooned. "Come inside."

She swept her arm toward the steps, inviting him into her Reading wagon.

Punita followed and sat on a low stool near the door. Her aunt shut the door and moved toward the table located in the centre of the kite. It was close inside, dim with lit candles and burning incense. Her aunt motioned for Stefan to take the available chair. She sat on the other side of the table facing him.

The table was covered with a deep blue cloth. Her crystal ball sat in its middle. On her right, at the corner of the table sat the square of black cloth covering her tarot cards. She carefully lifted the crystal ball and its base to her left, covering it with the black fabric. She then picked up the stack of tarot cards and started shuffling them. As she did so, she scrutinized the young man seated opposite.

Stefan twisted his body toward Punita.

"I feel like a bug under a magnifying glass," he whispered.

174

"You are a fine-looking young man," Punita's aunt said, recapturing his attention. "Have you been treating my niece well?"

"Y-your niece?" Stefan gulped, turning to look at Punita.

Punita giggled involuntarily and quickly covered her mouth with her hand. Her expressive face reminded him that she had described her family's business on other occasions.

"Ah. I believe that Punita may not have told you everything," she said, looking at him through long black lashes. "Let's see what the cards will tell you instead."

Punita's aunt placed some of the cards carefully in front of Stefan and the reading began. As the cards were exposed, her aunt interpreted for Stefan, dealt more, had him retrieve some himself.

In the end, the fortune was promising. Stefan would be successful in a business that he would build with his father. He would have a wonderful family—a boy and a girl, no the girl first—and his wife would bring him great happiness. All seemed very promising until the last cards. Her aunt paused, collected up the cards and set them aside.

She sat quietly for a moment and asked for his hands, palms up. She passed her index finger feather-light over the lines in his hands and frowned. Then she gently moved the crystal ball back to the centre of the table, placing the black square over the cards.

Again, Punita's aunt sat quietly, and when she began speaking, her voice sounded detached as if it was floating in and around the room.

"Danger comes," she said. "You must take great care and keep your wits about you. If you escape the danger, your life will be as I said. If you do not take care, all will be lost."

At her words, Punita felt the walls of the wagon close in on her. Stefan's next words steadied her.

"Will I know this danger when I see it?" he asked, leaning toward the table.

He had been listening in silence and smiling as Punita's aunt foretold his future. His smile was gone.

"Perhaps. You may hear of it before it finds you. Its shape may not be obvious. It will harm you. How you react will determine whether you live ... or die."

The words of Punita's aunt were said with certainty. Her dark eyes focussed on Stefan.

"You must leave now. You and your father must go. Danger comes. You are not safe here."

She rose and stepped toward the door. The door to the kite opened, letting in blinding daylight.

"Go now. Find your father!" she insisted.

Punita and Stefan flitted down the stairs, both of them stunned by her aunt's harsh words.

"What did your aunt mean with that last bit?" he asked. "I thought she was having a bit of fun with the cards, but when she started talking about danger, she became so serious. She is certainly dramatic. Almost scary!"

He was laughing as he looked at Punita, but she was not laughing.

"Stefan, we must find your father at once!"

Punita grabbed Stefan's hand and began to run. They found their fathers sitting on a bench outside the Kota ledge. They were deep in a conversation. It was rare that her father smoked, and she had never seen cousin Alexi smoke, but each of them held a cheroot from which vapours rose and curled around them on the lazy breeze. She knew that when her father held a cheroot, the situation was serious.

When the men looked up at their children, their eyes were seeing something else. They each took a moment to mask their thoughts before they welcomed Punita and Stefan.

Punita waved her hand to clear the lingering smoke.

"Papa, what is it?" she said, her wrinkled nose expressing distaste. "Mama won't like that you're smoking. You know she gets ill from the smell."

The two men dropped the cheroots and stomped them under their boot toes.

Stefan found two stools and they sat with their fathers, sharing their adventures.

"It was a little troubling, Papa, the way Punita's aunt spoke at the end. About the danger, I mean. I can't imagine what she meant. I am not aware of any danger."

The fathers glanced at one another.

"Perhaps," Alexi said, "we should leave now, Stefan. Take some minutes to say good-bye to Punita. Then we must be off. Be back in, say, fifteen minutes."

Nicolai listened as his cousin spoke and interrupted before Stefan and Punita departed.

"My sister is correct. Trouble is coming. We must take the wagons away." His look was serious.

"We will leave before daylight. Go now and say your good-byes. Alexi and I have a few more details to sort through," he said, dismissing them.

✧

Stefan let Punita lead him to a quiet place on the far side of the horse paddock. They sat in the shade of a sycamore tree, on a fallen log overlooking the lake. They talked about their life together and their two children, first a girl and then a boy.

"A year seems such a long time," she said.

"Yes, but it is a small price to pay for an entire lifetime together," he answered.

"Promise?"

"I promise," he said.

They held each other close and he kissed her with enough kisses to last the year. Separating to catch their breath, Stefan looked into Punita's tear-filled eyes.

"Your eyes glisten like melted chocolate."

He kissed each salty eyelid and then her quivering mouth once again, then they rose from the log and hand-in-hand went in search for their parents.

"Stefan, what do you think this danger is that our fathers speak of?"

"Truthfully, I can't imagine. I will spend the next year in the youth military but, given the current political climate, that's not a complete surprise. I'm disappointed about university, of course. But there will be time afterward for that. Besides, there's no real danger with the youth military. It's just training," he mused. "Your aunt's warning puzzles me too. This danger is likely the imaginations of old men. I'll be fine. We'll be fine."

He shrugged the concern away, putting his arm across her shoulders and kissing the top of her head with reassurance.

They were quiet for a moment, then Punita asked, "So, did you spot the children playing the Game?"

"I don't think so. I thought for a moment that I spied something a while ago but can't be certain. What about you? After six years away, could you find it?"

"Yup! That boy there," she pointed to a boy leaving the nearby paddock, "has it just now."

181

She waved at the boy and beckoned him to come closer. In a whisper, she asked him to reveal the token. He stepped close to them, looked around to be certain no one else would see and with a deft hand retrieved the object from his pocket, which he quickly concealed again, before running back to the camp.

"Amazing!" was all Stefan could say.

✧

When they reached the ledge, Punita saw that Alexi was already climbing into his van, one foot in and the opposite hand holding the door. Nicolai's hand rested on Alexi's shoulder. Seeing Punita and Stefan approaching, Alexi stepped away from the van and opened his arms to Punita, inviting her to share a farewell embrace.

"Take care, my friend," he said to Nicolai. "Stay free of harm and we'll see you again in a year. My son will be ready for his beautiful bride by then. Punita, my dear, God keep you safe. Stefan, in the van, we must go."

Punita stood next to her father, mute, tears trickling down her cheeks. Together, they raised their hands in farewell, and the van drove off, leading billowing clouds of dust as it disappeared into the forest.

"Oh, Papa," Punita sobbed. "Oh, Papa."

She turned and buried her face into his comforting chest. His arms held her tight.

CHAPTER FIFTEEN

Nicolai went in search of the kris and asked him to call an emergency meeting of the vista as soon as the fair ended. When everyone was assembled, Nicolai addressed them.

"My friends, we had a visitor this afternoon who brought some disturbing news. The government has ordered that all non-citizens be rounded up and detained. Those without identification papers are to be seized and held indefinitely. Camps are being built for long-term detention. We must get away from here as quickly—and as quietly—as possible." He paused, allowing them an opportunity to absorb his words.

"You mean no rattling pots, I take it!" a woman remarked.

"Precisely!" he answered with a grin.

"Separate and travel in small groups. Small groups travel faster and, hopefully, won't merit notice. I won't tell you where to go. Nowhere is safe." He paused again. "If you have papers, keep them safe and with you at all times."

He gazed upon the crowd, trying to convey the peril that faced them.

"Expect to be travelling for some time. And be careful! Trust no one," he warned.

"How can you be so trusting of the information you were given?" a wary male voice enquired.

"Herr Puchinski brought us word himself!" Nicolai answered. "For those of you who don't know, Puchinski's mother was one of our people. When she married his father, she stayed with him in Liegnitz and they built a life there. Puchinski has always been a friend of our people. His word is reliable and trustworthy. He would never betray us. In fact, he took great risk speaking with me today."

Nicolai peered into the eyes of each man and woman for emphasis.

"We must hurry. But be discrete."

Before the gathering dispersed, Nicolai stopped them again.

"Before dark, we will meet one last time. Each family will receive its share of the treasury and the horses, and we will pray."

The vista burst into anxious activity, pulling down entertainment alley, packing wagons, collecting treasury shares and horse allotments and praying. As darkness settled on the grove, the caravan fractured. Parties began to roll out, alone or in small groups.

Nicolai's wagon would be the last to leave. He wandered through the circle offering words of encouragement to each family as they withdrew. He embraced Hanzi, his long-time friend, and dispatched words of advice to Samson and his wife.

When the camp was empty, he hitched one of his horses to Rosalee's kite and, by the light of a half-moon, drove it deep into the forest. Rosalee and Punita helped him cover it with an old tarpaulin, branches and brush, until they could no longer see it.

"Good-bye, my friend," Rosalee placed her hand lovingly on the side of the kite. "Stay safe until we meet again."

She buried her face into Nicolai's chest and sobbed.

"Punita," he said, take the horse. "We'll walk back."

He cupped his hands. Punita grabbed the horse's mane, stepped into her father's hands and bounced upward landing just behind its withers. Nicolai handed her the reins and smacked the sleek rump. Punita and the horse trotted off toward the camp, while Nicolai and Rosalee embraced their sorrow, and returned walking hand-in-hand.

The ledge rolled through the forest with barely a creak. Rosalee had fastened anything that rattled or clanged, and Nicolai had oiled the axles and tack. Some noises could not be stopped, but, where possible, they had been muffled. The Kota share of the horses, including Bang, had been secured to the rear of the vardo and trailed behind.

They skirted cities and towns and headed northeast, toward Schinawa on the Oder River. They travelled in the dark, thankful for the heavy clothing that protected them from the icy night. If they spoke at all, it was in whispers.

As the sky turned blood orange in the frosty morning, Nicolai looked for a hiding place. He drove the vardo as far into the forest as its width would allow, and covered it with branches, thankful that its earthy colours made it easier to hide than Rosalee's red and gold kite. Punita hobbled the horses nearby and blindfolded them to keep them quiet. They ate cold food and drank icy water—no fire, no smoke, no cooking odours.

Rosalee tucked Punita into her bed, rubbing her feet to warm them first, then covering them with socks—something she had done when Punita was small—and gave her extra blankets to keep her warm through the chill of the day.

"Nicolai, where are we going?" Rosalee whispered as they snuggled into their cold bed.

"I won't tell you much, just yet," he whispered back. "The less you know, the safer you'll be. What I can tell you is that I hope to connect with my cousin Konstantin Anker, or his brother Zabar. They operate coastal freighters along the Oder River. At this time of year, one of them should be nearing Schinawa. Overall, our destination is Amsterdam."

He kissed his wife on the forehead and held her in his arms. He slept little, as did Rosalee.

They rested through the daylight hours, dozing when they could, worrying when they could not. At twilight, they rose again. Nicolai permitted a small fire and Rosalee prepared a warm meal. In the meantime, Punita helped her father hitch a horse to the ledge for another night's travel. By moonrise, they were rolling through the countryside.

Near sunrise, Nicolai searched the forest for another safe place, where again they hid the ledge, hobbled and blindfolded the horses, consumed a cold meal, and crawled into their beds. At twilight, they rose and Rosalee prepared a warm meal, while Nicolai prepared to leave for Schinawa in search of Konstantin and Zabar, and a buyer for the horses.

"Cook only after dark," he warned them, "and do it quickly. If you speak, do so in whispers. And, if you must leave the vardo, be careful. Anyone could be watching. If I'm not back in five days, walk into Schinawa and look for Konstantin or Zabar, and the freighter. Be careful. Note your surroundings."

"But, how will we find you?" Rosalee asked.

"My dear," he said, caressing her face in one hand, "if I am not back in five days, there is a strong chance I won't be back."

His thumb caught the lone tear that trickled from the corner of her eye.

"Be brave," he said, "for all of us."

Nicolai hugged Rosalee and Punita to

him for a long moment, then mother and daughter clung together, watching as he led the string of horses into the dark.

The women tidied up the remains of their meal, ensured that the ledge was camouflaged as best they could, then climbed back inside.

For three days, they huddled together in the heatless wagon, venturing out only when necessary or to cook the evening meal. Their rations were running low, and they worried for Nicolai's safety.

Early in the morning of the fourth day, Punita and Rosalee froze at the sound of crackling branches and heavy footsteps. Rosalee reached for a cast iron frying pan and handed a heavy pot to Punita. She crept to the side of the door and braced the iron skillet over her head, ready to strike the intruder. Punita stood further back waiting to reinforce her mother's first blow.

They heard measured footsteps on the stairs, felt the wagon shift with the intruder's weight, and watched the handle of the door turn. Hearts pounding, they steadied their weapons. They exchanged one last terrified look then focussed on the door. The door opened slowly, providing Punita a clear view of the doorway. Rosalee raised the skillet higher, preparing to swing with weight behind her motion.

❖

"Papa!" Punita screamed in a loud whisper, dropping her pot on her bed and running into her father's arms.

Rosalee set down her skillet and embraced her husband and daughter.

"We've been so worried," she said.

Nicolai squeezed them both firmly, quietly expressing his relief to find his women safe. He reported that he had found Konstantin, and sold the horses, and that it was time for them to leave for Schinawa. He told them to take only those things that were necessary.

He left the wagon and returned a few minutes later with an armload of clothing.

"What is this?" Rosalee asked.

"Do we not have clothing enough?"

"The roads are not safe, my dear. Especially for beautiful women." He looked lovingly at his wife and daughter. "The farmer who bought the horses loaned us one of his carts. We need to look like poor farm hands."

"But Nicolai, these clothes are torn and filthy."

"Precisely. We want to look like farm hands who have been working in a field." He held up his arms and turned around. "Have you not noticed?"

"Well, yes, I did," Rosalee said, her voice flat, "but I thought you might have had to sell your clothes too. I've never seen you so unkempt. Your beard is a mess!"

Punita covered her mouth as if to suppress a giggle. Catching her eye, Nicolai shoved two straw hats at her, and dropped boots on the floor.

"Farm hands," he said more firmly. "Now! And tie your hair up tightly. You're to pass as young men."

✥

He left the wagon again, giving them space to prepare for the journey. When they emerged a short time later, he bit the inside of his cheek so as not to laugh.

"Somewhere under those hats, I think I have a wife and a daughter. Did I not know it, I would be looking for a grain field and a pole on which to hang the two of you." Chuckling, he took the bundles they carried. "Well done, my little scarecrows!"

"Punita! Why is your parcel so heavy?" he asked. "I said a few items."

"Papa, please. I can't leave my birthday clothes behind. Alexi bought me a beautiful wool suit and a matching hat, so I look smart when I apply for work. Stefan gave me shoes, gloves, and a handbag to match. I'll need them, Papa!" she begged.

Nicolai groaned, and stowed the parcels under the bench of a rickety cart waiting near their vardo.

"One last thing to do," he said, "but we need to be inside."

He gestured toward the ledge's staircase. The women climbed in behind him. From a bag he carried with him, Nicolai withdrew three cloth belts, then he retrieved the treasury box from the cupboard and took a leather bag from a pocket in his jacket. He handed each of them identification papers, then counted out the money that was their share of the treasury, which he then divided into three portions. He slid a portion and a belt across the table to each of them. Next, he emptied the contents of the leather bag.

"The horses," he said forlornly, watching the money fall from the leather bag.

"The farmer thinks he paid a good price for them, but he has no idea of their true value. Bang alone is worth more than what he paid. If only we could take them with us ..." he lamented.

Then he took a deep breath and split the farmer's money into three portions as well, dealing a portion to each.

"Between us, we should have enough money to start again when we reach

Amsterdam. But, I want each of us to carry a share. That way, if anything happens to one of us, the others will still have money. Put your jewellery in the belt as well. We don't want to attract attention of any sort."

He showed them how to put the money and the jewellery into the belts, and to tie their belts around their waists.

"Keep your papers handy, in a secure jacket pocket. You don't want to lose them."

When Punita released the clasp of her necklace, she hefted the weight of the emerald in her palm and held her hand toward her mother.

"No, child," Rosalee said, curling her fingers around Punita's. "The necklace is yours. You carry it in your belt."

When the belts were securely fastened, they tucked their shirts into their trousers and tied their trousers tightly with a piece of rope, then donned a heavy wool jacket.

"Oh, I feel so ..." Rosalee lamented, pausing as if searching for a descriptive word. She scratched her arms and shuddered.

"Dirty? Itchy? Stinky?" Punita offered suggestions.

"Enough, you two. Let's go," Nicolai said, biting the inside of his cheek again, "my little scarecrows."

Mother and daughter both glared at him, then huffed down the stairs.

"A rickety chariot for my little scarecrows!"

Nicolai bowed low from the waist and, in answer to their questioning glances, swept his arm toward the farmer's cart. He helped them into the cart, and showed them where he had stowed their bundles, in a cupboard under the bench.

"The farm hands use the cupboard to stow shovels and other tools. Keep this space clear," he told Punita, indicating the remaining space under the bench.

"If we are challenged in any way, you are to hide in there," he pointed under the seat, "and do not come out until I say so. Sit on this crate for now, but ... if you do need to hide, pull the crate across the opening and your hiding place will be concealed."

"Yes, Papa," Punita said, shivering.

The bed of the cart held crates, mostly empty, except for loose bits of cabbage— dregs of a crop that had likely been transported to market recently.

"Nicolai!" Rosalee protested. "Could you not have found a cleaner, sturdier wagon?"

"The worse we look, the less likely we are to be challenged," he said, flicking the reins.

The nag, not one of his own, leaned into the pull and the rickety cart rambled into the road. Rosalee sat beside Nicolai on the bench, her countenance bearing an expression of despair.

CHAPTER SIXTEEN

The family sat in silence, swaying with the movement of the wagon as the horse's heavy hooves raised dust clouds in the sun-dried dirt road, until Nicolai interrupted their meanderings.

"I spoke with Konstantin," he said.

"He will help us get to Amsterdam. We are to meet him at the dock in Schinawa tomorrow. If we do not arrive by then, he will wait two more days and then he will head north again. He can't linger too long, or the authorities will become suspicious of his activities. We are all in danger. As Alexi warned, the roundup of non-nationals is underway, especially in the cities and towns."

"Dear God, keep us safe," Rosalee prayed, clasping her trembling hands near her heart.

"If we miss Konstantin in Schinawa, we are to travel north along the Oder River. He will look for us at every dock for as long as he can. But, the ship will travel faster than we will be able to travel by foot or wagon, and each time he lingers, he and his crew will be at risk. Konstantin has a licence to work the river, but he must do it in a way that he does not attract attention." He turned to his daughter. "Punita, you were small the last time we met with Konstantin. Do you remember what his freighter looks like?"

"I think so," Punita contemplated. "It's all white, except for the lower part of the hull, which is a deep red, like drying blood before the crust. All of the trim is silver. And the name is painted on the bow, something to do with a shell."

"Well done, my daughter! You have always had a quick mind and a good memory. I'm proud of you!"

He paused to capture his thoughts.

"Many coastal freighters have a similar shape and white is a common-enough colour. The name will help you distinguish her from others. Konstantin's ship is the *Silver Oyster*, hence the shell. There is one other distinguishing feature to keep in mind. He usually flies the flag of our people, two stripes: green on the bottom representing earth and blue on the top representing heaven. In the centre is the red chakra. When you look for the ship, make certain you see the flag. If you don't see it, trouble may be afoot. You'll need to proceed with caution."

The horse plodded along, the creaking of the wagon the only sound for several minutes.

"Can you describe Konstantin, Punita?" Nicolai asked.

"Yes, Papa. He looks just like you, except that his hair and beard are lighter than yours, and he is not so handsome as you!"

"Ah, the loyalty of a wise daughter! I appreciate your sentiments, my dear, but we all know that Konstantin is the better-looking one. Not by much though," Nicolai said, one side of his mouth turning upward in a half-grin.

Nicolai slid his hand into the pocket of his pants and retrieved a scrap of paper. On it, he had drawn a map of where they were going and the safest route for travel, by wagon and by foot. He reviewed with his wife and daughter all things necessary to keep them safe and help them reach Konstantin in the event they encountered any trouble along the way.

Nicolai reminded them both of the hours that he had spent training them to defend themselves, how to hide and how to run. Danger had been part of their life style and he had done all he could to ensure that they would always be safe, especially if he was not with them for protection.

Focussed on Nicolai's words, Punita was slow to notice the tears trickling down her mother's cheeks. Rosalee's sniff startled her.

"Mama, why are you crying?"

Rosalee shook her head as if to say it

mattered not. Nicolai reached over and cupped Rosalee's cheek, stroking the tears with his thumb and leaving a dirty streak in their place.

"You both look so worried … and so sad," Punita said, her voice quivering.

Several minutes later Rosalee confirmed Punita's suspicion.

"Nicolai, I am so afraid," she said, her words barely audible.

Punita had been anxious since they broke camp and fled in the night, but there was something in Rosalee's voice that escalated her fear. Nicolai reached his arm around Rosalee and hugged her to him.

'We'll be fine," he said, seemingly without conviction. Punita too was unconvinced.

⁜

Nicolai kept the horse moving northeast along dirt farming roads, pulling off into the trees if they heard anything or saw anyone. Progress was slow but steady, and by late morning they could see the spires of the Schinawa churches on the horizon.

Not long after, Nicolai was alerted to
something amiss when the horse's ears
perked forward, its head nodding time with
soft anxious snorts. He slowed the horse to
a quiet plod, signaling for Punita to duck
into the cupboard below the bench. It was
too late to avoid an encounter with the
uniformed men, who soon came into view.

Three military trucks were parked at
the side of the dirt road and nine armed
men milled about, drinking bottled bev-
erages and eating bread and cheese. The
approach of the rickety cart startled them
into action.

Three of the men whipped their rifles
from their shoulders and took aim at the
two farmhands seated on the cart. A fourth
man, older and more authoritative, set his
beverage and bread aside. Standing, he
brushed the crumbs from his uniform and
narrowed his eyes at the intruders.

"Who are you!" the officer demanded.

Nicolai, having been forewarned by
the horse, nodded and removed his hat

deferentially, clutching it to his chest. Rosalee lowered her head, allowing her hat to obscure her face.

"Good day to you, officer! Just a couple of farm hands returning a wagon," Nicolai slurred in the local dialect.

The officer indicated to two of the other men to inspect the wagon. They sauntered around it and peered under it.

"Nothing untoward," said one of them.

"Just some rotting cabbage leaves."

"Well enough," said the officer. "Be on your way. But take heed. It's not safe to be travelling these roads."

"Yes sir. Appreciate the warning."

Nicolai replaced his hat, flipped the reins and clucked to the horse to move off.

Half an hour later, Nicolai knocked on the seat and Punita slowly unfolded from the hollow beneath.

"Oh, Papa, that was f-f-frightening!" she said, shakily resuming her seat on the crate.

While they discussed the experience and how important it was to be ever vigilant for danger, the time and distance to Schinawa passed quickly.

An hour later, Nicolai found another sheltered spot where tall trees encroached the edge of the road on both sides, their great bows reaching across the road forming an arch of autumn colours. The air crackled with the dust of decaying leaves. Nicolai stopped the wagon long enough to stretch and eat. It was then that he told the women of his plan to leave them with Konstantin while he returned the horse and cart to the farmer in the morning.

A while later, the wagon rattled past Schinawa's red brick train station, through the town, and down a gradual slope where the road wound toward the river. Nicolai's family was well within the time needed to keep Konstantin free of suspicion from the port authorities. The three of them relaxed knowing that soon they would be safely aboard the *Silver Oyster*.

"Remember: vigilance!" Nicolai cautioned again, as the horse lumbered toward the river.

CHAPTER SEVENTEEN

Twice a year, Captain Konstantin Anker met with Gerhard Lange, a farmer from Liegnitz. He would moor the freighter at the dock in Schinawa and await the arrival of Herr Lange and the farm goods he would bring: canned fruits and vegetables, jams, cheese and Schmidt sausages. On alternate occasions and also twice a year, Konstantin's brother Captain Zabar Anker would meet Herr Lange's brother-in-law, Otto Schmidt, for the same purpose. Konstantin and his brother welcomed the trade with Lange and Schmidt. The tasty sausages made by the Schmidt family were favourites in Dutch markets.

Konstantin paced the deck of his ship, anxious for Gerhard to arrive before he returned north. He did not want to miss the last trade of 1934, not knowing whether there would be another opportunity, given the current political climate in Germany.

He barked at the crew to hasten the stowing of goods while he waited. The chill of the October day made their labour easier.

✧

Late in the morning, Gerhard's truck rolled to a stop above the dock, and Konstantin rushed to greet him.

"What is it, my friend? Are you in a hurry?" Gerhard asked, spying the industrious activity on the freighter, and extending his hand to the Captain.

"Unfortunately, I'm pressed for time this trip," Konstantin accepted Gerhard's hand and gave his right arm a friendly jab. "We are returning north tomorrow morning, so I have the crew working double time to ensure our cargo is sorted and stowed. I can't tell you how pleased I am that you've arrived as you have. I would hate to return to Amsterdam without Schmidt's famous sausages. The distributors would have my hide!"

The men shared a knowing chuckle.

"You must promise never to tell Schmidt how desirable his sausages are. He would increase the price and I would never be able to afford them!"

"I won't. My brother-in-law's head is fat enough with the demand by our local suppliers! He raises the price for them, but I insist that the price for you be kept reasonable," Gerhard said.

"Paul, my boy!" Konstantin said greeting Gerhard's son. "You've grown since last year. You're turning into a fine young man."

Paul glanced at him shyly.

"Here," Konstantin said, flipping a coin in Paul's direction. "You have time to find a sweet. Off you go, while your father and I do some business."

Paul thanked him in a squeaky adolescent voice, looked to his father for permission to leave, and disappeared quickly up the ramp.

"Have you any lace with you, Konstantin?"

"I set aside a few bundles, and some other items that your family might like. Come below."

⚜

Konstantin and Gerhard stood on the deck, watching Paul meander along the road from town. Gerhard checked his pocket watch and waved to hasten his son's return. Paul jogged toward the dock, almost colliding with a dilapidated cart that had drawn to a halt on the road way above. At sight of the cart, Konstantin tipped his cap to Gerhard.

"Excuse me. This fellow will need directions." He nodded toward the cart.

Marching along the ramp to the dock, Konstantin steadied Paul as they passed midway. Konstantin rumpled the boy's ebony hair.

"Look like your father, you do! You'll have the girls chasing you soon enough."

Paul's cheeks burnt crimson in response.

⚜

On the dock, Konstantin greeted Nicolai and his family with affection. He then

directed Nicolai to a nearby barn where the
horse and cart could be stabled for the night.

"We'll have a meal at a tavern up the
road," he said pointing, "while we wait
for the sun to set. It will be safer to unload
the wagon after dark when prying eyes are
hampered."

Nicolai nodded and flipped the reins,
putting the cart in motion once again.

"Ladies," Konstantin whispered to
Rosalee and Punita, "follow me."

As he escorted them along the ramp, he
described his vessel.

"The *Silver Oyster* is a coastal freighter,
built to carry fifteen hundred tons of cargo
in her holds."

He pointed to the name painted on the
bow—bold writing inside a gaping oyster
shell of mahogany and silver. The same
work was artfully repeated across the stern.

"She employs a crew of six, all experienced in the sailing of a motor vessel one
hundred metres long. She has two masts,"
he said, again pointing as he described the

layout of his ship, "one towering over each of the holds and supporting an intricate web of rigging and booms for loading and discharging cargo. The wheelhouse and cabins sit midships at the top of the super-structure, forward of the smoke stack. And, her profile is low enough to allow safe passage under the bridges."

"She's lovely," Rosalee said, "and I can hear in your voice that you are proud to command her."

"I am that, yes!" Konstantin said, then stopped at the end of the ramp and handed them onto the deck.

Once aboard, Konstantin lead them toward two men who had been watching their arrival.

They were tall men with the stature of soldiers, although the younger one looked too young to actually be enlisted in the military. Their appearance seemed to make Rosalee jittery.

"Gerhard Lange, may I introduce my cousin-in-law, Rosalee Kota, and her daughter, Punita?" Turning to his guests, he introduced Gerhard and Paul.

Paul's gaze held Punita's until she blushed and looked away.

"Paul!" Gerhard interrupted the stare, at the same time giving Konstantin a look of enquiry.

"My cousins have been travelling through the countryside, which, as you can well appreciate, is currently unsafe. They thought it best to use the disguise."

Turning to Rosalee, Konstantin suggested that she and Punita go below-deck.

"You'll find my first mate, Tomas, working down there. Introduce yourself and he'll help you. I'll be along presently to explain things."

"Well, we must be off," Gerhard said. "We'll leave you to your business. Paul ..." Gerhard gave his head a side-ways jerk indicating that Paul should precede him up the ramp. Paul said good-bye to Konstantin and departed.

"Konstantin, I won't ask what the business is, but I caution you to take great care. Life is too uncertain these days. Your journey on the river may be in danger," Gerhard said in confidence. "Be mindful of port authorities, dock crew, and especially Sturmabteilung."

"Sturmabteilung?"

"Yes, they're still Hitler's thugs, but they're travelling in small packs now. People have been referring to them as 'Brown Shirts'. Regardless of the name, they can be sinister and vicious."

"Thank you, my friend. I will heed your warning as we return north. Safe journey to you."

"And to you, Konstantin. Fair winds and following seas. Till we meet again."

They shook hands affectionately, then Gerhard followed in Paul's wake.

On the dock, Gerhard put his arm around Paul and turned him toward their old farm truck.

⚜

"Punita, do you recognize those men? I think we've met them before," Rosalee whispered below deck.

"No, Mama, but we've met so many people at fairs that it's hard for me to say."

"Yes, but they stand out somehow. They have an obvious family resemblance—tall, blue-black hair, almond-shaped charcoal eyes. They could be brothers, but for the bit of grey at Herr Lange's temples. They look like gentry, or soldiers. Perhaps they are just farmers, as Konstantin said, given their tanned arms."

"Wait! Did you say Lange?"

"I believe so. Do you know the name?" Rosalee asked.

"The other day, when Stefan and I rode out for the picnic, Stefan mention a friend as we rode past his home. I think Stefan said his name was Paul." She tapped her lip with a dainty forefinger. "Yes! That's it! He said his friend was Paul Lange. How curious that Konstantin should know him."

Then, mercurial, she changed the subject.

"Mama, I wish I could wear my new suit ..."

"No, you can't. You heard what Konstantin said. It's safer for us to stay as we are. We can worry about our clothes tomorrow."

"I heard," Punita said with a petulant grumble.

"And then he said 'Besides, if you smell a little, folks will be less inclined to approach you!'"

She wrinkled her nose and sniffed at her armpit.

"Do we really smell?"

"Punita, stop!" Rosalee snapped. *Why, he's the young man who came for a reading the last time we were in Liegnitz! I remember now ... I warned him about war, and brown eyes.* Her gaze rested on Punita's dark brown eyes. *That's it! Somehow there is to be a connection. The paths of our families will cross again! I will have to ask my tarot cards later.*

⊕

"This tavern is so dark, and it reeks of stale ale and tobacco smoke," Rosalee hissed quietly as she walked next to Punita. Her nose twitched, and her hand rose swiftly to stifle a sneeze. "I prefer fresh air!"

"Compared to Cousin Alexi's beautiful hotel, this place is simple, unwelcoming and stale," Punita said, agreeing with her mother.

From her thought of Alexi's hotel, Punita's mind wandered to Stefan and the days before the fair. She allowed herself to dream briefly of the life they would begin together, now less than one year away.

Konstantin led them to a table in the back of the tavern, away from windows and prying eyes. As they wove between tables, Konstantin paused to speak with a serving girl. He asked her to bring "four servings of rabbit stew and bread, three ales and something for the young lady." He cast a look back, indicating Punita. The server nodded and turned toward the kitchen.

Lost in thought, Punita almost missed Konstantin's explanation of the travel yet to come.

"When the sun sets, we'll unload the wagon. The dark will provide the cover we need to avoid prying eyes. Once your things are stowed, we'll turn in for the night. Tomorrow will be a busy day. The crew and I still have lots to do before we push off, including the stowing of Herr Lange's goods."

"I'll be leaving at sunrise to return the wagon to the farmer," Nicolai interjected, "the one you recommended as a trusted friend—and I should be back by mid-morning. What time will you push off?"

"Before noon, if we can manage," Konstantin replied. "Even my old friend, Gerhard, whom I would trust with my life, warned me to take care. Considering his standing in the community and his military experience, I must take his warning seriously."

"Did he speak of the round-up?"

"Yes, he said to be wary of military trucks and Brown Shirts."

Their dinner arrived—bowls of delicately seasoned rabbit stew and fresh baked bread. The welcoming aromas quickly replaced the offensive staleness of the pub's atmosphere. Their mouths watered in anticipation. After a hasty sampling of the stew, Rosalee marvelled at the exotic spices and the sweetness of the vegetables. In response, the men critiqued the ale.

"I'm particularly pleased that it has quenched my parched throat," Nicolai said, sharing a wink with Konstantin.

Punita was thrilled to see a glass of lassi placed in front of her. *It's not pink,* she thought. *I suppose they can't get raspberries here at this time of year.* She sipped it, expecting it to be tart and plain, but noted immediately that it differed from the one her mother made. She offered the glass to Rosalee for a taste.

"That has been flavoured with mashed vanilla beans, and topped with cinnamon," she said.

"Finding vanilla beans and cinnamon is a hard thing to do when we travel all the time, especially these past years. How

219

lovely it is. I wish I had that instead of the ale."

"Konstantin, Punita and I would like to do some shopping in the morning," Rosalee interrupted the men's quiet discussion. "If there's time, that is."

"There will be time. In the morning, I'll give you some suggestions," Konstantin said, pushing his chair away from the table. "Stay and enjoy your meal. I'm going to mingle with the locals to glean the latest news on river conditions and find out what's happening in the city. And...tomorrow, Nicolai, when you return the horse and cart to the farmer, you will be careful, yes? Watch out for those trucks?"

"We ran into some this morning," Nicolai responded, "but we had a plan and it worked. We were waved on."

"Hmm, that concerns me. Have another plan ready for tomorrow too."

"Of course," Nicolai said. "I would do nothing to jeopardize myself or my family." He turned to his wife and daughter.

"Rosalee and Punita are everything to me. Remember that. No matter what befalls us in our travels."

The three ate the remainder of their meal in moderate silence.

"This food is settling nicely in my belly," Punita said.

"Mine too," said Rosalee.

"It has been many days since we last ate so well. But, I can eat no more."

She pushed the bowl of stew from her.

"My stomach is too jittery to enjoy the last."

"I'll just finish my drink," Punita said. "It's so delicious. I hope we find lots of vanilla beans and cinnamon and raspberries in Amsterdam. And I hope the next eleven months pass quickly, so I can be with Stefan again!"

Nicolai and Rosalee exchanged a knowing glance. They had done their best to shelter Punita from harm, although she had been disciplined to handle danger. Except for the long-ago conflict with Samson, she had never been exposed to the serious risks of living as a nomad. Often in the moments before sleeping, Rosalee and Nicolai whispered their hope that Punita would never live to know danger.

CHAPTER EIGHTEEN

The hull of the freighter was broad and deep. Most of it was stacked high with cargo that Konstantin had collected on his journey south along the Oder River, but, during the past few days, he had instructed the crew to shift the cargo and create two discrete rooms, one for Punita and the other for her parents.

"I apologize for the humble accommodations but hope you will be comfortable for the next several days," Nicolai said, a frown shadowing his face. "I thought about giving you cabins, but that would leave you exposed in the event we're challenged."

"I've heard that some folks are so nervous about round-ups, abductions, and Brown Shirts that they're willing to tell lies about their neighbours just to keep themselves and their families safe," Konstantin elaborated.

"I've heard that too," Nicolai said. "And, I've noticed more than one individual avert their eyes when talking to me."

"Like they've something to hide," Rosalee said.

"Precisely! Few can be trusted these days," Konstantin said. "Once we're at sea, you may move to a cabin below the wheelhouse. For now, I hope you can be comfortable below."

He gave them each a torch to light their way along the unusual footing.

"We are grateful for your help, Konstantin," Nicolai responded. "We'll manage."

The smell of hemp, creosote, and spices permeated the artificial rooms. Drafts from the open hatches were blocked by the cargo, but enough air circulated that they were comfortable.

"Sound travels on the water," Konstantin added. "As an extra precaution, keep your voices low. We don't want to attract any attention."

Three heads nodded, acknowledging

Konstantin's instructions and concerns. Konstantin left them to organize their spaces as suited them and went above deck to arrange for their departure by noon the following day.

A while later, Konstantin beckoned them to join him on deck.

"It's time to collect your things from the cart," he said.

Confirming Nicolai's earlier remark, emptying the wagon did not take long. When their few possessions had been stowed, the family returned to the deck to bid Konstantin good night.

Following the day's labour, the captain had released his crew for the evening. Together with his three guests, they watched the men return, their way lit by moonlight.

Konstantin introduced each crewman as they boarded, informing them that the Kota family would be accompanying them to Amsterdam.

"Each of my crew can be trusted,"

Konstantin assured his cousins. "They all have Roma roots."

To a man, they acknowledged their responsibility to the captain and his guests, before bidding them good night.

"The officers and I each have a cabin amidships," Konstantin informed his passengers. "The crew share accommodation in the forecastle."

"We'd best retire as well," Nicolai said, indicating to Rosalee and Punita that they should precede him into the hold.

He shook hands with Konstantin and descended through the hatch, into the darkness.

⚜

As Punita's body relaxed in the safety of the hull, she heard the muffled sounds of her parents. Sounds she now knew well. Despite their movement, the freighter remained steady. Tears slid from the corners of her eyes and tickled past her ears. One hand on her breast and the other on her belly, her thoughts were of Stefan and she yearned for him.

Following the ordeal of their recent travels, the three slept soundly that night, lulled by the river water rhythmically lapping against the ship's hull.

At sunrise, Konstantin rapped on the hatch.

"Nicolai," his voice cast low into the hull, "it's time!"

Rosalee caressed Nicolai's freshly shaven cheek, before he kissed her quickly and clambered up the ladder. He had a brief discussion with Konstantin, accepted a cup of coffee, and headed for the stables.

"The wagon ride to the farm won't take long," he told Konstantin, "but I'll have to walk back. I'm guessing my return could take an hour. I think there's enough foliage left on the trees that the natural colours of my clothes will blend in, providing me with good camouflage. I'll be safe enough."

Regardless, Konstantin warned him once again to go with caution. When the women stepped onto the deck, he invited them to enjoy a more leisurely breakfast. They sat in

227

the galley with him sharing coffee, cheese, and bread, while the morning sun burnt away the chilly river fog.

When the crew began appearing for breakfast, Captain Konstantin gave them orders for stowing the remaining goods. Then he suggested that Punita and Rosalee take their leave, pointing them in the general direction of the bathhouse and dress shops that they had enquired about. He recommended that they purchase clothing that would keep them warm and comfortable both on the river and at sea.

"Trousers might serve you better on the ship," he noted, "and it will be cold on the open sea. While you're in the town try to blend in. Do nothing that will attract attention."

He also told them to either tie their hair securely or cut it.

✥

The bathhouse was near the dock, strategically placed for the convenience of river travellers. It was early enough that Punita and Rosalee were the first patrons. The shop smelled of clean. Steam wafted from behind a door that led off the storefront.

They followed the shopkeeper through the door and down a short hallway. She pointed them toward a room that, after Herr Puchinski's hotel, was rustic, but Punita appreciated it for what it was. She thanked the shopkeeper and closed the door.

Filling the bathtub with hot water, Punita suggested that Rosalee bathe first. While her mother bathed, she washed Rosalee's chestnut hair. When it was Punita's turn to bathe, Rosalee did the same in return.

Punita was excited to finally wear the clothes that Alexi and Stefan had given for her birthday: a smart wool suit in a rich blue colour, brown leather walking shoes with a matching handbag and gloves. The suit came with a blue wool overcoat, and a cloche hat—blue like the coat with a brown ribbon that matched her gloves. The weather did not justify the need for the coat, hat, and gloves, so she had left them on the ship. In contrast, Rosalee donned a simple skirt and blouse, and a heavy sweater. They stuffed the farm clothes into the paper bag that had recently held the clothes they wore.

"These clothes are beyond repair," Rosalee said, jiggling the bag at her side. "I see you have a fire in the yard. Would you mind if we burnt them?"

"Of course," the shopkeeper said. "I'll take care of it, if you like."

"Oh no," Punita said, taking the bag from her mother. "We wouldn't want to trouble you. Mama, why don't you pay the bill and I take care of these." Punita disappeared down the hall and through the door that lead to the garden.

"Can you suggest any nice clothing shops?" Rosalee asked, drawing the shopkeeper's gaze away from Punita. "We'll have to replace those items."

"You must have had some challenging times recently," the shopkeeper suggested. "Have you been travelling?"

Rosalee smiled at the shopkeeper. *Careful what you say!*

"Uh, no. We ran into some weather the other day, and one thing lead to another. It was most unfortunate." She fought to maintain her confidence and resisted dropping her eyes at the lie.

Both women jumped when the garden door banged and grinned bashfully.

"All done," Punita said gaily, as she rejoined them. "Ready to go, Mama?"

CHAPTER NINETEEN

Nicolai stepped from the trees just as the first of three military trucks began to lumber past. He jumped back behind the nearest tree, hoping that he had not been seen. He whipped his fedora from his head and peered around the gnarled bark for a second look, then ducked back again. The second truck slowed, then stopped.

An armed guard jumped from the truck's runner and another exited the passenger's side door.

"Hey. What's this about?" the driver of the third truck hollered.

The first guard held up his hand.

"Wait," he commanded, raising a palm toward the impatient driver.

Nicolai tucked himself tightly behind the tree hoping his leather jacket provided the needed camouflage. His heart pounded. He recognized the trucks as the same ones that had stopped his wagon the day before. *I've been seen. God help me!* Seconds passed: an eternity of not knowing and imagining the worst.

"You there, behind the tree," barked the first guard. "Come out. Now! Hands in the air."

Nicolai did not move. Time passed, measured in his heart beats. He heard a snick as a bullet was loaded into the barrel of the guard's rifle.

"Come out now! We have no time for play," the first guard growled, his voice menacing.

Nicolai hesitated.

"Now! Or I shoot!" The third demand was more threatening.

Nicolai stilled his heart and his hands, weighing his chance of escape against being shot. Knowing that his family waited for him at the pier, a mere ten-minute walk away, any decision he made was risky. *If I run, I'll likely be shot. If I do as ordered, I might have a chance.*

He placed his fedora on his head and tugged the brim low, then stepped away from the tree. Hands in the air, he stood tall, and took cautious steps toward the road. *I'll explain who I am and my intentions*, he thought, *and hope for the best. I can't put my family at risk.* He quickly assessed his situation, determining the best persona to adopt. He was grateful that he had shaved off his beard and changed his clothes before he left the freighter.

Grinning at the armed men, he exuded all of his charm.

"Good morning, gentlemen," he said. "Please forgive my hesitation. I was startled by your convoy and did not want to impede your journey."

His dialect suggested local gentry.

"May I lower my arms?"

"What are you doing hereabouts?" demanded the second guard, using the muzzle of his rifle to indicate that Nicolai's arms were to remain in the air.

"I am returning to town. I've been to a farm up the road. Just doing some business."

Stay to the truth, avoid being tripped up, he cautioned himself.

"Why is a gentleman such as yourself walking in the woods alone?" whined the second guard.

"Papers," his comrade demanded.

"Ah. Well," Nicolai hesitated, then began patting his pockets. "I wanted to speak with a farmer down the road about his fine racehorses, and decided a walk was in order. My daughter's getting married, you see, and I thought—"

"Papers!"

"I don't seem to have them with me."

Nicolai apologized and continued patting his clothes.

"How odd. I had them when I set out for the farm. I must have dropped them along the way."

He turned toward the path he had just walked, trying to sound sincere.

"I see. *Sir,*" sneered the first guard.

He peered toward Nicolai, pondering the unexpected delay.

"I'm thinking," he said, "that we've met before. And I'm wondering where that might have been?"

"I don't believe so," Nicolai said, shaking his head and hoping the guard's memory was not good enough to recall their encounter of the day before. "I'm sure I'd remember ..."

"Hmm. I'll think on that," the guard said, scraping stubble on his chin.

"If you were looking at racehorses, you should have some money with you," the other guard interjected.

Greed lit his eyes.

"Let's see your purse," he said, winking at his comrade.

"Yes. Uh. I have a small amount with me," Nicolai's stomach clenched. *I'm glad I left the money belt behind.* He fought to steady his nerves. "A few coins in my pocket."

"Let's have a look then."

The first guard waved the barrel of his rifle to encourage Nicolai. Nicolai lowered one hand and put it in his jacket pocket. He pulled out a leather pouch.

"Hand it over."

The second guard snatched the pouch and weighed it in his hand, tossing it slightly as if the weight might reveal the value of the contents.

"I doubt this is enough to buy a race-horse, but I think we can help you spend it."

He winked at his companion again.

"Well, certainly, officers. I'm happy to share. How much—" Nicolai reached for the pouch.

The butt of the first guard's rifle smashed into his outstretched hand with such force that he felt small bones fracture. Nicolai gasped at the suddenness of the action and the spontaneous pain. He grabbed the injured hand with his free one, and guarded it close to his chest, gasping through the burning of broken bones and torn flesh.

"Oh. We'll share all right. Just not with you. *Sir*," the second guard mocked.

"No papers. No money. Must be a dirty Jew," he spat the last word.

Then, in a business-like fashion, he stepped back to clear a path.

"Get him in the truck," he ordered.

"About time!" the driver of the third truck hollered. "Get a move on. We're going to be late!"

Nicolai tried to protest.

"I'm not a Jew," he screamed, trying to shake their hold on him, but they held fast and manhandled him into the second truck.

With a last shove, he landed on his hands and knees at the feet of several other unwitting passengers. The collision of his broken hand on the floorboard of the truck shot searing pain up his arm, leaving him breathless and nauseated. As his breathing slowed and the pain ebbed, he raised his head, cradling his injured hand.

Nicolai's eyes adjusted to the dim interior and he looked around the inside of the truck. *Families. Men, from youth to middle-age, and a few women huddled together, many still wearing their night clothes, some barefoot.* One of the men reached out to help him up, as others slid along a bench making space for him.

The trucks lurched and began to roll again, dust clouds roiling behind them.

Guarding his broken hand, Nicolai finally regained enough composure to ask the others who they were and what was happening.

One middle-aged man still in his night clothes, blood trickling from a nasty gash in his temple responded.

"We are Jews one and all."

He let his statement dangle long enough for Nicolai to recognize that his earlier protest had been repugnant to them.

"We were rousted out of our beds earlier this morning, just past sunrise."

"They won't tell us where we're going, or why they have taken us," another man, in trousers and shirt but no shoes, said. "I'm Benjamin, by the way. Benjamin Goldhirsch. He's Eli Mendelsohn."

"We're both businessmen in Schinawa," Eli muttered, brushing self-consciously at his night clothes.

"These," Benjamin gestured to the others, "are our neighbours—Mordechai Wirth and Zev Riese, and our wives. The boys are my sons."

Some of the women sobbed with fear, one stared out the back of the truck in a glassy trance. The young men huddled with their parents.

"Friend?" Eli asked.

"Nicolai. Please. Call me Nicolai."

Eli nodded.

"Nicolai, have you any idea what's going on?"

"I think so," he gasped, hugging his injured hand to his chest and wincing at the pain. "I am of the Roma people. Several days ago, our vista—our caravan," he added for clarity, "was warned of a roundup of displaced persons—their term, not mine."

"What means this 'displaced person'," Mordechai asked.

240

"I don't know for certain, but I suspect it will mean anyone they find unsavoury, anyone that could be labelled an enemy of the state, especially criminals, homosexuals, Jews, Romani, and any folks without legal citizenship papers. I heard the leader of the guards say something about radically undesirable elements. I can only guess that that means something similar."

He shook his head.

"My family has been travelling by night to avoid being seen," Nicolai told them. "I was careless this morning. I should have been paying attention, instead of dreaming of freedom. My wife and my daughter are waiting for me this very minute. We are trying to leave the country."

His shoulders sagged in despair.

"This news you have is not good, my friend Nicolai," Mordecai said. "Do you know where it is they take us?"

"I can only guess that it is to one of those sites where the camps are to be built," Nicolai said, "but, no, I don't know where they

241

are. I see you have sons with you but no daughters or young children,"

"That is so," Benjamin responded.

"If we are expected to build a camp, that explains why our daughters and younger children were left behind."

The woman who stared out the back of the truck keened loudly.

"My children! My children! Who will care for them?" She wrapped her arms around her body and rocked in anguish.

"There, there." Eli tried to comfort his wife. "There are many good people in the village who will see to our children while we are away. We will be home soon enough. Shhh ..."

"I have to get out of here," Nicolai said, wiggling to the edge of the bench.

"Nicolai. Wait," Benjamin said. "You're injured. You won't get far. And the men in the third truck will see you. My wife, Noya, works with a doctor. Let her look at your hand."

He motioned to Noya to move next to Nicolai.

Nicolai lowered his hand toward Noya. She held his wrist and gently palpated his hand. A sudden intake of his breath told her that she had found the source of his pain.

"The heel of your thumb is splintered, and these small bones," she carefully drew her finger across the back of his hand, "they are broken too. Already the site is hot with inflammation."

She looked at the others, then back to Nicolai.

"There is little I can do without medical supplies. Yael? Might I ask for a bit of the ruffle from your nightdress, so I can at least bind his hand for stability in the meantime?"

The other woman released her hold on her husband's arm.

"Of course," she said, ripping the eyelet trim from her nightdress and handing it to Noya.

"This will hurt," Noya warned. "Are you prepared?"

Nicolai nodded and winced one hissing breath as she bound his injured hand.

"At least this will give enough support that you won't feel as if your hand is held on only by skin," she said, returning his hand to his own care.

"Thank you, Noya," Nicolai gasped, trying to control his shaking body.

"Your body is suffering from shock. In time the shivering should stop," she said.

Nicolai nodded acknowledgement and leaned back into the wall of the truck, closing his eyes and willing the pain to pass. *I can't stay here. I must get off this truck! Open your eyes, fool. You can't devise an escape if you can't see what's happening.* Nicolai's eyes shot open and he sat rigid. He looked at each of his fellow passengers and felt hopeless. *I can't save them all,* he fretted, *but I can try to save myself. My family needs me.*

CHAPTER TWENTY

The flap over the back of the truck had not been closed. Through the opening, Nicolai watched the movement and spacing of the truck behind, noticing that it disappeared from view when the truck in which he was held captive rounded a curve. He began counting from the time the rear truck went out of view until it returned again. After several such curves, he realized that the rear truck could be out of view for up to three minutes. As he calculated the timing, he also observed the landscape. They were passing through forest. The roads were narrow, and on either side lay a ditch. He recognized the area. If he was going to escape, he would have to do it soon.

Through the easing pain, Nicolai studied the path of the road. He felt confident that, if he timed his jump well, he could roll into the ditch, wait until the third truck rolled past, then scramble into the forest. With any luck, he could make it back to Schinawa before dark.

He rose from the bench and crouched in a corner, near the tailgate.

"Nicolai, what are you doing?" Benjamin hissed. "They will see you."

Nicolai turned his eyes from the road and looked at Benjamin in sadness.

"I apologize that I cannot help you," he said, "but I must get back to my family."

He turned back to the road just as the truck rounded another curve and the third truck disappeared out of view.

"God be with you all," he said as he jumped over the tail gate, hung for three heartbeats while the road passed below him, then let go.

Nicolai landed on bent knees and rolled into the ditch, clutching his injured hand to his chest and trying to slow his breathing. His heart beat wildly. He heard gravel crunch under the tires of the third truck as it stopped just above him. *They can't have seen me*, he thought, and pressed himself tighter into the ditch. For seconds, all was quiet. Then he heard rapid footsteps.

"What now!" shouted the driver of the third truck.

"We heard a noise from the back of the truck and think someone jumped."

The voice was angry.

"Count the ones inside," the voice commanded.

"The farmer is missing," said a second voice.

Nicolai recognized both voices as those of the guards who had captured him.

"Did you see which way he went?" the angry voice asked.

"No! I was behind the curve," said the driver of the third truck.

"Give us a hand. He can't have gone far. The rest of you watch the trucks. Make sure no one else tries to jump."

Nicolai heard the scramble of footsteps on gravel, then quiet. The snick of a bullet being loaded into its barrel startled him, but he did not move. He held his breath and squeezed his eyes shut, willing himself to be invisible.

"Get up now and I won't shoot," snarled the angry voice.

"You two, get down there and bring him up. Make it quick."

Nicolai heard two bodies slide into the ditch, one landing near his head, the other near his feet. His body went limp with resignation. He knew then that he would have to be a very lucky man indeed if ever he was to see his family again.

"Get up now!" shouted one of the guards.

Nicolai hesitated too long. He was not expecting the heavy boot that kicked into his ribs. He raised his head as a second kick struck. The crunch of breaking ribs sucked his breath away and sent him into immediate shock. He tried to lift himself, but his body failed to respond.

"I said get up!"

Rough hands yanked him to his feet and he screamed at stabs of new pain.

"Put him in the last truck and tie him," the angry voice said.

"And hurry it up," said the driver of the third truck. "We're running late, and we still have one more stop!"

Nicolai lay on the floorboard of the third truck. He had fainted when the handlers threw him in. He tried to sit up, but the pain in his right side took his breath away. Broken ribs. Broken hand. He moved his left hand to check the damage, but it felt weighted and would not move. Pain shot through his right hand again, and he realized that it had been bound to his left. When his breathing slowed, he opened his eyes and peered around the inside of the third truck—more people, mostly men, two women, no children.

"Who are you?" he asked no one in particular, his voice husky with pain.

"Nicolai!" a familiar voice called to him.

"Wh-who calls my name?" Nicolai asked between heavy gasps.

"Samson. Nicolai, it's Samson."

"Samson! What are you doing here? You're supposed to be safe away?"

"We were," Samson said, his voice was heavy with despair. "We'd been on the road for days, hiding during the day as you said. Only travelling at night. My eldest was ill. I had to go into a town for medicine. They stopped me just outside of town. It was dusk. I thought I'd be safe."

Samson began to sob. "My family. They are alone and wait for me. God help them!"

"And the rest of you?" Nicolai asked, searching their faces.

Slowly each identified themselves. Most were petty criminals collected from police cells during the previous evening. Nicolai's gaze rested on the two women huddled together in a corner.

"Those two don't like men," sneered one of the scruffier men. "They work in a brothel, but only really like each other's company. If you know what I mean."

He inhaled and expectorated a wad of

250

saliva in the direction of the women. The wad fell short of its target and rolled toward Nicolai's captive hands.

"What is to become of us?" one of the women wailed, ignoring the insults.

Nicolai repeated the dismal news that he had shared with the captives in the middle truck.

To his frustration, he realized that his hands were not only tied together but tethered to a metal loop secured in the floorboards. He could do nothing but lay stretched out or curled in a ball.

"What time is it?" he asked.

"Hard to tell," one of the men said. "The flap is tied down, but from what little I can see through a rent in the fabric, it will soon be dusk."

"I heard one of the guards say that we have one more stop," Nicolai said.

Within the hour, the trucks stopped again in the centre of a small village. It was dinner time. The aroma of evening meals filled the street. Bellies growled.

251

Nicolai heard a heavy banging on one of the doors, screams of protest, bellowing and crying. Then the trucks began rolling again, not stopping until sunrise of the following day.

Nicolai shivered with the pain of his broken bones. Shock, Noya had called it. In the end, he escaped the pain in a heated delirium.

CHAPTER TWENTY-ONE

"Get up, you lazy cur."

Nicolai felt the prod of a baton in his thigh and tried to rouse himself. The truck had stopped. Every muscle in his body protested against movement. He groaned. He was cold and hungry. He had not eaten since he had left the tavern in Schinawa. With the thought of that meal and his family, panic seized him. He tore his mind from his worry to focus on his misshaped hand and broken ribs, letting the pain distract him. *I must get free.*

"You need to release my hands," he said to the guard with an undertone of defiance. "My hands ... are tethered."

"Eh?"

"My hands," Nicolai panted through pain. "They're chained to the floorboard."

The guard reached in and released the clamp that bound him to the floorboard.

"Now ... get up."

The baton poked Nicolai's thigh again. He struggled to his feet, gasping through the pain and effort. On his knees, he scanned the faces and condition of those who sat on the benches. A light of realization flickered behind his eyes. They were all bound, hands and feet. The binding at their feet was linked to clamps in the floorboard, fastening them in place. *No wonder no one tried to help me. He saw hopelessness in Samson's eyes and looked away.*

Nicolai slid from the truck, and willed himself to stand erect and independent, while the others were hauled out and lined up next to him. His swollen hand throbbed within a purple-red encasement and he resisted the impulse to hug his injured hand and protect his side. He coughed to clear his dry throat, wishing for water.

As they stood in the chill of the morning, wavering from hunger and thirst, another guard appeared.

"Welcome to Dachau," he sneered,

eyeing each of them, as if daring them to defy him. "You are here as guests of the state, and in exchange for your keep, you will work. Work makes you free!" He shouted the camp slogan with enthusiasm. "Follow me."

The line of men and women from the trucks followed the guard, too weak and befuddled to resist his command. He led them to a building where he released the men to the care of other guards, then led the women elsewhere.

"Ben!" Noya screamed, fighting to escape.

"Shut up you!" a nearby guard shouted, silencing her protests with a back-handed slap to her left cheek.

Tender flesh below her eye tore and bled.

"Noya!" Benjamin cried, watching his wife disappear around a corner with the other women.

The men were unchained and instructed to strip. Their heads were shaved and then they were forced to shower with lye soap.

They were given striped uniforms and shown to a bunk house that smelled of lye soap and unwashed bodies.

"Here you will receive your meals and sleep," their captor told them. "Each morning you will be directed to your work detail."

"What about food?" one of the petty criminals asked. "We have not eaten for days."

"You'll eat with the others," grunted the guard.

By the time the men found an unoccupied bunk they could claim as their own, the work detail from that day was returning for the evening meal. Empty eyes searched through the new arrivals, relieved that they knew none.

An exchange of questions and answers ensued. The current tenants reported on the conditions of the camp and daily activities, while the new arrivals shared news of their capture and activities of the state.

As the sun lowered in the evening sky and a chill settled in the bunk house, a clatter arose at the door. Men jumped from their beds and began lining up outside the door, each carrying a tin cup and a bowl. Outside the door, three guards stood. One doled out a mushy broth and a piece of hard bread, while the other two watched to ensure no misbehaviour. On the return to the bunk house, each man filled his cup with ice water from a standing tap.

Huddled around wooden tables, the men sat on benches, slurped the bland broth and chewed the dry bread. Samson sat on a bottom bunk next to Nicolai who was slow to eat the food. Nicolai had begun to shiver again and found it difficult to eat. Samson finished his own food quickly and took the bowl from Nicolai, bracing him with one arm and raising the bowl to his lips so he could drink.

"Drink, Nicolai," he encouraged. "You must keep up your strength."

Nicolai did as Samson bid, but he no sooner took the last sip then vomited the entire mess into the bowl again. Nearby

257

bunk occupants looked away. One man gagged and slapped his hand over his mouth in response.

"I-I c-can't-t," Nicolai shivered, collapsing into the bunk.

"Here," one of the workers said, "take my blanket and cover him. He looks unwell. What happened to his hand?"

Samson explained Nicolai's injuries, putting a hand to Nicolai's forehead.

"He's feverish," he said, to no one in particular.

Another worker approached.

"I'm a doctor," the thin man said. "Let me have a look."

The doctor removed the soiled rag that held Nicolai's broken hand and examined the damage. Nicolai moaned through delirium as the doctor probed and tsked.

"This injury does not look good," he said to Samson. "His hand is too swollen and stretches the skin taut. And burns to the touch. See here, bruising has started. And these two fingers don't lay straight."

He shook his head.

"If I had the tools, I could fix this. As it is, there is little I can do, but I will try."

He called for help and, while others held Nicolai still, he straightened the broken bones as best he could.

"Now all we can do is hope against infection," the doctor said.

"What about his ribs?" Samson asked.

The doctor lifted Nicolai's jacket and probed the bruised site.

"Indeed, two appear to be broken." He turned to the workers.

"I need strips to bind him. Does anyone have something that will suffice?"

Two men stepped forward proffering strips of fabric and the doctor wound them around Nicolai's chest.

"That is all I can do for now. Let us all pray that he survives his injuries," he said, lowering Nicolai's jacket before shuffling wearily to his own bunk.

A siren sounded and one of the criminals jumped.

"What's that? Has someone escaped?"

"No. It means lights out."

No sooner were the words spoken than the men heard a loud snap and the building went dark. And quiet.

✥

In the morning, the lights snapped on at moonset and the hum of generators began again. The newly arrived men followed the other workers to the toilets—a row of metal receptacles positioned side by side, no walls for privacy. After responding to their morning urgency, they returned to the main room and awaited another meal of mush and dry bread.

The doctor who had treated Nicolai's injuries the previous evening appeared at Nicolai's bedside. Nicolai had yet to rise. He thanked the doctor for his aid while the doctor felt his forehead and briefly inspected his injuries.

"You'll live," he said, lowering Nicolai's jacket. "Come now, we must wash before our morning meal is served."

Samson supported Nicolai to the toilet, then followed the doctor to the wash fountain.

"Why bother, doctor?"

"I beg your pardon," the doctor said while he scrubbed his neck with a scrap of fabric and cold water.

"Why bother washing? Who cares?" Samson asked.

"We do, my boy. Washing and keeping to a daily routine keeps our minds focussed and provides us with hope. The moment we surrender hope and our respect for ourselves and others, we will have nothing to live for." The doctor looked kindly upon Samson. "Have you a family?"

"Yes, sir."

"Do you not wish to see them again?"

Samson nodded, tears threatening to spill from his hazel eyes.

"Then you must wash!"

As the doctor's words reached the souls of the men at the fountain, they cupped their hands in the icy water and scrubbed harder.

"Good men!" the doctor said. "Come along. Our delicious breakfast will arrive shortly. We must eat every drop of the tasty gruel if we are to manage the tasks we're set today."

On his last words, he returned to the room with the rows of bunk beds and sat on a bench to await his meal.

✧

"How are you, man," one of the workers asked Nicolai.

Nicolai shrugged.

"Think you can handle the heavy labour?"

"I hope I can," Nicolai shuffled through the doorway behind him.

When the men were marshalled out of their quarters, Nicolai saw for himself what the others had described the evening before. The quarters were located in an old gunpowder and munitions factory that had been converted in 1933, with the intention of housing those deemed to be radically undesirable elements, including anyone labelled unsavoury or an enemy of the state, or found without legal citizenship papers. He survived the day, with large thanks to his fellow workers who understood his difficulty. Through the day, they tried to deflect the lighter work toward him while they managed the heavier tasks. It was to the credit of all that they managed the day without the guards becoming any the wiser.

And so, the days passed, and Nicolai's broken ribs began to heal. The progress of his hand was slower. Because of its instability and the injured ribs, he was forced to use his left side and hand while he favoured the right. His right hand burnt and turned a deep purple. After a time, the burning passed, and his hand too began to heal.

CHAPTER TWENTY-TWO

Carrying their bundled purchases, Punita and Rosalee returned to the freighter shortly after eleven o'clock. Their shopping had taken a little longer than anticipated and they hastened out of a side alley, making their way toward the dock. The wind blew briskly near the river, tugging their hair loose and whipping it about their faces.

Konstantin paced the deck. The crew appeared ready to cast off. As Konstantin handed the women onboard, Rosalee's eyes searched the deck.

"Where's Nicolai?"

Konstantin looked grim, his mouth cutting a flat line of concern on his sea-weathered face. His dark eyes shifted toward the sky.

"We have had word," he said. "Nicolai returned the wagon to the farmer, but he was seized on the outskirts of town. A number of people were rousted from their sleep early this morning and loaded into three military trucks. Nicolai was spotted by the guards as he stepped out of the forest at the town gate. He was forced into one of the trucks. No one knows where they're headed, but we can't risk more time at the dock to find out."

He returned his attention to the crew.

"Cast off!" he commanded.

Punita looked to Rosalee, eyes wide and mouth gaping. Rosalee grabbed at Konstantin's sleeve.

"But ... Nicolai!" she pleaded.

Her knees buckled, and she collapsed to the deck, dropping the packages she carried.

"Mama!" Punita reached to help her.

Konstantin took Rosalee's arm and helped her rise.

"Nicolai will understand. He and I talked of this. We have a contingency plan. If he is able, he will find us. If not soon, he will find us in Amsterdam." Konstantin tipped his forelock. "Now you must excuse me. The ship is underway. Go below and change. You must fit in with the crew."

Fretting, the women did as they were bid. As they descended the ladder into the hold, they heard Konstantin shout to the crew.

"Erik, lower the Roma flag! Hoist the German colours."

❖

When the freighter docked at the next port, Konstantin ordered that the room created for Punita be dismantled to allow for storing of more cargo. Punita moved her few possessions into her parents' space and shared it with Rosalee.

Nicolai's absence was a constant worry for Rosalee and Punita, and they prayed that he could manage the contingency plan. They found a comfortable spot on the forecastle where they spent anxious hours scouring the shoreline for him. The journey along the Oder should have been beautiful and tranquil, but they were too worried and too frightened to notice.

Konstantin guided the freighter north at a slow, steady pace, allowing Nicolai the best opportunity to reach it. The crew kept watch through the night, maintaining a vigil for him and any signs of danger.

⚜

One night, the chief engineer, Hans, knocked on the door of Konstantin's stateroom, rousing the captain from a light sleep.

"Enter."

Hans removed his cap as he entered, revealing a shock of red hair laced with white streaks. Konstantin lit a small candle near his bunk.

"What is it, Hans?"

"Sorry to disturb your rest, captain. I've heard loud voices from across the river and the puttering of a small motor. Sounds more alcohol-induced than a threat, but I thought you'd like to know."

Hans' weathered face frowned with his own concern.

"Thanks, Chief. You're right, as usual. I'll join you in a moment."

"Skipper," Hans acknowledged, and excused himself from the room, replacing his cap as he closed the door.

Konstantin watch the small man depart, grateful for his wisdom and decades of service. He grabbed his trousers and dressed for the evening chill.

On Konstantin's instructions, the ship's speed was increased for the following thirty minutes, to put distance between it and the merrymakers.

⚜

At each port along the river, Konstantin moored the ship and conducted his usual trading. He felt it important to continue in his ordinary course so as not to attract unwanted attention.

Konstantin instructed Punita and Rosalee to stay below and remain quiet when they were docked. He and his crew had papers that allowed them to trade up and down the river. Punita and Rosalee did not. The German government considered them to be non-citizens, and they were fleeing a Nazi round-up. It was imperative that they not be spotted by anyone who could betray them to officials.

Each night, new cargo was shifted to form higher walls around the small space shared by the women. Eventually, the only way to access the space was to crawl through a small hole on one side.

Once they were inside for the night, one of the crew blocked the hole for privacy using light-weight cargo so the women could easily move it themselves, if necessary. During the day, if their safety was threatened, the women were told to retreat to the hiding space; otherwise, they moved freely about the ship, dressed as crew, and helped where they could.

Nearer the mouth of the river, port agents were more officious and insisted on checking Konstantin's papers, including the crew and cargo manifests, his ownership papers, and his business and trading licence. Occasionally, they boarded and kicked and prodded the cargo. Konstantin knew them all and was able to assure them that the papers were in order.

At the last stop before the city of Stettin, Konstantin encountered a port agent whom he had never met. The agent boarded the freighter and insisted that all cargo be checked against the manifest.

"We received orders from the Sturmabteilung yesterday," the agent advised Konstantin. "Every ship is to be inspected for stowaways, refugees, and contraband. No more rubber-stamping."

The crew lounged on the deck, smoking and chatting amongst themselves, covertly watching the agent and keeping a lookout for any trouble that might come from the bustling dock or the steady river. As Konstantin descended into the forward hold with the agent, he caught Hans' eye and gestured for him to alert the women.

"I see that the cargo here is organized and your paper work is legitimate," the agent informed Konstantin, as he climbed the ladder to the main deck. "Now, let's have a look aft."

Eric quickly descended into the aft cargo hold and alerted Punita and Rosalee. In low whispers, he cautioned them not to speak or move. He then moved the cargo around, blocking access to their space. He had one hand and one foot on the ladder preparing to ascend to the deck when the agent looked down at him, blocking the little daylight that penetrated through the hatch.

"What are you up to?" the agent barked.

Eric grinned and shifted a weight in his left hand.

"Flour, sir. Cook's making biscuits."

"Good enough. Come up then, so we can get below and finish the inspection, and get this vessel underway."

Rosalee held Punita close, feeling the sweat of fear trickling between her breasts and under her armpits. Punita's breathing became a rapid hiss in her ears.

She heard the men's voices, but the conversation was muffled. She fretted that the cargo walls might cave in on them. Then, she heard a change in her daughter's breathing, her body shifted.

"Mama, look!" Punita whispered, raising her curled hands. "I can't straighten my fingers! Mama, I don't feel w—"

Punita fainted, slumping against Rosalee. Rosalee embraced her daughter's limp weight, fighting the curl of her own fingers. She heard the ringing in her ears grow louder, and felt her mind spinning out of control. Then all went black.

⚘

"What was that?" the agent said, spinning toward a noise.

"Rats." Konstantin answered quickly. "Damn things. No matter how hard we try to control them, a few still evade us. I suppose it's better that we have some on board. If we see them jumping, we'll know that the ship's in trouble!"

272

Konstantin hoped his levity would distract the agent, but the agent simply nodded and continued his poking, prodding, kicking, and checking of the cargo. The inspection seemed to take hours, although it was only twenty minutes.

"Your man had best clean that up before your rats get into it," the agent said, pointing to a spot where, Konstantin surmised, Erik had left deliberate telltale evidence of flour near a barrel.

"I expect he'll be back for more ingredients, but I'll remind him when we get topside."

The banter became more companionable as the agent completed his inspection, and they returned to the main deck. As soon as the agent stepped onto the dock, Konstantin gave orders to cast off.

When the ship was well away from the dock and once again motoring along the Oder, Hans and Konstantin went below to dig the women out of their hiding space. They found Punita and Rosalee groggily folded in each other's arms. Hans, being the smaller of the men, crawled into the hiding space and handed first Punita and then Rosalee through the opening. Each man hoisted a woman on their shoulder and climbed the ladder to the deck.

The women were assisted to a bench outside the galley. Under the setting sun, they gulped fresh air. Their heads seemed to clear, and they visibly began to relax.

"The danger has passed," Konstantin said. "Can you manage on your own while I check with the crew?"

"We will," Rosalee answered.

A few minutes later, Erik brought the women water and a cloth.

"Hans says a cool, wet cloth and ample water will bring you 'round," he said, his brow wrinkled with concern.

During their next meal, Erik expressed regret for sealing the hiding space so tightly, but Konstantin quickly minimized the apology.

"I would have done the same thing," he said, peering at the women. "You understand that it was necessary?"

"We understand very well, Konstantin," Rosalee said, looking first to her daughter, then to the captain and his crew. "It was necessary for everyone's safety, not just ours. Besides, I don't think you sealed the space too tightly, Erik. I think we may have caused our own fainting. We're not accustomed to this level of fear."

⁂

Near the mouth of the river, wind from the north caused swells that rocked the ship from side to side. Both women, never having spent a significant duration on water, complained to Konstantin of queasiness. He assured them that it would pass.

By the time the crew tied the ship to the dock in Stettin, it was almost time for the evening meal. Konstantin dismissed the crew, encouraging them to enjoy an evening in town. Then, he invited the women to accompany him for dinner at a nearby tavern.

"Try not to look obvious," he told them when they asked whether they could change their attire.

"It's best that you still blend in as crew. I've received word that the search for refugees has been extended to the northern ports. You won't want to draw anyone's attention."

The dock was a hive of activity, even at such a late hour. Derricks swung cargo on and off ships, under the supervision of industrious stevedores and dockers.

Following Konstantin, Punita and Rosalee wove their way through the chaos on the quayside, toward the tavern. While they waited for their meal to be served, Konstantin continued to enlighten them about his business and their travel.

"Stettin is an important port for us. It will take two days for the cargo to be reorganized. Some will be discharged and sold here, while additional cargo will be loaded onboard and stowed. Once the cargo transfer concludes, we will sail to Amsterdam."

In answer to questions posed by Rosalee, the captain continued.

"When our work is finished in Amsterdam, we load the ship with more cargo and return to Stettin, then we repeat the journey on the Oder. This has been my family's business for many years.

"If you'd like," Konstantin said, "I can arrange for you to stay in a room above the tavern while we're in port. However, if you choose to do so, you will have to be very cautious. The Fuhrer's ever-evolving rules make everyone nervous. You two are not familiar to the locals, and —"

"Konstantin, thank you," Rosalee interrupted, placing her small hand on his arm. "We would welcome a few nights on solid land, but we would not feel safe."

She gazed at her daughter for agreement and was rewarded with a nod.

"On the other hand," Punita said, "would it be safe for us to walk through the old town before we depart?"

Punita's question dangled between them while the server removed the remains of their meal.

"While we transfer the cargo," Konstantin suggested, once the server was out of earshot, "you are welcome to go ashore, but don't wander too far from the ship. I'll send one of the crewmen with you for protection. Wear your sea clothes so you don't appear obvious, and keep an eye out for Nicolai."

⚜

The following day, Konstantin asked Milosh to accompany the women ashore, with strict instructions to all of them to blend in with the activity on the dock and in the town.

"Look like crewman with a few hours leave!" he said.

The party of three wandered about the city square, looking in shop windows and stopping to inspect goods offered by street vendors. The women bought nothing, except a mid-day meal for themselves and Milosh.

Milosh, Rosalee speculated, *must be in his late twenties. For a young man, he seems quite clever and observant.* Milosh's head turned in her direction as if sensing her attention. Rosalee blushed.

"How long have you been sailing, Milosh?" she asked.

Milosh smiled, turning his unremarkable face into a source of light. His pale brown eyes shone.

"I worked in the Anker warehouse part-time while I was in school," he said.

"As soon as I graduated, I asked for a position on one of the ships. Captain Buduly, the warehouse manager, arranged for me to sail with Captain Konstantin."

"So ... you enjoy sailing then," Rosalee asked, noting that his compact stature probably made movement about a ship easier than that of a larger man.

"I do," he responded with enthusiasm, removing his cap, running his fingers through sandy hair, and replacing the cap again.

Milosh gazed at the position of the sun, as grey stratus fractus clouds scudded across the pale sky, on a brisk salty breeze.

"We'd best get back to the ship," he said, "afore the skipper starts to worry."

The women agreed and fell in step behind him.

"Mama, I'm worried about Papa," Punita whispered. "Where do you suppose he is? Do you think he's safe?"

"I don't know," Rosalee answered. "Perhaps we can watch for him from the ship's forecastle, while the loading continues."

In a sea of people, they searched for Nicolai, hoping he would walk from behind a building or a horse cart, his lovely weathered face smiling, teasing them for worrying unnecessarily. But they did not see him in Stettin, and two days later, the *Silver Oyster* motored out of the harbour on a course charted for Amsterdam, without him.

CHAPTER TWENTY-THREE

During the third week of Nicolai's residence in the Dachau concentration camp, a guard noticed that he failed to work as hard as the other men and challenged him. Nicolai was forced into an awkward position—carry a heavy load as others were doing, or risk that the others would be punished for helping him. Nicolai joined the men in the heavy work, trying not to tax his healing hand.

The work that day involved lifting and carrying cement blocks, four men to a block. Nicolai laboured with the others, bearing the weight of the block with his left arm and supporting it with his right. As they shuffled the load to the construction site, one of the other men slipped on a patch of ice, losing his balance. The block shifted toward Nicolai and he was forced to take the brunt of its weight on his right hand. Nicolai groaned loudly at the impact, feeling small bones crack in the back of his hand, but held the weight firmly with his left hand and arm.

That evening, the doctor removed Nicolai's bandage and examined his injuries.

"I am concerned about this new damage," he said.

Nicolai's hand had swollen throughout the day and the skin on the back of his hand stretched hot and red.

"You must be careful tomorrow."

"I'll try, doctor, but you know I'll be expected to pull my own weight. I won't have any of you held responsible for my weakness."

Beads of perspiration pearled on his forehead as he spoke.

"You could ask to be taken to the infirmary," one of the workers offered.

"No!" another snapped. "You know full well that no one returns from the infirmary!"

It was not Nicolai who was taken to the infirmary the following day. Two others were carried off before mid-day, complaining of headaches and flu-like symptoms. That evening, the workers discussed concern for their comrades.

"How long have they been here?" one of the petty criminals who had arrived with Nicolai asked.

"They arrived about two weeks before you," the doctor answered. "They woke up with fever and chills yesterday. I told them I thought they might have a flu, but they refused to go to the infirmary."

Three days later, word began to spread throughout the camp. The men who had been taken to the infirmary had been diagnosed with epidemic typhus. By noon, all of the workers were ordered back to their bunk houses. In groups, they were taken to the infirmary, examined by medical staff, deloused and returned to their barracks with instructions to scrub every inch with sand and lye soap, while others boiled all of their clothes and bedding in an attempt to halt the spread of the disease.

Those who were not sick prior to the scouring avoided illness. Others were not so fortunate.

Nicolai had been fighting similar symptoms, but never complained about the headaches. He presumed that the fever and chills, sensitivity to light, and delirium were all related to the ongoing injuries to his hand. It was not until a doctor in the infirmary noticed the rash that covered his trunk and extremities that he knew he had typhus. He resisted the guards who dragged him to the quarantine building, insisting that he was well and able to work.

Jerking within the guards' grasp, Nicolai glimpsed Samson's face. Tears trickled from his worried eyes.

"Nicolai!" he mouthed.

Nicolai collapsed, no longer resisting the guards. *I haven't the strength to fight. What will happen to my family?*

The guards dropped him on a hospital cot in the infirmary, and hurriedly escaped to the showers when a doctor warned them to thoroughly clean themselves before they were bitten by the lice.

Nicolai's fever rose rapidly. In his delirium, he told his wife that he loved her, and spoke of the horses that he and Punita would raise and race. He saw Punita perched atop a filly sired by Bang, her long brown tresses flowing in the morning sun. On the third day, he looked upon Rosalee's beauty one last time. Feeling his life seep from his lips, he raised his broken hand toward her, calling her name with his last breath.

CHAPTER TWENTY-FOUR

The *Silver Oyster's* cargo was significant, and as she moved away from the dock she sat at her marks, fully loaded. Once the pilot had manoeuvred her beyond the harbour limits and disembarked, the skipper navigated her north across the Dannscher See, into the West Oder, across the Stettiner Haff and onward to Swinemunde. When the *Silver Oyster* cleared the coastline at Swinemunde, her captain went in search of his passengers, and found them sitting on the main deck in the lee of the superstructure.

"Konstantin," Rosalee asked, "what is that flag at the top of the aft mast? It differs from the German flag that was hoisted after Schinawa?"

"Rosalee! I'm impressed. You're already picking up nautical terminology!" Konstantin praised her. "And that is a good

observation. That's the flag of the Netherlands. When we're on the river, I like to use
the Roma flag or the German flag, sometimes both. The Roma flag is a signal to
any of our people who might want to share
news. We collect information up and down
the river. It's a way for all of us to stay connected." He gazed at the flag flapping at the
top of the mast. "When we left Schinawa,
I worried that we might jeopardize folks if
they approached or, worse, put us at risk, so
I had it lowered, and ordered the German
flag hoisted instead."

He scrubbed his chin in thought.

"I'm not so sure it will be wise to continue using the Roma flag during the round
up," he pondered, "it will make our folks
vulnerable. I can only hope that they remember our schedule and can identify our ships
without the flag." Konstantin cast his eyes
to the sky and squinted. "Now we sail to
Amsterdam on the open sea. The flag today
expresses a different message: the *Silver
Oyster* is a commercial vessel conveying

287

cargo. Compared to the river, our sea journey will be different in many ways. We will have no commercial stops. We sail directly to Amsterdam via the Kiel Canal, and should arrive in two or three days, depending on the wind, and presuming we do not encounter any difficulties."

"Difficulties?" Rosalee repeated.

"This time of year, there can be storms, and if the wind blows against us, it will slow our journey. Then, of course," he said, his dark eyes serious. "we could be boarded by the German coastguard."

Rosalee gasped.

"I don't want you to worry. The ship is safe and quite seaworthy, but I learned this morning that the coastguard is now diligently patrolling the German shoreline. They are asserting their authority and searching vessels for refugees and stowaways. A freighter such as the *Silver Oyster* usually hugs the coastline, but, given our current concerns, I have altered course to swing wide of it. I'm hoping that, by doing so, we will avoid such a boarding. Should anything come amiss, however, one of the crew will be sent to assist you."

Rosalee frowned. Konstantin placed his hand on her arm and peered into her chocolate eyes.

"Rosalee, we know these waters. You need not worry," he said. "Now, if you'll excuse me, I must consult the charts and confirm the new course." He made a small bow and headed up the ladder to the wheelhouse.

⚜

The *Silver Oyster* sliced through the gentle swells with a constant, hypnotic rhythm. The women stood in the bow, four hands wrapped around the railing, hair streaming in the wind, trousers flapping about their legs. They laughed as sea spray caught them in the face and licked the salty residue that misted their lips.

The ship's pace quickened, as the bow cut through swells that rolled her gently from side to side. Several minutes later, Punita's smile disappeared.

"I think I'm going to be sick!"

She spun and found an empty wooden bucket just in time to capture what expelled from her squirming stomach. With the second heave, she fell to her knees, her mother by her side. Rosalee gathered her daughter's hair from her face and placed a hand on her shoulder for comfort. Punita hugged the bucket and heaved again.

Rosalee dropped to her knees, unintentionally catching a whiff of the bucket's contents. Her stomach clenched and, in the next instant, the two women heaved together, tidily hitting the bucket despite the rolling motion of the ship. As one, they sat back on their heels, each wiping her mouth with the back of her hand.

"Bleh!" Punita moaned. "That was awful."

Rosalee jerked forward and heaved again, lingering over the bucket, and spitting into it. After some seconds, she sat back on her heels and wiped her mouth again.

"Bleh!" Rosalee reiterated her daughter's earlier sentiment.

Together mother and daughter managed a feeble giggle.

"We have a lot to learn about sea travel, I think."

"Mama, can we just sit there and rest for a bit," Punita said, pointing to a sheltered spot below the break of the forecastle. "I'm feeling too shaky to stand."

"Yes. Good idea. But leave the bucket here," Rosalee suggested. "Tuck it into that coil of rope so it doesn't spill. The taste of vomit is one thing, having to smell it is another. I'd rather not heave again."

The two sat panting and gulping, trying to still their rebellious bellies. When they felt more settled, they moved aft of the superstructure, pulling their coats tightly for warmth, and huddling together out of the wind.

Once his work with the charts concluded, Konstantin sought the women. Tomas led him to the main deck, aft of the superstructure. Squatting before them, Konstantin examined their condition.

"How are you feeling?" he asked in earnest.

Four eyes blinked as if to focus on him.

"Here, rinse your mouths with this, then drink. It'll help."

He held two glasses of fizzing water before them.

"Tomas prepared this for you and brought you a clean bucket. I should have warned you," Konstantin apologized. "I know it won't help you now, but your experience is not uncommon for first time seafarers. In fact, I know several sea captains who are regularly seasick—sometimes for days—each time their ship gets underway. They get over it. It's just a matter of time and individual constitution."

He stood and stretched, looking out over the railing toward the distant horizon.

The women rinsed their mouths, spat the mixture into the clean bucket, then drank the remainder of the beverage.

"Better?" Konstantin asked after a few minutes.

They each nodded, forcing a smile.

"The cook is preparing food, so you might want to stay clear of the galley. I'll ask Tomas to bring you another drink in a while, and some dry bread. If you can keep that down, you should be able to enjoy the next meal. In the meantime, midships is the best place for you. There's less motion here, as well as being out of the wind. And, try to keep your eyes on the horizon. It should help settle your stomach."

Four owl eyes blinked at him again.

"Tomas," he said, "keep an eye on them, while I take the helm."

"Aye aye, Skipper," Tomas responded, before departing with the bucket and empty glasses. "I'll just rinse these first."

By the next meal, Rosalee said that she felt recovered and that she intended to eat with the crew. Punita was still feeling queasy and declined. Tomas suggested that she might feel better outside rather than in her cabin and rigged a mat and blankets on the wheelhouse deck, where she could rest. She moaned as she lowered herself and rolled into a fetal position, holding her belly, eyes closed tight.

"I'll check on you in a while," Tomas assured her.

Rosalee checked on Punita after dinner and sat with her while the crew tended to their evening chores.

Tomas joined them at sunset.

"When the sun is gone, it will get colder out here. May I suggest that you move down to your cabin now?"

He posed his question to Rosalee in deference but looked to Punita for a decision.

Punita nodded her response.

"Th-thanks," she stammered. "Can we open the window, so I can get fr-fr-esh air at least?"

"Certainly," Tomas said, stooping to collect the mat and blankets.

※

The next morning, Rosalee and Tomas guided Punita to the main deck, and encouraged her to walk aft of the superstructure. Colour returned to her cheeks, and she kept a piece of dry bread in her stomach. By midday, Punita felt restored and agreed to try eating a light meal.

While they sat with Konstantin in the galley, he explained the revised chart.

"Our journey will take longer than we planned," he reported. "As I mentioned earlier, our usual route is to stay close to the shoreline and pass just outside Rugen Island. However, we believe that route now poses a risk. The Germans are indeed boarding transient vessels.

"We are going to swing wide of Rugen Island and sail closer to Denmark. Our journey may take a few more days, but not many. The breeze is steady, and the sea is kind. We will make good time," he assured them.

Punita clamped her hand over her mouth and raced out of the galley. Just outside the door, she reached for the bucket that Tomas had left as a precaution. Kneeling on the deck with her head over the bucket, she overheard Rosalee speaking with Konstantin.

"I don't understand how this sailing can still affect one of us and not the other."

"Some adapt quicker than others," Konstantin said, sharing the wisdom of his experience. "She'll be fine. Eventually."

CHAPTER TWENTY-FIVE

The *Silver Oyster* motored on, swinging wide of Rugen Island, heading toward the small islands south of Sjaelland.

Late in the afternoon, a rogue wind started to build. In its infancy, it pushed the ship forward and hastened her journey. Dark clouds gathered rapidly, swirling and building, black and ominous. The north easterly wind collided with the outflow winds from the Kattegat, fed from the North Sea. Rain began to fall in salty drops and the temperature dropped rapidly. When gusts began driving ice pellets horizontally, miniature needles pricked exposed skin.

At the southern tip of Sweden, a rare storm blasted the *Silver Oyster*, tossing her about like a cork in a dishpan. In the wheelhouse, Konstantin ordered the ship's speed reduced, and directed the women to return to their cabin.

"Hold onto the rails securely as you descend, and don't venture forth until the storm has passed," Konstantin told them. "Someone will come for you when it's safe to come out again."

Filled with fear, the women left the wheelhouse immediately.

"Hans," he barked at the Chief Engineer, "switch on the clearview screen."

Immediately, the high-speed rotations began dispersing the rain and spray from the fore-end window of the wheelhouse, providing a better view for studying the tempest bombarding the ship.

"Order the crew into foul-weather gear!" Konstantin issued his next command.

Tomas grabbed the radio and repeated the captain's order. Below them, on the main deck, the crew donned foul-weather gear, fastening their cuffs and pant legs tight against the gale force winds. The ship tossed on the waves and rolled with the deep swells.

"Don body-and-soul lashings and rig the life lines to the forecastle," he shouted into the storm's din. "Batten down the hatches!"

Once again, Tomas repeated the orders.

"Captain," the first mate yelled to be heard, "they'll need help."

Konstantin's eyes followed Tomas' pointing finger.

"Go!" he shouted in reply. "Hans and I will manage here."

⚜

From the galley, Tobar, the ship's cook, spied deck hands Erik and Milosh scramble to carry out the captain's orders. The two men slipped and slid across decks made treacherous by accumulating ice pellets. Together, the men fastened the wooden battens over the hatches and secured them with tarpaulins to ensure no water entered the holds. As they struggled with the aft covers, Tobar hastened into his own slicker and lashings and dashed to help.

The sea swelled and churned, and the wind screamed. The writhing current pushed the *Silver Oyster* north and east, off the charted course. Her bow dipped under the waves then reared to the sky, crashing down into the sea again, each time sending a great shudder through the ship. Streams of frothy water raced across the decks, careening off the superstructure in unchecked waterfalls.

❖

Tomas hastily descended to the main deck to inspect the hatch lashings. He handed his way down the ladder, grabbing at anything that would keep him safe until he was properly hooked onto a lifeline.

The ship rolled, caught broadside by a six-metre swell. Tomas lost his handhold and slipped on the reverse roll. When the bow of the ship dipped below another frothy wave, he slid forward across the deck, and collided with a stanchion. The residue of the wave roiled across the deck, slipping its icy fingers under Tomas and carrying him toward the ship's rail.

Tomas reached for Erik, but slid past the crewman, his flailing arms coming up empty. He heard Milosh holler loud over the roaring storm alerting the others that the first mate was free-falling into the scuppers. As if in slow motion, he watched Milosh hand himself through the rigging, likely intending to intersect his path toward the rail before another powerful wave claimed him for the sea.

Tomas continued to scramble, reaching again for Erik's outstretched arms.

"Grab on!" Erik screamed, but once again Tomas missed Erik's extended hands.

A moment later, the bow of the ship rose suddenly out of the sea, rolling Tomas directly into Erik's embrace. Erik held onto Tomas and locked his fists. Together, they anchored their feet against gear and rails.

"Push toward Milosh!" Erik shouted.

Rain lashed at their hands as if trying to break their grip.

"Milosh, grab on!" Erik shouted again.

Milosh lunged toward them and intercepted the two men as the bow dipped to receive another giant wave. The three men held fast together sliding and rolling toward the superstructure, searching for purchase.

Tomas felt his heart beating wildly as he struggled to catch his breath. A panicked thought over took him. *If these men lose their grip, I'm gone!*

The ship pitched and rolled, plunging forward and hammering hard each time its bow dropped into the sea.

Breathing hard, the men encouraged each other to thrust amidships. Suddenly, the galley door banged open, and Tobar grabbed two of the men by the scruff of the neck. Adding his weight as additional leverage, he hauled them inside.

The men braced themselves within the galley while outside the turbulence hammered at the ship. Puddles of water pooled at their feet and rolled around the small space in time with the ship's contortions.

"Riding out a storm is tough at the best of times," Tomas panted, eyeing his crewmates. "Erik. Milosh. I can't thank you enough. My wife would have been greatly displeased, if I missed her birthday at the end of the month." His feeble levity broke the tension.

"She still might have something to say about that shiner marring your pretty face, though," Erik teased.

Tomas raised his fingers to his throbbing eye and nodded.

"Right, then," he said, bringing the respite to an end. "Let's get back to work, or none of us will get home."

Erik and Milosh left the wheelhouse and returned to their tasks, wind and raining flogging them mercilessly, while Tobar helped Tomas struggle into his body and soul lashing.

"I'm ready," Tomas said, maintaining a grip on the galley door as he exited, then turning to shove it closed again.

Through the door's porthole, Tomas saw Tobar add his weight and the latch caught. Then he hooked his safety line and struggled toward the hatches to ensure they were securely battened.

✣

In their cabin, Rosalee and Punita clung to each other. The plunging and jarring tossed them about the bed on which they had huddled. They pressed their bodies into a bunk, trying to steady themselves, and screamed to no avail. Their fearful cries evaporated into the wind that screeched along the alleyway outside their cabin.

An hour later, as quickly as it had struck, the storm dissipated. All on board heaved a collective sigh of relief, seeing the shoreline of Sweden loom in the path of the *Silver Oyster*. Punita thought she heard Konstantin issue orders and felt the bow of the ship slowly turn. They would cruise west toward Sjealland before heading south, sailing closer to the small southern islands than first planned, he had said.

As the storm abated, Rosalee and Punita once again heard the comforting sound of the sea swishing against the hull. They collapsed together in exhaustion and fell asleep, still clinging to one another on the lower bunk.

✣

Once the crew had checked the ship for damage and reported to the captain that her structural integrity was good, Konstantin ordered the ship's speed increased, and went below to check on the women.

He found them huddled on the lower bunk bed, assured them that they were safe, and encouraged them to join him in the wheelhouse. He watched them pry their fingers loose one-by-one leaving welts on each other's arms. Fear seemed to have made them stiff. Their movements were slow as they staggered along the passageway and up the ladder.

On the deck outside the wheelhouse, Konstantin waited while the women gulped fresh air, then enquired about their welfare. Punita and Rosalee looked at each other and started to laugh. Konstantin knew it to be the edgy laughter that follows fear, the release that dissipates adrenaline. Those within earshot paused in their duties and looked on with curiosity.

The women's clothes were rumpled, and their hair frizzed around them like wayward halos. When their laughter calmed, Rosalee answered Konstantin's question.

"W-we're fine," she hiccupped, observing her daughter, as she regained her own composure. "As a matter of fact, despite all that we've been through, Punita never puked. Not once!"

The onlookers chuckled and praised the women for their courage.

CHAPTER TWENTY-SIX

The women continued to rest on deck outside the wheelhouse, under Konstantin's watchful eye. The fresh air seemed to revive and settle them.

"Captain," First Mate Tomas interrupted. "We have a radio message from Captain Zabar. The German coastguard boarded the *Silver Pearl* as it transited the Kiel Canal. They had their papers checked and the cargo was inspected. Apparently, this is the new routine. The captain just wanted you to know in advance to ensure our cargo is stowed well and that we have papers ready to hand."

Konstantin thought for a moment and issued a command.

"Tomas, send a response to Captain Zabar. Thank him for the information and tell him that we will chart a different course home. He'll understand and will let father—uh, Captain Buduly—know that our arrival in Amsterdam will be delayed. We'll sail northeast of Sjaelland to Kattegat Sound and onto the North Sea. I'll be along presently to review the charts."

"Aye aye, Captain!" The first mate acknowledged and headed for the radio room.

Konstantin stood contemplating for a bit longer, rubbing his index finger across the day's stubble beneath his lower lip.

"Well, ladies," he said, "I doubt you intended to have such adventures when you signed on with me. Prepare yourselves. We will be at sea several more days and the further north we go the rougher—and colder—the sea will be."

Examining the horizon, he clarified his thoughts.

"When we reach the top of Denmark, we will head south to Amsterdam, staying close to the coast, and enter the shipping channel at Borkum. From there, we'll motor into the Wadden Zee."

"The North Sea," he added, "can be wicked this time of year, but should be nothing compared to the storm that just struck. This is a good ship. She's tight, staunch and strong, and she's built to ride the swells that we'll encounter. Now, if you'll excuse me, I must see to the charts again."

He tipped his cap and left.

The women wandered the deck, coming to terms with the next leg of their journey. They reflected on how far they had travelled and shared their worry about Nicolai, wondering where he was and what had delayed him.

Nausea continued to plague Punita. Konstantin told her that it was rare for seasickness to last so long and hoped the nausea would pass before the ship reached the North Sea.

The sea between Denmark and Sweden was calm and the breeze light despite the time of year. The ship motored north through the Kattegat. Unseen risks hid below the frothing waves, though. The captain had to plot his course to avoid reefs and shallows, and checked bearings against lighthouses along the way to ensure clearance of obstacles that might damage her hull. Staying the course kept everyone alert.

⚜

The winds changed as the ship neared Skagen at the northern tip of Denmark. The temperature dropped. The currents swirled, and the wind whistled.

As the *Silver Oyster* departed the Baltic Sea and entered the North Sea, the water's temperament transformed. The swells became deeper and the freighter plowed into waves that rose and broke over the forecastle head, then drifted away on a misty sea breeze. At the precise point where the Skaggerak meets the North Sea, the waves of one roiled and roared against those of the other. The women covered their ears against the deafening sound. Random snowflakes twirled in the wind, some melting on their rosy cheeks, others threatening

310

to enshroud the ship. The twisting winds snatched words and breath away, leaving emptiness behind.

The ship corkscrewed in the frothy, merging currents, driven by a steady north-easterly wind. The captain ordered the power reduced to steady the *Silver Oyster's* passage, and she cut cleanly through the turmoil that marked her entry into the North Sea.

"Konstantin," Rosalee said, "we're worried about our safety in the cabin. Will you permit us to stay in the wheelhouse?"

The captain agreed to their request, and the women did their best to stay out of the way of the crew.

While anxiety plagued mother and daughter, they quietly discussed whether, indeed, the journey past the tip of Norway and into the North Sea was worse than the rogue storm, or perhaps slightly better.

❖

Once the ship had plowed through the chaos of the churning seas, the weather

311

over the North Sea moderated. Konstantin ordered the engines full ahead and set the course for Borkum.

Tomas brought the women warm drinks and invited them to share a hot meal in the galley. Seated at a table for only the second time since departing Stettin, Punita nibbled at dark rye bread and sipped weak tea. Rosalee's belly gurgled with hunger.

"Fresh sea air certainly fosters a healthy appetite," Tomas said, acknowledging the gurgle.

Punita glared at them, putting an end to further discussion about food. The aromas of the warm meal might have evoked her hunger on another occasion, but, at that moment, Punita cared only that her wayward stomach remained still.

⚜

Konstantin entered the galley a short time later to deliver a brief update. To the crew, he noted that their course would take them near Ringkøbing, Denmark, following the coast south to Borkum, and home. The men knew the ship's usual route home via the Kiel Canal and Ostfriesische Inseln to Borkum, then onward to Waddeneilanden. Near Texel Island, she would enter the Ijsselmeer, motor into the Markermeer and dock at the Amsterdam deep-sea port. As their captain spoke the familiar names, they appeared relieved.

For the benefit of the women, he elaborated.

"As long as the wind and weather hold, the ship should dock in Amsterdam within the next forty-eight hours."

Rosalee and Punita sighed their own relief, knowing that their sea journey would soon end.

"How are you two faring?" Konstantin asked.

"I'm feeling much better, thank you," Rosalee responded. "It's amazing how quickly a person can become accustomed to the pitch and roll of a ship at sea. In the beginning, I staggered everywhere. Now, I feel steadier on my legs—sea legs, I think you call them. Yes?"

"Indeed." The captain smiled at her. "You will find, however, that when we put to land again you will continue to feel the pitch and roll for a few days. The sea does not so willingly give up its influence."

"Oh, no," Punita groaned and sank further into the bench on which she was perched, "and I was praying just to be normal again."

"You will ... eventually." Konstantin tugged his forelock and disappeared.

"I'll certainly be happy to be on land again," Punita mumbled. "I desperately want to eat something, but don't dare."

She wrapped her arms across her belly.

"Just the thought of eating more than bread and tea makes me queasy all over again."

CHAPTER TWENTY-SEVEN

M id-morning of the following day, news echoed throughout the ship that Texel Island was in sight. The ship's new course was adjusted to pass by the island, and, late in the afternoon, a pilot vessel approached near Edom. Once the pilot was on board, he guided the freighter through Markermeer to the dock. Hawser lines were finally dropped, and the *Silver Oyster* was securely moored in her berth.

To that point, life aboard the ship had been tranquil in comparison to what the women now observed around them. The ship and dock had become a hive of busyness. The stevedores boarded to orchestrate the discharging of cargo, while the dockers prepared to receive it. The women watched with curiosity as the bustling men used steam-driven mechanical cranes and simple manpower to accomplish their work.

Konstantin was nowhere to be seen, but Tomas stopped to speak with the women briefly, suggesting that they should prepare to leave the ship when the captain came for them. They nodded and went below to tidy their hair and collect their few belongings.

When the women returned to the deck, they spotted Tomas waiting for them. He took their bags and guided them to the pedestrian ramp leading to the dock.

"The captain has been delayed," he advised. "I will take you to the warehouse to meet him. Hold fast to the railings, you don't want to misstep and end up in the drink."

Still rolling from the ship's movement, they did as he suggested and stepped unsteadily onto the dock. Swaying and clinging together, they waited for Tomas' next direction, and followed him, weaving amongst the dockers, cargo, and gear, then up a wooden stairwell to the road.

Tomas tipped his head right and led them across the quayside to a red brick building that towered four storeys above them. A bold white sign hung the height of the second and third storeys with the name *Oyster Pearl Imports* carved into it, painted burgundy and silver. Printed at the foot of the sign, in neat black letters, were the words *Buduly Anker–Proprietor.*

Tomas held open a bright green door in the lower left corner of the building, indicating with his head that the women should enter.

On the other side of the green door was a small office, sparsely furnished. Four mismatched chairs sat waiting for use. Leaving their bags with them, Tomas indicated that the women should sit and wait. Then he disappeared through another door, the opening of which permitted scents of spices, rope, tar, and sea to seep into the room before it banged shut.

Opposite them sat a young woman, perhaps twenty-five years old, behind a battered old desk. Her fingers bounced up and down across an odd machine that made a clacking sound each time a finger hammered a small circle, depressing it and allowing it to pop up again. Clack, clack, clack, the sound continued without interruption, not even when she glanced up at them, and watched Tomas pass through the door.

"That's a typewriter," Punita whispered to her mother. "Alexi's assistant has one at the hotel."

"Yes. I saw her use it when we were visiting," Rosalee acknowledged.

❖

The women waited politely for some time, hands clasped on their laps, before the young woman disappeared through the interior door and returned with a tray of tea, cheese, and biscuits.

"Captain Konstantin sends his apologies." She spoke German with precision. "He has been delayed a little longer than expected, and offers this refreshment, which he hopes will keep you well until he collects you. He shouldn't be much longer."

Rosalee and Punita gawked with surprise.

"Your German is perfect!" Punita exclaimed.

"Thank you," the young woman replied. "My mother is from Germany. She insisted that my brother and I learn her native language, so we could visit relatives and be able to communicate properly."

Dismissing the distraction, the young woman returned to her desk and resumed her typing.

The tea was refreshing, and the cheese and biscuits filled a void that neither woman realized existed until their bellies rumbled when the tray arrived.

"I feel I can safely eat again," Punita said, biting into a biscuit layered with cheese.

"Mmm," the women sighed together in appreciating of the refreshments.

⚜

Their tea was not yet cold when Konstantin appeared.

319

"Rosalee. Punita." He nodded to each. "Come."

He picked up their bags and led the way through the interior door.

"I had to review the manifest with the warehouse manager," he said, "and, of course, explain the detour of our journey and the need for two stowaways."

As the women followed, he waved his arm in an all-encompassing stroke indicating the warehouse through which they passed. The smells of spices, fruit, cured meats, and other sea scents assailed their senses once again.

"Here is where we receive and ship cargo," he shouted to be heard over the din of activity. "Our ships—the *Silver Oyster* and the *Silver Pearl*—sail between here and Stettin, but we have connections with other ships that sail to northern and southern Europe, Africa, Asia, the Americas, and so on. The cargo is sorted here and marked for delivery elsewhere."

The women's gazes followed the sweep of his arm. The space within the walls of the building was vast.

320

"Do these stacks reach the top of the building?" Punita asked, raising her voice as Konstantin had.

"No. The ceiling here reaches only to the second floor. The two floors above store other cargo." He indicated the ropes and pulleys dangling intermittently about the space and odd-shaped carts. "The dockers deliver the cargo to the warehouse, then our men take over. Some goods are wheeled in here and stacked using the ropes and pulleys. Other goods are taken directly up to the higher floors using a similar system, but on the outside. You may have noticed the long jibs—the cranes—and platforms jutting from the outside of the building. From the street, our men hook the cargo. The cranes are used to lift it up to the platform, where it's hauled into the floors above."

Without waiting for a response, he led them across the warehouse. As they stagger-walked and listened, the women tried to fathom the process Konstantin was explaining.

On the opposite side of the warehouse, Konstantin opened yet another door and the three stepped into a roadway where a weathered green truck sat idling. After the noise inside the warehouse, a sense of peace enfolded them.

Tomas jumped out from behind the wheel, leaving the door open for Konstantin. He then opened a door on the other side indicating that the women should slide in next to the Captain. Konstantin deposited their belongings in the back of the truck and slid into the driver's seat. The women had only a moment to thank Tomas for his kindness before the truck rumbled away.

⚜

"I arranged for a message to be delivered to my wife as soon as we docked," Konstantin said, keeping his eyes on the road. "She will be expecting us shortly. Tonight, we shall enjoy a good home-cooked meal and a soft, welcoming bed. Tomorrow, we can talk of your long-term plans."

Rosalee and Punita looked at each other with a mixture of sorrow and bewilderment.

"What is to become of us?" Rosalee asked. "Without my husband to rely on, how will we survive? I know how to live in a vardo that moves constantly through the countryside, but I have no idea how to survive in a city."

Punita linked her arm through her mother's.

"We'll find a way, Mama," she said.

"You mustn't worry," Konstantin said. "We'll organize everything tomorrow."

"Cousin, you have been so kind and generous to us these past several weeks," Punita responded, "and we are grateful for your wisdom and guidance."

"Konstantin, I can't help but worry about Nicolai," Rosalee lamented. "It's been so long since we saw him. How will we ever find him again?"

"Your husband is a resourceful man," Konstantin replied confidently. "He knows where you were headed. If he is able, he will find you. I asked my brother to watch out for him. The *Silver Pearl* is now working its way south along the Oder River. Zabar will make enquiries too. I won't tell you not to worry, because you'd do it regardless. We must pray and think positively that he will find his way."

The women bowed their heads and rode in silence for the remainder of the ride.

CHAPTER TWENTY-EIGHT

K onstantin's home was a short drive
from the dock. The backside of the
house faced one of the many canals in
Amsterdam and a small foot bridge. The
front faced onto a city street. It was tall, not
unlike the warehouse, but narrower than the
warehouse, and located at the end of a series
of large townhouses that had been built
around 1750. They listed slightly to the left
with age, reminding Rosalee of her tendency
to stagger with a list since leaving the ship.

Rosalee drew Punita's attention to the
pleasing façade of the house. It was finished
in a cream-coloured stone, each townhouse
distinguished by the colour of its finishing
stone. Small rows of windows wrapped
across the front of the townhouse and along
its exposed side, indicating at least four
levels. Small additional windows under the
eaves indicated the possibility of a fifth level.

The two windows on the lowest level, at the top of wide ascending staircases made of white stone, were considerably larger and separated by a set of carved double doors. The twin staircases ascended under the windows and merged to form a broad landing outside the ornately carved doors. The staircases and landing arched over a pair of blood red doors. From the street, a staircase descended to the red doors beneath the house.

Konstantin parked the truck on the street and collected the bags from the back. The women climbed out, leaned into one another for support, and followed him to the foot of one of the grand staircases.

"Have you lived here a long time?" Rosalee asked.

"Yes. My family has lived here for decades," Konstantin answered, heading up the stairs.

"Where do the red doors lead?" Punita asked, pointing toward the lower entrance.

"Those doors lead to the servants' quarters and storage," he answered, ascending slowly, waiting for the women to catch up.

One of the red doors opened, and a man in uniform stepped up to the street. He nodded to Konstantin, climbed into the idling truck and drove away.

The women followed Konstantin, with Rosalee expressing appreciation for the decorated bannister. The solid stone offered stability.

Konstantin placed his hand on the knob of one of the carved doors, but before he could turn it, the door popped open and two young, towheaded boys flew at him.

"Papa, Papa!" they shouted in harmony.

Rosalee and Punita hung back, enjoying the boisterous welcome. Konstantin set the bags on the floor inside the door and bent to acknowledge his children.

The bags disappeared during Konstantin's brief exchange with his children.

"Come in, please," he said, extending

the invitation to Rosalee and Punita, while he ushered his sons through the doorway.

Two small girls stood back, waiting for him to enter, tethered by his wife's firm hands, one placed on the shoulder of each. The girls bounced for joy as Konstantin leaned forward with an affectionate kiss for his wife, followed by a playful tweak of each of the tiny noses pointing up at him.

As they entered the doorway, an older boy politely bowed to Punita and Rosalee. Startled, Rosalee gasped and took a step back.

"This is my eldest son, Ambroos. He's fifteen," Konstantin said, placing an affectionate hand on the shoulder of a brown-haired boy who resembled him in a remarkable way.

"Mama, are you all right?" Punita asked. "You've gone awfully pale."

"I'm fine," Rosalee answered. "A-Ambroos, I'm pleased to meet you. You resemble your father and my husband. The similarity caught me off guard. I thought I was seeing a ghost."

She smiled feebly, hoping to minimize the shock of her reaction.

"Of course, he does!" Konstantin said, translating her comments to his son. "I never gave it a thought, until you said so. Ambroos' hair colour is closer to Nicolai's than mine. I see now why you were surprised."

Konstantin spoke further to his eldest son, pointing upward. Ambroos acknowledged his father's instructions and reached for their bags. Taking the stairs two at a time with his lanky legs, Ambroos disappeared up a tall dark staircase that rose to the side of the dim hallway.

"This is my wife Anika, sons Braam, aged eleven, and Casper, aged seven, and the twins Dora and Drika," Konstantin said lifting a tidy braid from each to show the comparison. "Drika's hair is a little redder than Dora's."

The tiny girls giggled. The young boys stood formally beside their mother, waiting. All four younger children were fair skinned, and strongly resembled Anika, except that the boys had Konstantin's bearing.

The twins spoke in unison, each holding up four fingers of their right hand.

"They're four years old," Konstantin said translating the twins' declaration into German.

Thumping footsteps on the stairs announced the return of Ambroos.

Konstantin spoke further to his family, then repeated to his guests in German.

"I've just told them that you are the family of my cousin Nicolai Kota."

The children and their mother bobbed at the introduction, which gesture was returned by Rosalee and Punita.

Konstantin removed his hat and coat and handed them to a servant.

"We are so grateful for your hospitality," Rosalee responded, and Konstantin translated.

"Nonsense. Please come in," Anika said, allowing her husband to translate again.

She stepped back, allowing her guests space to remove their coats. The servant waited as they did so, then disappeared with their outerwear.

"I'll take you directly to your rooms," Anika said as she stepped on the first of many stairs leading up into the dark. "You will want to freshen up before our meal, and perhaps rest."

Konstantin translated again, and Punita and Rosalee followed Anika up the staircase.

They ascended first one narrow staircase, then another. As they did so, the atmosphere changed from a warm main floor with smells of fresh polish and baked bread to cooler floors and fresh sea air. A fourth staircase led higher, but Anika stopped at the third level and led them down a dimly lit hallway, passing several closed doors. At the end of the hall, she turned the knobs of two adjacent doors simultaneously, and gave each door a shove.

"Rooms are same. You choose, yes?" Anika said in halting German.

331

She entered one of the rooms, walked toward a partially open window and closed it, before moving to the second room to do the same. Anika allowed them time to peruse each room before beckoning them to follow again.

"Here," she moved to another door, turned the knob and shoved, "is bath, and here," she turned to the door across the hall, "is water closet. You like bath? Sleep? Come salon one hour, ja?"

On a gush of thanks from the two women, Anika left them, disappearing as discreetly as her son had, down the dark narrow staircase.

CHAPTER TWENTY-NINE

"Oh, Mama! Wouldn't you like a nice, hot bath?" Punita asked as she walked into the bathroom, leaned over the tub, and turned the taps.

The pipes rattled and clanged, announcing the rise of water from floors below. Soon, it began to spurt out of the water spout.

"I would, indeed," Rosalee smiled.

As the water filled the tub, they wandered across the hall and Rosalee marvelled that they would have their own indoor toilet and would not have to use an outhouse or a ship's head. She pulled on a chain and watched as the water flowed from a white porcelain reservoir into the bowl of the toilet.

"Yes," she said, "I think I will enjoy a bath very much."

Punita returned quickly to the other room, closing the taps on the almost-full bathtub.

"There you are, Mama," she gestured to the tub. "Hop in. Here's some soap and towels. If you want to wash your hair, I can help you with that."

"Tomorrow, I'll wash my hair," she said. "It will take too long to dry, and I'd like to rest a bit. My legs are still uneven."

"All right," Punita said. "I'll check out the bedrooms."

She closed the door behind her, leaving Rosalee to enjoy the warmth of the cocooning bathroom.

Punita discovered that the bedrooms were mirror images, except that one was decorated in pink roses and white lace. The other was blue delft and white lace. Punita selected the pink room, thinking of Stefan and her room at the hotel.

With the thought of Stefan, her hand rested intuitively on her belly. She was not certain, and it was probably too soon to tell, but she did wonder whether some of the nausea and cramping that she had suffered on the *Silver Oyster* might have been from another source. She let her mind wander with the romance of it, remembering her time with Stefan.

When the reality of her situation crept into her thoughts, she closed her mind to it and set to sorting through and organizing the few possessions she now had. She shook out the blue suit and dusted the matching shoes.

Her mother knocked on the door jamb, breaking into Punita's reverie.

"I'm done. Will you bathe too?"

"Yes, quickly," Punita said with a nod. "I could use a little rest from my uneven legs too."

Rosalee smiled and closed the door to the blue room.

In the bathroom, Punita drained the tub and ran fresh water, spying a small bottle of bath oil on the ledge of the tub. She dribbled a few drops into the water as it flowed from the taps. The warmth of the water released the scent of lavender, reminding her first of Mathilde, then Stefan.

When she closed the door to the bath-room, she noticed a full-length mirror mounted on its back. She shed her clothes in a heap on the floor and looked in disbelief at the woman whose reflection stared back. *Who are you? Certainly not the robust young woman who lay in Stefan's arms not so long ago!*

The mirror in the hotel had told her that she was young and healthy, brown from the sun, muscles round and firm. After almost six weeks of travel and nausea, she was now skeletal. Her muscles were no longer round and full. Her legs were like sticks. Cheekbones defined her face. Her eyes were dull.

Punita's hands drifted once again to her belly. *Still flat. If life stirs within, it's too soon to see.*

Stepping into the hot, fragrant water, Punita's reverie filled with images of Stefan. She allowed her fingers, slippery with the oil, to wander over surfaces Stefan had brought to life.

"Oh, Stefan," she sighed, "I pray the months pass quickly, until we are together again. I can't bear to be without you."

Salty tears trickled from Punita's eyes, and she dashed them away, replacing them with streaks of scented oil. She rested her head on the back of the tub and fell asleep in the warm oily waterbed. Not long after, she awoke smartly to the shock of cold water and pulled the bath plug. She rubbed herself briskly with a fresh towel and paused once more for a look in the mirror before fastening the towel under her arms. She collected her discarded clothes and padded toward the pink room to dress.

Punita and Rosalee met a few minutes later as they each stepped into the hallway, refreshed, if still a little wobbly. They held fast to the railing and wall as they descended the steep staircase.

"Did you sleep a little, Mama?"

"I did," Rosalee answered over her shoulder. "You?"

"Yes. I fell asleep in the tub. The cold water woke me up!"

The women giggled as they descended to the main floor, where delightful aromas filled the hallway in promise of the meal to come. From a room along the hallway, they heard a mixture of voices—Konstantin's deep and reassuring, the children speaking over each other, Anika's lighter, and others.

"The salon must be this way," Punita indicated.

CHAPTER THIRTY

"Ah! Ladies!" Konstantin greeted them heartily at the doorway, offering each an elbow in which to insert their hands. "Come and meet everyone.

"Children, enjoy your gifts quietly, eh! The adults would like to be heard too."

The children quieted and collected their new toys, scurrying to another part of the salon, out of the way of adult feet.

Leading them further into the room of heavy woods, fine furniture, Turkish carpets, and exotic ornaments, Konstantin introduced Rosalee and Punita to his neighbours Franz and Rachel Rothwell, his father Buduly, his mother Walentyna, and his sister-in-law Gaeta.

"I was just about to tell our guests how brave the two of you have been," Konstantin said. "A sea journey from the Baltic Sea to the North Sea and on to Amsterdam is not for the weak of heart. Under the circumstances, you both managed very well indeed!" He grinned at Punita, wrapping his arm around her shoulders and squeezing affectionately. "It is most unfortunate that young Punita was not as seaworthy as her mother."

At that moment, a servant appeared with a silver tray of fine glasses filled with a golden, bubbly beverage.

"Is-is that—Champagne?" Punita asked.

Surprised that Punita guessed correctly, Konstantin replied, "Yes. You know it?"

"I had the opportunity to try some not so long before we met you in Schinawa," Punita replied.

"Ah, yes," Konstantin responded, then changed the topic, not wanting to divulge the reason for her champagne sampling. His neighbours would not understand.

"What news have I missed in the past weeks?" he asked, and the conversation shifted to the news of the Dutch economy and the creeping depression.

"At least we don't suffer like some of the other countries," said Franz. "We will recover soon, without ever having lost much! Take that Hitler, on the other hand, he scares me. Him and his government. They are not to be trusted!"

"Franz, I don't think now is the time to speak of politics," Rachel cautioned her husband. "That is a conversation for later. Shall we not stick to pleasantries?"

Walentyna hooked her arm through Punita's and led her to an empty corner.

"My dear, you are so thin. We must fatten you up! We have a lovely dinner ahead of us. A good place to start, I think." She gave Punita an encouraging smile. "My, what a beautiful suit. The fabric is of fine quality."

Walentyna fingered the hem of Punita's jacket, and skillfully changed to a more comfortable topic.

⚜

Buduly placed his hand in the centre of Rosalee's back and led her in another direction for a private conversation.

"Konstantin tells me that Nicolai was taken by Hitler's men," he confided in a deep but quiet voice. "I've had word from my son Zabar. He is at this very time guiding his ship south along the Oder River. Security has tightened since you left. At every port, he spreads the news of the danger and enquires about those who are taken. He has not yet reached Schinawa, but he will tarry as long as he dares and try to find out what happened."

For a moment, Rosalee's eyes filled with hope, then she hung her head and swiped at her tears.

"Rosalee, we will do our best to find Nicolai, or find out what has happened to him. Is there anyone you can write to? So long as we are able, we will continue to deliver messages. And look for him."

Rosalee lifted her head. With sadness and embarrassment, she told Buduly that she wrote only a little German. Nicolai was the one with the advanced schooling.

"But Punita is well-schooled too," she

342

said cheerily. "She can converse and write in German."

"That will be quite suitable. Do you know anyone to whom you could write?" he asked again.

"Perhaps," she answered, "I will have to discuss that with Punita. She may have more and better connections, since she's lived in Liegnitz for the past six years."

"Very well. If we can help in any way, let us know. I have lived in Amsterdam for a long time, and my wife and daughters-in-law come from old Dutch families. They are all very clever and will be able to help you send letters to whomever you think can help." He gazed about the room. "We can talk more of this tomorrow. For now, come, let us rejoin the party, shall we?"

Again, his hand found the centre of her back and he escorted her toward the gathering.

Not long after, a servant whispered to Anika, and she announced that dinner was ready for serving. Konstantin invited the adults and Ambroos to the dining room and the servant escorted the younger children to the kitchen.

"Don't spill your dinner on your good clothes," Anika warned them.

"No, Mama," the four young voices chimed.

⚜

Rosalee's attention was drawn to the fineness of the dining room, its size, the length of the table covered in the most delicate of white lace. Delft dishes and silver cutlery spaced equally to mark a place for each diner. Crystal glasses captured candlelight casting colourful bars of light about the room. Brightly woven Persian prayer mats hung on the walls.

The men gallantly pulled the carved and polished chairs from the table for the women, before taking their own seats. They were no sooner seated, then three servants paraded in trays of food. Each servant appeared to have their own responsibilities and tasks which they managed proficiently.

The meal passed smoothly with small talk and tantalizing tastes.

After the simple fare that travellers ate, Rosalee marvelled that ordinary flavours could be blended in such a way to create new flavours and heady aromas. As delicious as the food was, she cautioned Punita to sample carefully.

"Your stomach was overtaxed on the sea voyage and overeating and drinking now could cause discomfort through the night," she whispered discreetly.

"You need not be concerned, Mama, the nausea has not yet passed. I will eat only a little."

To Rosalee's surprise, she too was unable to eat much of her meal and took only small sips of the burgundy wine poured in the beautiful glasses. She determined early in the meal that the rich food made her queasy as well.

By the time dessert was brought from the kitchen, both Rosalee and Punita were showing signs of fatigue and discomfort, a condition that did not escape their hostess.

Discreetly, Anika enlisted Konstantin's aid to determine whether they would prefer to be excused from the remainder of the evening.

Embarrassed, they nodded.

"Come," said Anika, "I take you up."

She rose, making polite excuses to her guests.

On the landing of the third floor, the women assured Anika that they could manage and that she should return to her guests. With a swish of her silk skirt, Anika bid them good night and left them to retire at their leisure.

At the entrances of their rooms, mother and daughter hugged good night. It had been a while since Punita had a room to herself. Her mother could not remember ever sleeping alone.

"Good night," they whispered one to the other.

Rosalee's hand cupped Punita's cheek. A look of longing and sadness filled her eyes.

"Sometimes you look just like your father," she said, her eyes abruptly filling with tears.

346

CHAPTER THIRTY-ONE

The next morning found the two women curled together in Punita's single bed. It would take time for Rosalee to learn the ways of a city.

On Konstantin's instructions of the evening before, they rose and prepared themselves for the day, then descended the narrow staircase to the main floor where they met Konstantin in the dining room.

"Good morning, ladies," he said, lifting his eyes from a newspaper. "Did you sleep well?"

"Yes, thank you," Rosalee responded as she followed Konstantin's invitation to help herself to rye bread, cooked eggs, a selection of Dutch cheeses, and home-made jams.

A servant appeared with a coffee canister and a questioning face.

"Yes, please," she answered, moving her cup toward him.

The same offer was then extended to Punita.

"The children have gone to school and Anika is assisting our Dr. Henrik with a challenging birth," Konstantin said, breaking the quiet of the repast. "After you've eaten, we should discuss plans for your life here in Amsterdam."

They acknowledged his remarks, not knowing what to expect. Life in a city was as foreign to Rosalee as sleeping alone.

"When you've finished your meal, join me in my office. It's the last door on the right, at the end of the hall."

He collected his newspaper and excused himself. Moments later, the sound of Konstantin's footsteps stopped at the end of the hall and a door closed.

"Mama, what is to become of us?" Punita asked.

"I don't know, Punita. I'm at a loss to imagine. Your papa was always the one to make decisions. For all of us. The last he said to me was that if anything happened to him, we were to trust Konstantin. Papa did, so we must. He is all we have," Rosalee said, wringing her hands. "Just now, I am more concerned about the money. We have German money, not Dutch. I hope that Konstantin can help us exchange it. Also, I don't know the cost of things in a city."

"We'll need to find work," Punita added, "and we have few skills."

"We don't know the language either."

"Do you think Konstantin would turn us into the street?"

"No. He's a good man. We are safe for now," Rosalee assured them both.

They ate the remainder of their breakfast in silence.

"How are you feeling today," Rosalee asked as she set her empty coffee cup onto its saucer. "Still nauseous?"

"A little, it's not as bad as it was at sea. Look!" Punita said as she pushed her plate toward the table centre. "I've managed to eat bread and cheese, and, so far, it's sitting quietly."

"That is a good sign," Rosalee said, trying to sound encouraging. "By tomorrow, we two should be whole again. Provided our legs co-operate!"

"Did you feel how the mirror above the bathroom sink leaned in to have a better look at you this morning?" Punita marvelled. "I thought the wall would collapse on me. It must be part of the sea motion too."

"I'll be happy when we are normal again," Rosalee agreed. "Come. Konstantin is waiting for us."

⚜

They found Konstantin seated behind a carved mahogany desk in a room that was both masculine and nautical. Unlike the rest of the house, which reflected Anika's influence in the decorating, Konstantin's room was organized for business. It was an extension of his office on the dock, he told them, and it helped him focus above the distractions of a busy household and rambunctious children.

In front of the desk sat two chairs of the same carved mahogany, the cracked green leather seats and backs telling of regular and long-time use. Konstantin directed the women to the chairs.

"We have much to discuss and organize before I sail again. I've a list here of what I think may be your primary concerns, but if I've missed something, let me know."

He placed a sheet of paper in front of them and with a twist of his fingers turned the page so they could read the words.

"I hope, Konstantin, that one of the things on this list is learning to read and write the language of Amsterdam," Rosalee said, reminding him of their limitations.

"Ah! How foolish of me!" He reached for the list and placed it in front of him, scribbling more words at the bottom of the list.

"I will read it for you, then," he said, running his finger down the list.

"Money. Lodging. Employment. Nicolai. And the last, language."

He looked at them questioningly. Rosalee nodded.

"We can add more, if necessary," she said.

Working their way through the list, the women shared with Konstantin that they had money, but it was in German currency. It would have to be converted to guilders. They also needed to understand how long the money would last.

"I can certainly arrange for the money to be converted, and, as far as determining how long it will last, we have two things to consider.

"So long as you live under this roof, you need not spend any except for personal needs. However, there will come a time when you will wish to be on your own and for that you will need income. Plan to stay with us for the next several months," he encouraged.

"My wife speaks a little German and she will guide you. One of the servants, Baldev, is fluent in many languages, including

German, Dutch, and Romani. He can inter-
pret as necessary until you have a better
command of Dutch."

Rosalee sat back into her chair, visibly
relaxing as Konstantin began to provide
tools necessary for their survival.

"At some point, we can discuss employment, but we have time for that. As you
travel about the city, observe those who
work, and what talents are compatible with
yours.

"Finally, my mother will tutor you in the
voice of Amsterdam, and help you send letters of enquiry through the community to
see if Nicolai can be located. If you write
letters before I leave, I will pass them along
the Oder River."

He folded his hands over the list as he
concluded the review of his concerns.

"A thousand thanks, Cousin Konstantin.
We will always be in your debt," Rosalee
stated with sincerity. "I would like to prepare those letters today. How will we find
your mother, and when are you leaving?"

"You need not rush off. I am in port for another week or so," Konstantin advised. "My parents live within walking distance, but, until you are familiar with the area, I suggest you ask Baldev to escort you."

Rosalee and Punita rose and left Konstantin to his business. Punita returned to her room claiming nausea, and Rosalee went in search of Baldev.

CHAPTER THIRTY-TWO

Near midday, Rosalee knocked on Punita's door, and let herself into the pink room. Punita was resting in an armchair, a book splayed open in her lap.

"How are you feeling, my daughter?"

"I am well, Mama. The nausea seems finally to have passed." The relief in Punita's voice was audible. She closed the book and set it aside. "Where have you been?"

Rosalee sat on Punita's bed and propped the pillow behind her back, as she explained that she had arranged for Baldev to take her to the home of Buduly and Walentyna. She was invited to pass the morning with them and Baldev was asked to return before midday to guide her back to Konstantin's home. Over coffee and fresh cakes, she had learned a great deal about Buduly's family and how they came to be in Amsterdam.

"Their story is very interesting," she said. "I'll try to tell you Buduly's story in his words."

Punita shifted her position and listened with interest.

"His life began as a nomad and followed a course similar to ours. He and his family lived in wagons until he was twenty. Then things began to unravel.

"One particularly bad winter, an illness passed through the camp. Very few survived. He saw to the burial of his grandmother, his parents, his younger brother, and two sisters. According to tradition, most of his family's possessions were burnt with their vardo. What little he kept, he carried with him in a tattered valise. The few survivors of his vista separated to search for relatives or another vista to join.

"Buduly had no one and wandered for months, living off the land. When he neared a city or town, he worked for a few coins to buy food.

"Eventually, Buduly found himself in Stettin, wandering along the docks. Someone asked whether he would be interested in working as a deckhand on the *Silver Oyster* bound for Amsterdam. 'Why not,' he said, 'I have nothing better to do.'

"On that first voyage, he discovered a passion for sailing and the sense of adventure that came with it. He made the return run from Amsterdam to Stettin on many occasions, each time learning more about sailing and the shipping industry.

"He developed a healthy interest in the owner's business and proved to be a reliable crewman. Eventually, the captain took him under his wing and trained him not only in managing the business, but in sailing the ship. The captain was a quiet man who spoke little of his family. Perhaps that is why he became fond of Buduly. He saw in him a kindred spirit.

"On one occasion, as the *Silver Oyster* prepared to dock in Amsterdam, the captain invited Buduly to dine with his wife and daughter. Buduly accepted, surprised to hear that the old captain had a daughter."

"The captain must have been a very private man," Punita said, interrupting the tale.

"Indeed!" Rosalee responded. "Buduly did not know what to expect, but, when he looked upon the captain's daughter that first time, he saw his future clearly. Before they set sail for Stettin, he had asked the captain's permission to marry Walentyna. The captain shared that he had been secretly hoping Buduly would fancy his daughter. Walentyna was a clever girl, and more than a little appealing to the eye.

"The captain refused to marry his beloved daughter to just any man. He was impressed with Buduly and thought the match worthy. Although Walentyna was older than any woman that Buduly would have married had he stayed with his vista, he had eyes for none but her. When the *Silver Oyster* returned to Amsterdam, the two were married."

"What a sweet story," Punita said, clasping her hands together.

"But wait!" Rosalee said, stopping her daughter. "There's more!"

She took a deep breath and continued the story.

"Buduly and Walentyna lived with her parents for the first years of their marriage. When they learned that she was pregnant, they cast about for a home and eventually settled on the townhouse now occupied by Konstantin. Having lived his early years in vardos and then at sea, Buduly could not imagine living in a walled-in structure. The compromise was to purchase the townhouse and replace the exterior walls with as many windows as possible.

"From 1918 to 1929, Buduly and his family watched as the Netherlands resisted a financial recession. Any country involved in World War I had suffered similarly, because of debts incurred during the war. The Netherlands had not been directly affected by the war, but it suffered nonetheless when

Germany, one of its primary trading partners, was afflicted with its own economic downturn.

"Fortunately, running an import/export business kept financial concerns at bay for the Anker family. A further recession had started creeping into the Dutch economy in the early 1930s, but so far, the effect on the family was small.

"When Walentyna's parents died, she and Buduly inherited a large estate. By then, their two sons, Konstantin and Zabar, were both married and starting their own families. The smart thing to do, they decided, was to ensure that their sons' families had homes in which to grow.

"Buduly and Walentyna located another townhouse that suited the needs of Zabar and Gaete and bought it for them. Then, at the request of Konstantin and Anika, the family home was deeded to them. Walentyna and Buduly purchased an apartment on a quiet canal where they could watch the daily comings and goings of their neighbours, but still had views of the sea. 'Once a sailor, always a sailor,' Buduly said."

"Such a lovely story," Rosalee said, ending the tale.

"What a remarkable story of success and determination," Punita said, smiling at her mother. "Truly inspirational!"

"I agree," Rosalee said. "By that time, I was feeling very comfortable with our new friends, so I asked whether Walentyna would be interested in schooling us. We discussed the need to learn the language, including reading and writing, and she seemed sincerely pleased to be asked to teach us.

"Buduly suggested that we should learn numbers too. If we are to run a business, we should know how to keep records. I told him that you are clever with numbers and helped Papa with the treasury."

Rosalee brightened and clapped her hands.

"Our first lesson starts tomorrow after the morning meal ... provided your nausea is manageable."

"How exciting, Mama. Buduly and his wife are so kind to spend time with us. And Konstantin and Anika are very generous to allow us to stay here without cost, even though the economy falters."

"Yes. We must make the most of the opportunity, so they will be proud of us," Rosalee said. "Come, Punita, I believe the mid-day meal is being served. Can you eat?"

"Yes! I am starving!" Punita responded, surprising herself with her enthusiasm.

❖

As arranged, the tutorials began the following day and continued for many weeks. Both women were keen students, eager to learn the language of their new home.

One of the first goals, however, was to write the letters enquiring after Nicolai and his whereabouts. Rosalee wrote the simple letters.

Punita wrote letters too, one to each of Stefan, Alexi, and Mathilde. She told them of their safe arrival in Amsterdam and their proposed plans. In her letter to Stefan she told him how much she missed him and how she looked forward to becoming his wife. In her letter to Alexi, she begged him to help find her father, telling him that Konstantin had recommended he speak with Herr Lange.

There's that name again, she thought. *It seems Mama is right to wonder about the connection between the Lange family and ours.*

It tugged at Punita's heart that she was unable to say she was pregnant. She would tell him another time, when she knew for certain. Of Alexi, she begged his help locating her father, sharing as much of the incident in Schinawa as she knew.

When the *Silver Oyster* next set sail, Konstantin carried the packet of letters with him.

CHAPTER THIRTY-THREE

Within a week of Nicolai's death, the gates of Dachau were opened to admit a cream-coloured Rohr driven by Retired Major Gerhard Lange. Major Lange asked for directions to the administrative offices and slowly rolled the Rohr to a stop outside the entrance of a three-storey white-brick building. He unfolded his length from the vehicle and stretched as he surveyed the compound. What he saw did not impress him. Hundreds of skeletal men clothed in striped uniforms engaged in heavy labour. *They look like automatons*, he thought, disgust and compassion rising in his gorge.

Not in uniform, the staff in the administrative office were slow to respond to Gerhard's presence until he cleared his throat and knocked on a wooden countertop.

"Pardon me," he said in a loud, clear voice, "I'm looking for the commander of this camp."

Six pairs of eyes turned to him, seemingly bewildered by the volume, but before any of them could speak, a chair in an adjoining room grated on the wooden floor and heavy footsteps carried the commander into the front office.

"I am Inspector General of this camp ... Theodor Eicke," the man said with authority.

"Who are you?"

"Retired Major Gerhard Lange, formerly of the Regiment of King Wilhelm the First," Gerhard said, showing his credentials.

"How may I help you, sir?" Eicke responded.

"I am enquiring after an individual," he said, "a cousin of a friend of mine."

Gerhard assessed Eicke, suspicious of whether he was a trustworthy fellow.

"The individual goes by the name of Nicolai Kota. I understand that he was

365

detained outside of Schinawa, perhaps a month or so ago. I believe he was brought here, and I'm wondering whether you can confirm the information I've been given."

"And who gave you this information, sir?" Eicke asked suspiciously.

"As I mentioned," Gerhard continued to assess Eicke, "a friend of mine mentioned that his cousin was missing and asked whether I might help. I asked about, and it became more of a word here and a word there. Nothing particularly concrete. I've driven from Liegnitz trying to track Herr Kota's journey and thought that—since I'm in the area—I'd ask here. Have you any record that might indicate whether he's passed through this camp?"

"Kota, you say. Hmmm. Let me check."

Eicke turned toward the staff, caught the eye of one, and asked for the register.

"You said within the past month or so?" he asked, returning his attention to Gerhard.

Gerhard nodded.

"Bring me the register for the last quarter," Eicke specified over his shoulder.

A momentary flurry resulted in a leather-bound register being deposited on the counter between the two officers. Eicke opened the register and scanned the names of entries since September. Well along the list, he plopped a finger mid-page and looked up.

"Kota, you said. Nicolai Kota?"

"That's correct."

"This entry shows that a Nicolai Kota, a Jew from Schinawa, was brought into the camp in early November," Eicke said. "He had a broken right hand and broken ribs."

"My God!" Gerhard mumbled apprehensively. "Your record is mistaken. He's not a Jew. Herr Kota is Catholic. A good Catholic! He is also a German horse trainer, and his skills are invaluable. I demand his immediate release."

"Can't do that, sir," Eicke glared at him.

"And why not?" Gerhard stood to his full height, holding Eicke's glare.

"Because he's dead!" Eicke said, gloating.

"Dead! How?" Gerhard exclaimed.

"We had an outbreak of epidemic typhus. Still do," Eicke said. "It's almost under control, but Kota was one of the first to die."

Gerhard tried to contain his rage at a needless death. His sense of disgust choked him.

"And his body? Where can I find it? I'd like to at least take it back with me for a decent burial."

"Can't do that either," Eicke replied irritably.

"And why not?"

"Anyone who has died from typhus has been burnt to reduce contamination."

"And his possessions?" Gerhard asked.

"Says here," Eicke ran his finger across the page, "that he had none. They seldom do. They usually come in here with only the clothes on their backs. No papers, no money, no possessions."

Eicke snapped the register closed and leered at Gerhard.

"Will that be all, sir?" Eicke sneered. "Any other missing bodies you'd like to enquire after?"

"No," Gerhard said quietly, turning toward the door. "Thank you for your time, Inspector General."

Outside, Gerhard scanned the camp again, seeing in more detail the misery that resided within its gates. His shoulders sagged with realization of the hopeless situation before him. It was December. Christmas would be in a few weeks. *Nothing feels right. There is no hope here.*

Icy flakes of snow swirled about him. He tugged his collar up to his ears and donned his leather gloves before sliding onto the icy leather seat and starting the Rohr.

As Gerhard drove back to Liegnitz, he chewed on the words he would use to deliver the sorry news to his old friend, Alexi Puchinski.

CHAPTER THIRTY-FOUR

W eeks passed and Punita's appetite resumed. Slowly, she regained the weight she had dropped during the sea voyage. When she examined herself before the bathroom mirror she still saw a flat belly, but felt small changes occurring elsewhere. Her breasts were tender, her clothes fit a little tighter at the waist. When the third month passed and still she had not bled, she resolved to speak with her mother.

Knocking lightly on the door to the blue room before their morning meal, she turned the knob and entered to find her mother sitting on her bed, both hands on her belly and tears streaming down her cheeks.

"Mama!" Punita rushed to her mother, kneeling at her feet.

"Mama, what is it?"

Rosalee turned her wet eyes to Punita, slowly returning from her dream-like state.

"Punita, child, I was afraid to believe it. Your father and I tried so many times to give you a brother or sister, and now—it appears we've been given another chance. I'm fairly certain that I'm pregnant again!"

Her face was ethereal as she spoke, her voice solemn.

"I pray to God that this child will survive and be a testament to your father," she said.

Punita looked in awe at her mother. Slowly, a smile crept over her face.

"Well, then, I think our lives are about to become very interesting, Mama. I think I'm carrying Stefan's child."

It was Rosalee's turn to be surprised.

"Oh, Punita. My darling child." She reached for Punita and hugged her lovingly.

"I have been so distracted by my own circumstance, that I didn't notice yours. I should have known. You haven't bled since you returned to camp. And the ongoing nausea! Of course, you carry Stefan's child!"

371

"What a curious situation we have," Punita mused.

"We will be mothers, sister, daughter, and grandmother all at the same time!"

Rosalee hugged her daughter to her and together they laughed. With hands on her daughter's shoulders, Rosalee set Punita apart from her once again and looked deep into her daughter's dark chocolate eyes.

"We must look after each other," she stated, her shadowed gaze fixed somewhere in the future. A fleeting frown passed over her countenance.

"The next months could be difficult. Pregnancy can be a dangerous matter for a woman."

"*Hallow, hallow. Goedenmorgan,*" Anika said in her sing-song voice from the hallway. "*Ontbijt, ya?* Hun-gree?"

"Good morning to you, Anika. We are both very hungry and ready for breakfast," Rosalee replied.

Rosalee and Punita ate their breakfast quickly, anxious to be on their way. They

372

wanted to share their news with Buduly and Walentyna. They released Baldev from his obligation to escort them, confident that they could find their own way. Bundled against the bite of the sea wind and swirl of snowflakes, they stepped cautiously over crunching snow and ice, linked arm in arm.

The women chattered as they walked, discussing their future ahead with children created by the men they loved. For the first time in months, they had happiness to share. When Nicolai and Stefan finally rejoined them, they would be the happiest of families, and in the years ahead they would realize all their dreams.

Rosalee and Punita shared their joy with Buduly and Walentyna before their daily lessons began. Walentyna expressed concern that Punita was unmarried and so young to be having a child. With Buduly's help and knowledge of their culture, Walentyna was enlightened to the importance of the pregnancy and Stefan's promise to marry Punita the following summer.

❖

More weeks passed. Punita and Rosalee teased and encouraged each other as their waists thickened and their bodies expanded and altered to accommodate the advancing pregnancies. Konstantin's home bustled with the excitement of two births, and the studies with Walentyna continued.

Each time the *Silver Oyster* or the *Silver Pearl* returned to port, the women eagerly awaited news of Nicolai and Stefan. And each time the ships sailed, they carried a packet of letters.

Within a month, a letter came. Alexi wrote that Stefan was in good health, still in military service, and that Punita's letter had been forwarded on to him. He also wrote that he was making enquiries about the folks who were collected from Schinawa. He heard that they may have been detained at a holding area called Dachau. As suggested in her letter, he had asked his long-time friend, Retired Major Lange whether he might investigate. Until he heard further from Herr Lange, he cautioned the women not to set their hopes too high.

"Retired Major Gerhard Lange," Punita repeated. "Mama, he's a German soldier. Do you think we can trust him?

"He must be trustworthy," Rosalee said. "Konstantin would not have recommended him otherwise." She chewed her lower lip in contemplation. "Our paths cross so frequently with Herr Lange that I'm beginning to accept that destiny has indeed entwined our families. We must pay closer attention to the connection." Rosalee then enlightened Punita about her reading for Paul Lange in 1928.

"From time to time, I have asked the cards about the connection. So far, they give me nothing, except the constant reference to brown eyes—the colour of melted dark chocolate—which, of course, you and I both have. Regardless, I always have a sense of foreboding after a reading. Punita, when you have time, see whether the cards tell you anything."

"Yes, Mama," Punita responded

375

dutifully. "In the meantime, I think I should write letters—one of thanks to Alexi, and another letter to Stefan. It is time I told him of my pregnancy!"

The next letter from Alexi expressed delight to know that soon he would be a grandfather and that Stefan was elated to hear the news of a child. He also reported, at Stefan's request, that Stefan was counting the days until he and Punita were married and they were all together again.

Nicolai, Alexi wrote, *has been detained at Dachau as I suspected. Herr Lange is en route to learn more. I can only await his report regarding the detention. I'm sorry to say that the situation appears dire.*

In early summer, the women returned from their lessons with Walentyna and entered the large doors of Konstantin's home. In the dim hallway, they were startled by the voice of Ambroos.

"Good afternoon, ladies," he said from

the shadows of the hallway. "A letter has come for you. Shall I fetch it?"

In unison, they turned toward him. Their bulging bellies collided. Giggling, Punita stepped aside to allow him passage.

"Yes, please. There's not much space left in this hallway to navigate when the two of us are here at the same time!"

The young man ducked between them and snatched a pink envelope from the post tray on the hall table. He held it out to Punita.

She accepted the envelope and examined the handwriting. She expected Alexi's bold script, but the letters she saw were small, fine, and deliberate.

"Thank you," she said absentmindedly, then turned to Rosalee. "I don't recognize the hand, Mama."

"I need to put my feet up, Punita. Let's go upstairs and read it, shall we?"

They waddled up the staircase, using the railing as support. In the last trimester of their pregnancies, the child-weight burdened their ascending steps.

In the pink room, Punita sniffed the envelope before she opened it.

"Mmm, this smells wonderful!" she pondered as she tore through the flap of the envelope, extracted the letter and read the signature at the end.

"I know this scent! Mathilde! Mama, it's from Mathilde!"

Punita quickly scanned the words on the page, then looked to her mother. Mama, her mouth said, but no sound followed. Punita sank to the bed. Rosalee snatched the letter from her hand and read,

My dear Punita,

I was so delighted to hear from Alexi the news of your impending joy. He was very excited about the future.

You are wondering why I am writing to you, instead of him. It is such sadness that brings me to this task.

Three weeks ago, your dear Stefan was shot during a skirmish in a small town not

far from here. The bullet entered his head just above his right ear. He died instantly.

The shock of Stefan's death pierced the heart of my dear Alexi and he too died instantly.

The grief is overwhelming for all. My heart is broken. The town is broken – Alexi was such a commanding presence. And now you too, my dear, will suffer with the sadness of it all.

I pray you have strength to deliver yourself of a fine healthy child who will celebrate the lives of these two wonderful men. Your child is their legacy.

I wish I could at least temper this blow with news of wealth to come your way, but the economy suffers in this sorry place and the government has seized Alexi's hotel against unpaid taxes.

Life here is so different. I know not what will become of me. Perhaps you will see me at your door one day, and hopefully

*not hold against me the sad news I write
here.*

*Your faithful friend,
Mathilde*

Tears filled Rosalee's eyes as she sank
next to her daughter, holding Punita, while
sorrow escaped their broken hearts.

❖

A light rap on the door broke the sobbing
silence. Rosalee looked up at Anika's concerned face.

"How may I help?" she offered. "The
servants heard your crying and expressed
concern."

Rosalee shifted, encouraging Punita to
rest on the bed, and left the room, closing
the door behind her. In the hallway, Rosalee
told Anika of the letter.

"Such distressing news." Anika said. "I will
have a tray of calming tea sent up at once."

With a foot on the top stair Anika
hesitated.

"Konstantin has just returned from the dock," she shared. "A storm is brewing outside the harbour. The ship will not sail until it passes. I will inform him of this sad news."

⚜

The following day, the *Silver Pearl* returned to port, its arrival having been delayed by the same storm. Baldev brought a message from the warehouse, addressed to Punita once again.

"Mama, you open it. I couldn't read more bad news."

As she had seen her daughter do the day before, Rosalee tore the flap, removed the letter and read the signature at its foot.

"It's from Alexi" she whispered, and she read the letter aloud.

My dearest soon-to-be daughter-in-law.

Stefan and I are overjoyed to hear of your pregnancy. Soon Stefan's training will be over, and we will embark on our journey

*to Amsterdam to see the two of you safely
married and to meet the new child you
carry. Our happiness has no bounds.*

*I am also writing with news of your
father. Herr Lange visited me to report
on his findings at Dachau. Nicolai was
indeed detained in that heinous camp. It
is with a heavy heart that I tell you of his
circumstance.*

*During his capture, Nicolai's right hand
was injured quite badly. He also suffered
broken ribs. Herr Lange felt that he could
have healed from those injuries in time.
However, some weeks after his entry
into Dachau, the camp was afflicted with
epidemic typhus. Nicolai was one of the
first to succumb to that horrid disease.
Likely due to his weakened condition,
Herr Lange thought.*

*Please accept deepest sympathy from
Stefan and me. Herr Lange also asked that
I extend his sincere condolences as well.*

The impact of Alexi's words permeated Rosalee's thoughts as she read the final lines. She collapsed where she stood, gasping for breath. The sheet of paper fluttered from her hand, falling to the carpet. Punita sank to her side.

"What is it Mama? The baby?"

Tears pricked at Rosalee's eyes. Shaking her head, she pointed at the fallen paper.

"My Nicolai," she moaned. "My Nicolai."

"Oh, Mama," Punita wailed, embracing Rosalee fiercely. "All of our men are dead!"

CHAPTER THIRTY-FIVE

As she descended the stairs from the fourth floor, one of the staff heard the women sobbing. She paused and peered through the open doorway, then scooted down the remainder of the stairs in search of her mistress.

Moments later, Konstantin and Anika appeared in the doorway, and stooped to help Punita and Rosalee from the floor. Punita handed Alexi's letter to Konstantin and fingered the delicate gold bracelet made by her father as a gift for her eighth birthday. Konstantin silently read the letter with his wife. Stunned by the tragic news, the couple expressed their condolences and left the women to grieve in private.

⚜

"How can this be?" Anika asked no one in particular, as she closed the door to the blue room. "Such tragedy. God has not managed this one well. Those women have been through so much. They had such hope. And now this. Will it ever end? Are they never to be happy?"

"It is not for us to say. Life will happen as it must," Konstantin replied. "They have each other and they will have their children. Our task will be to help them heal so they can be strong for each other."

"You're right. Let's leave them for a while," Anika said.

Quiet steps carried them down the staircase.

⚜

An hour later, Punita screamed down the stairwell.

"Help, help. Oh, God, someone please help!"

Konstantin took the stairs two at a time, the others following on his heels.

"What is it, Punita?" Konstantin bellowed as he approached the landing on the third floor.

"Mama. It's Mama. Please help her!" Punita yelled from the blue room.

385

Konstantin's long strides carried him quickly to the room. He crouched by the bed where Rosalee lay writhing.

"Rosalee, what is it?" he asked, lifting her hair from her face.

Rosalee clutched her belly, rolling her head from side to side. Anika entered the room behind her husband and closed the door on her curious children. As she did so, she told Ambroos to find Baldev and send him up instantly.

"Yes, Mama," Ambroos said, and flew down the stairs, calling for Baldev.

Anika shooed her husband out of the way and knelt by the bed, noting the dampness of Rosalee's garments. She took Rosalee's wrist to check her pulse and felt her forehead for fever.

"What is it, Rosalee? Where do you hurt?"

She knew the answer before the question was asked.

"The child comes. Something is wrong. Help me," Rosalee begged. "You must save my child."

386

"I will do what I can, until the doctor arrives," Anika encouraged.

"Konstantin, we need clean towels and hot water, please."

In answer to the rap at the door, Konstantin gave Baldev instructions to bring Dr. Hendrik with all haste.

"Yes sir," Baldev snapped and was gone.

"Anika, I will arrange the things you need and settle the children. There is nothing for me to do here," Konstantin suggested.

Anika acknowledged his suggestion with a terse "thank you".

"Rosalee," he added with kindness, "I will pray for you both."

The door closed behind him. Punita heard him call the children away with him.

"Come, Punita, we must make your mother ready for the arrival of her child," Anika said as she started to remove Rosalee's street clothes. "Can you find a fresh bed gown?"

✤

On the other side of the bed, Punita held her mother's hand and offered quiet words of encouragement.

"The doctor will arrive shortly," Anika reassured them.

"Dr. Hendrik may be young, but he is a good doctor, and, as you know, has delivered many babies."

She mopped Rosalee's brow with a damp cloth.

"Breathe with me now," Anika said, when Rosalee gasped with another contraction.

Together, the women breathed to slow Rosalee's anxious panting.

CHAPTER THIRTY-SIX

Twenty minutes later, Konstantin ushered Dr. Hendrik into the blue room. He set his black medical bag on one of the Queen Anne chairs, and turned to the bed.

"Rosalee, you're a little early. I believe you're not due for another month."

"That's correct, Doctor," Punita answered for her mother.

The doctor's large hands pressed Rosalee's belly, moving with gentleness and experience.

"Something is wrong, Doctor," Rosalee said, grabbing the doctor's wrist and panting through her pain, eyes wide with fear.

"I must examine you further," the doctor said pushing her nightdress out of the way and leaning between her bent knees.

Keeping one hand on her belly, the long fingers of his free hand probed internally.

Rosalee's abdomen contracted in protest. The doctor's movements paused. Rosalee groaned as the contraction passed.

"Take a deep breath and let it out slowly. That's good. Repeat that a few times while I finish my assessment. Yes?"

Rosalee nodded, panting to control her pushing.

The doctor stood, arching his back. Anika handed him a towel.

"The child has not turned yet," he said, briskly rubbing the towel over his hands. "We will try to help."

"Punita, you may want to wait outside," the doctor invited.

"No!" she insisted. "I'm staying with my mother."

"All right," he agreed. "On two conditions."

"Yes?"

"Sit over there." He pointed to the vacant wing chair near the door. "And if I tell you to leave, you will."

Punita agreed and sat quietly on the blue satin chair, watching as the doctor and Anika helped Rosalee onto her knees.

"All right, Rosalee," Dr. Hendrik encouraged. "Let's see if gravity will help your baby turn."

Feeling helpless, Punita fingered the emerald at her throat, mouthing words without sound, trying to absorb her mother's pain and breathing with her.

Perspiration drenched Rosalee's hair and trickled into her eyes. Anika wiped Rosalee's face with a small towel and responded to the doctor's instructions.

Time passed. Rosalee's exhaustion bested her and she collapsed on the bed. Anika prepared her for a further examination.

The doctor stood and stretched his back again.

"Soft, slow pants, Rosalee," he said, "no pushing."

As he probed Rosalee's belly again, looking for progress, he turned toward the wing chair.

"Punita, it's time for you to leave."

"No!" Punita began to protest.

"Come, Punita." Anika placed her hands on both shoulder and helped Punita to her feet.

"Wait!" Punita said, skirting Anika and rushing to her mother's side.

"I love you, Mama. I will pray," she said, grasping the emerald again.

"I love you too, my daughter," Rosalee said breathlessly, stroking her thumb through her daughter's tears. "Go now. In a while you will meet your new brother or sister."

Punita kissed her mother's forehead and left the room. Konstantin met her in the hallway and guided her to her own room.

⚜

Anika closed the door gently and returned to the delivery bed.

"The child hasn't turned," Dr. Hendrik said quietly. "We'll have to deliver it breached."

"Doctor," Rosalee grabbed his wrist again. "My husband had to turn Punita. I've lost many children since."

"I'll do what I can," he said, "but the child appears determined to deliver feet first."

"Please," she pleaded. "You must save this child."

"Fortunately, because the child is early, it's smaller and may come easier than if it were full term," he whispered to Anika, "but we have delicate work ahead of us."

Konstantin put his hand in the small of Punita's back and guided her to the pink room. "Rest here. I will sit with you and we'll leave the door ajar, so we can hear if we're needed."

Punita sank onto her bed, exhausted with worry.

"This is too early," she cried. "The child can't come now."

Taking her old green shawl from the end of her bed and wrapping it around her shoulders, she leaned into the bed and curled into a ball.

"I know," he comforted her. "Rest now. Worry is not good for you or your baby. Think of your own child now. Rosalee is in good hands with Dr. Hendrik and Anika. You know that Anika is a capable birthing companion, and, in her opinion, there is no doctor better than Dr. Hendrik."

Konstantin pulled a chair from the corner of the room, set it next to Punita's bed, and lowered himself into it. He watched her lips move silently while her small hand clutched the pendant around her neck.

"You wear that necklace always," he said. "It must have a special meaning to you."

Punita stopped rubbing the emerald set in gold and looked up at him with sadness in her eyes.

"It's an heirloom, passed from mother to daughter for many generations," she said. "The emerald signifies the wearer's green chakra. Our strongest chakra."

"Your heart." Konstantin looked at her small frame and reached to stroke her shoulder. "Is there not a chant to be said as well?"

"Yes, I've been repeating it for Mama since the doctor arrived."

"Let us say it together," Konstantin offered. "Will you teach me?"

"Of course," Punita shifted to sit on the edge of the bed.

"No, child," Konstantin said, placing his hand on her shoulder to still her. "Stay as you are. I can hear you fine."

"We must open our body and mind," she instructed. "Breathe in on the first part of the phrase and out on the second. The rhythmic breathing will bring calm."

Punita rolled onto her back so she could breathe unrestricted. She stilled for a moment and inhaled deeply. Konstantin followed her instructions and imitated her actions.

"My energy," Punita inhaled, "is free of blockages."

She exhaled slowly.

Konstantin copied her actions and words. Together, they repeated each of the chakra chants, breathing slowly in and out.

"My root chakra is deeply grounded. My sacral chakra juices are creative and bold. My solar plexus feels mellow and calm. My heart is filled with love."

Her lips quivered, and she began to sob. She reached for the emerald and clasped it tightly.

"Mama," she whispered, "my heart is filled with love."

When her sobbing lessened, Konstantin encouraged her to continue.

"My throat speaks the truth. My third eye intuits inner knowledge."

Again, she sobbed through quivering lips.

"My crown chakra projects inspiration."

Together, they repeated the chant several times until, calmed, Punita fell asleep. Konstantin tucked the shawl snugly about her shoulders and tiptoed from the room in search of a tray of coffee and biscuits.

✤

The passage of the day was long, and the evening even longer. In the quiet of the early hours of the following morning, Rosalee screamed once, long and painful, startling Konstantin and Punita from a weary doze.

"Wh-what is it?" Punita mumbled as she stirred to a sitting position on the edge of her bed.

"Shhh," Konstantin responded, "wait."

"Mama," Punita said, rising to sit on the edge of the bed.

Konstantin's hand held her fast, stopping her from standing. Swishing sounds came from the blue room for several minutes, then muffled words, then quiet.

Finally, the door to the blue room opened and Anika slipped out. Again, Punita attempted to stand.

"Mama?" she asked, her dark eyes pleading.

Anika's sad face could not hide the tragedy.

"Punita, I am so, so sorry. The child was larger than expected. He wouldn't turn

397

and delivered feet first," Anika explained. "Your mother was exhausted. She delivered her son with her last breath."

A sob caught in Anika's throat, but she continued.

"The child was in the birth canal too long. We couldn't make him breathe."

Anika withdrew a white lace handkerchief from her pocket, blew her nose making a small honking sound, then stuffed it into her pocket again.

"Your little brother chose to be with your mother and father. God have mercy on their souls," she finished.

Konstantin went to his wife and wrapped his arms around her, allowing her to shed tears of sadness and exhaustion.

"Punita, I am so sorry," she sobbed into his chest.

With tears streaming from her eyes, Punita sat silently on the edge of the bed, stunned in her grief.

"Everyone I have ever loved has died," she moaned.

She wrapped her arms around her belly, rocking her child.

"You are all I have left."

＊

Konstantin led Anika from the room, pulling the door knob behind him.

"Never has a person seen such sadness," he whispered. "Let the poor child have a few minutes to meet her grief."

The door knob abruptly left his hand.

"I must see them," Punita insisted, pushing past Konstantin and Anika.

She stumbled to the blue room and opened the door.

"Mama? Mama!"

＊

Dr. Hendrik had tidied the room and straightened the bed. Rosalee looked to be sleeping with her new son in her arms. Wrapped in his birthing blanket, only his little face was visible—perfect and blue-hued. His tiny eyes were closed. A dark fringe of downy hair framed his face.

JERENA TOBIASEN

Punita stood at the side of the bed. She did not see her brother, only the lifeless form of her mother. She dropped to her knees and took her mother's still-warm hand between hers.

"Oh, Mama," were her only words as she rested her forehead on her mother's hand.

Konstantin stepped into the room to collect Punita, but Dr. Hendrik intercepted him.

"Let her grieve. She will heal faster. Suppressing her grief is not good for her child. I will sit with her, if you'd like to see to your household," he offered.

Konstantin stepped into the hallway, closing the door behind him.

The doctor moved a wing chair next to the bed and encouraged Punita to sit next to her mother.

"Kneeling is not good for you," he said, helping her rise.

"My mother was my guiding star," Punita said forlornly, clutching the emerald hanging at her breast. "I can't imagine life without her."

Dr. Hendrik stayed with Punita while she grieved. He held her hand and spoke in hushed, reassuring words. He asked about Rosalee, encouraging Punita to remember and celebrate her life. Punita told him about her father, Nicolai, and about Stefan and Alexi Puchinski. He held her, providing the comfort she needed when her body quaked with sobs. When her sorrow was spent, he explained the deaths, how they occurred, and what needed to be done next.

"Will I die too?" she asked the doctor in a voice so quiet that the doctor almost missed the question.

"Every pregnancy is fraught with danger," he told her, "but few result in death. Medicine has come a long way. There is much we can do to save mother and child now."

Punita gazed longingly at her mother's pale face.

"On a rare occasion, such as this, complications are such that one or both may be lost." He took Punita's hand and held it while he searched her chocolate eyes for understanding. "I will do everything I can to ensure that both you and your child live. Your mother had a history of losses and we must keep that in mind. From now on, I will see you every week to monitor your baby's progress, and you must call for me immediately if you sense anything unusual."

Punita sniffled.

"Yes, Doctor."

"In fact," he added, "I will examine you before I leave today."

⬧

Despite his young age, Dr. Hendrik was a wise, capable, and unique individual. He was accustomed to helping people through their sorrow and loss, as well as their joy. He remained with Punita until she was ready to leave the blue room.

Punita welcomed the strength he offered, his quiet companionship, and his encouragement. During the term of her pregnancy, she had learned to trust him. Despite the death of her mother and brother, her trust remained strong. She placed no blame at his feet for their deaths.

Buduly and Walentyna insisted that they take responsibility for the funeral of Rosalee and her son.

"Punita, dear," Walentyna asked, "did your mother have a name for the child?"

"Not specifically, but sometimes she said that, if she ever had a son, she would name him after Papa," Punita said, reminiscing.

"Then we shall name him Nicolai," Walentyna said. "Do you agree?"

"I think she would have liked that," Punita said.

Punita had given Walentyna her mother's favourite dress and reading shawl, thinking Rosalee would be happy to spend forever dressed in bright colours. Rosalee's dark hair fanned over her shoulders. Baby Nicolai lay in her arms within the satin-lined casket. He was wrapped in a blanket of blue and green stripes trimmed with a red border—the colours of the Roma flag—that Rosalee had knitted the week before she died.

Punita hovered over her mother's peaceful countenance. She leaned into the casket and kissed her mother's cheek. Then she leaned further and kissed the forehead of her tiny brother.

"They look so peaceful. As if they will sleep forever," she said, turning to Walentyna. "Thank you for your kindness."

"My husband and I would have it no other way." Walentyna dismissed Punita's remark. "Now, let us leave so the lid can be fastened and the service concluded."

Walentyna led Punita away from the casket to join Buduly.

"Ah! Punita," he said.

"I am just finalizing the wording for the headstone. What do you think of this?"

He handed her a sheet of paper on which words had been printed in a fine hand.

At the end of an arduous journey, here rest Rosalee Kota and her infant son, Nicolai. Joined in memory with their loving husband and father, Nicolai. Missed forever by their devoted daughter and sister, Punita.

A tear escaped Punita's eye and trickled past her nose.

"Thank you, Buduly," she said, her lips quivering.

CHAPTER THIRTY-SEVEN

A week after the funeral and without complication, Punita delivered a healthy daughter and named her Mina Rosalee Kota Puchinski. Mina was delivered in the pink room by Dr. Hendrik, assisted by Anika. On the heels of sorrow, the Anker family was delighted to welcome Punita's child and share in her joy.

By the end of July, the house was returning to a routine, altered by death and birth, when the bell rang. Baldev opened the door and surveyed the beautiful woman who stood in the doorway.

"Madame?" he acknowledged, waiting for her to state her business.

"I understand that my friend Punita Kota may be staying here with her mother Rosalee," she said.

Baldev invited her into the salon, indicating a chair, and excused himself. Rather

than sit, the woman walked about the
room, admiring the furnishings. She had an
eye for beauty and order. After a long journey overland, she welcomed the comfort of
the elegant room.

⬧

Punita descended the stairs, wondering
who would ask for her. She knew only the
Anker family and few others in Amsterdam. Baldev had given no name when he
announced the visitor.

Punita stepped into the salon hesitantly
but recognized her visitor instantly.

"Mathilde!" she exclaimed, flying into
the woman's arms. "I know you said you
might come. But I never truly believed it!"

Baldev appeared in the doorway to
ensure the guest was of no threat. Seeing
the women embrace, he offered to take
Mathilde's coat and bring tea.

"Oh, yes please, Baldev," Punita answered.
"We would appreciate that very much!"

Mathilde slipped out of her coat and
handed it to Baldev with a gracious smile.

"We have so much to talk about," Punita said. "Sit with me. Tell me of your journey."

"Liegnitz was chaotic after you left. People were scrambling everywhere. Fleeing for their lives, protesting, enlisting in the military. Then Stefan was killed."

Mathilde's eyes filled with tears.

"And Alexi ... his heart ..." she said, swallowing sobs.

Punita slid from her chair to kneel on the carpet at Mathilde's feet, and took Mathilde's hands in her own.

"We have had so much sorrow, Mathilde. You and me. My mother and small brother died in childbirth two months ago." Punita's eyes filled with tears. "So much sorrow."

She lowered her head into Mathilde's lap, and Mathilde stroked her porcelain fingers through the long dark strands of Punita's hair.

"Most of my customers moved away and those who remained stopped coming to me," Mathilde said in her lilting voice.

"After Stefan and Alexi died, there was nothing left for me."

Punita lifted her head.

"Have you no family?"

"No. I was an only child and my parents died when I was young. I lived with my grandmother for a while. Then she died." A slow smile spread on Mathilde's face. "I was young. I had no skills or training and I was forced to be resourceful. It wasn't easy in the beginning, but eventually I reached a point where I could control my life, and not have to depend on others."

Awareness dawned on Punita, understanding what Mathilde must have had to do to survive.

"Ahem," Baldev interrupted, carrying a tray of tea things. "Shall I leave the tray here, or would you prefer the dining room."

"Here, please," Punita answered. "It's less bother."

Baldev left the tray for the women to serve themselves and departed.

As they shared the tea, Punita told
Mathilde of Rosalee's tragic delivery and
the funeral, and Mathilde shared the details
of her journey across Germany.

"Fortunately, I have papers. Many don't.
I watched the poor things being spirited away
to who-knows-what demise." Mathilde finished with a wave of her hand. "My only
worry was that you and your mother might
have moved on, and I wouldn't find you."

"I'm so glad you did find me," Punita
exclaimed.

"What will you do now?" Mathilde
asked.

"I don't really know," Punita answered.
"We had a plan when we left Schinawa and
had to revise that when we arrived here.
Then Mama and I discovered that we were
both pregnant and Konstantin invited us to
stay until the babies were born."

"Plans always change," Mathilde said,
nodding.

"Now all of my options have expired,"
Punita said. "I suppose I'll have to make a

new plan. What I know for certain is that I can't live here forever. Konstantin and Anika have been so kind. But Mina and I must find a home and a way of our own."

Their conversation was interrupted when Anika appeared in the doorway.

"Oh, hello," she said entering the room with her hand extended. "I'm Anika. Welcome to our home."

Punita hastily introduced her friend, translating as needed.

"I've brought your small responsibility," Anika said to Punita, handing an armful of fussing baby and blankets to Punita. "I think she's hungry."

"Of course! I've lost track of the time."

Punita took Mina and pulled the blanket clear of her face and hands.

"Mathilde, this is Mina. Proof of the love I shared with Stefan."

Mathilde admired the baby, commenting on those features that were Stefan's and those that were Punita's.

"Aside from me," Punita said sadly, "you are the only one who might ever see Stefan in the face of my daughter."

"I should be off," Mathilde said finally. "I don't want to delay your daughter's meal, and I need to find a place to stay."

Hesitating, she turned toward Anika.

"Perhaps, Madame, you might recommend accommodation?"

Punita repeated Mathilde's enquiry in Dutch for Anika's benefit.

"Of course," Anika thought for a moment. "Punita, dear, would you mind if we offered the blue room to your friend, until she finds her own accommodation?"

"That way you will have time to find appropriate, long-term accommodation," she added speaking directly to Mathilde.

Punita translated again and turned to her host.

"That is very kind of you, Anika. Mathilde would appreciate that very much."

It was arranged that Baldev would take the truck to the train station and collect

Mathilde's luggage, and that Mathilde would stay as a guest in Konstantin's home while she looked for lodgings of her own.

⚜

In the next few days, Anika came to understand the nature of Mathilde's work and expressed her concern privately to Punita.

"Don't get me wrong," she said to Punita. "I quite like your friend and I have welcomed her into our home. I am concerned, however, that should the Rothwells discover the nature of her work, they will be vocal about her place in our community and the risk that her type of employment might compromise the community's reputation."

"I understand, Anika. It was not her intention to stay more than a few days, and I know that she is actively looking for a location," Punita explained. "I will ask her to move to a hotel as soon as she returns."

"No need," Anika replied. "I invited her to stay. I just worry about the Rothwells. They are such busy-bodies."

On the third day, Mathilde returned from her search and announced that she had found a perfect home.

"You are welcome to share the apartment with me," Mathilde offered Punita. "There is space enough for both of us, and the child, of course. It's in the De Wallen District where I intend to set up my new business."

"Won't we be in the way?" Punita asked, flattered by the offer.

"Not at all," Mathilde said, beaming with delight. "I will have no problem finding a good patron and new customers."

On the fourth day, Mathilde arranged for her luggage to be delivered to the new apartment and invited Punita to accompany her. When Punita returned to the Anker home, she told Anika that she planned to move into the apartment with Mathilde.

"But, Punita, my dear. How will you survive?"

"I still have most of the money that Mama and I brought with us. Because of

414

your generosity, we have needed to spend only a little," Punita explained. "It has been almost a year since I arrived on your doorstep. Now it's time that I found a home and work for myself. Matilde has offered the home. All I need is employment."

"But, won't you wait until Konstantin returns?" Anika asked. "He will be disappointed to hear that I let you escape without discussing things with him."

"Anika, you are a wonderful hostess," Punita said, taking Anika's hands. "I am sincerely grateful. But it is time for us to go."

"Very well," accepted Anika. "I will arrange for Baldev to deliver your things once they're packed. We will be very sad, indeed, to see you go."

"I will come back and visit. If that's all right?" Punita said, softening the blow.

"Of course! And you will always be welcome," Anika said, hugging her.

⚜

Two days later, Mathilde welcomed Punita and Mina into their new home.

As the months passed, Mina grew strong and clever. Mathilde and Punita encouraged her and loved her.

Punita managed her money carefully, but, in time, she saw it dwindling and worried about the future and how she would provide for Mina and herself.

"Punita, I taught you well," Mathilde said one evening, before she headed off to her window. "Why don't you work the window with me? Remember what I taught you about listening? More often than not, customers only want an ear for their woes. It's usually the young or frustrated that want a little more."

Punita resisted at first, but saw that Mathilde had success. She had already found a patron who sponsored a private room for his entertainment, away from the window.

"When I'm with my patron, the window isn't working. You could work the window once in a while to decide whether the employment suits you. I'll always be available if you have questions." Mathilde encouraged. "Think about it. There're a lot worse forms of employment, and few that pay as well."

When Mina was a year old, Punita began working with Mathilde. Between them, Mathilde and Punita kept the window operating almost every night.

Soon, Punita found support from a most unlikely individual.

Dr. Eamon Hendrik, who had cared for her mother and her during the terms of their respective pregnancies, and had remained family doctor to Punita and Mina, had asked Punita to marry him soon after Mina's birth. Punita had thanked him and declined. When he had learned that Punita intended to work in De Wallen, he had suggested a patronage instead.

417

CHAPTER THIRTY-EIGHT

Punita shared an apartment with Mathilde for the next ten years. One of them was always available to watch over Mina, while the other worked. They may have earned less during the war years because the economy was poor, but they amassed a sizable sum because there was little to purchase. Basic foods such as milk, cheese, bread, and meat were scarce. Occasionally, they accepted a bag of berries that could be used to brew an imitation coffee, or bags of flour or sugar, or other items they deemed suitable payment for their services.

"This German occupation concerns me," Mathilde stated one afternoon as she prepared for an evening's work. "First, they invade the city and take over public buildings and private residences for their headquarters and billeting, then they confiscate food meant for our tables, reducing our supplies to almost nothing. Now, they're imposing curfews that restrict our business during evening hours! We'll have to be resourceful, if we're to survive."

"I heard last night," Punita responded, "that a group of window workers have been speaking covertly with the operators of restaurants and cafés within the De Wallen district. We are now able to meet our clients in their establishments, so long as we do our entertaining elsewhere."

"Well," Mathilde said, "if we're to entertain them in the *kamers* behind the windows, we'll have to be discreet and alert. Even though those small rooms are private, we have to get there first, and the patrols are monitoring all comings and goings in the red-light district."

"We can sneak in the back way," Punita agreed, "but we should take care not to be seen. About five minutes after we'd left the kamer last night, my client and I walked straight into a patrol. One of them pointed a rifle at us, for goodness sake! I thought I'd be abandoned right then and there. Instead, the good fellow put his arm around me and we staggered off as if we were drunk. He has a bad leg and walks with an odd gait ordinarily. I was afraid that he'd fall, and they'd beat him up. I think the charade was more about me keeping him upright. As soon as the patrol presumed we were drunk, they lost interest and let us pass." Punita appeared to be contemplating the condition of her fingernails as her mind rambled. When she spoke again, anger salted her words.

"I hate them!" she hissed vehemently. "First, they killed Papa, Alexi, and Stefan. Then Mama and little Nicolai died because of what they did. Now, they'll starve the entire city of Amsterdam until we are all dead! Someone has to do something! They must be stopped!"

"God help us," Mathilde agreed.

❖

"Mathilde! Great news!" Punita said in a breathy whisper as she bustled through the door at the end of her shift.

She hung her hat and coat on the hook inside the door and turned to grin at her friend.

"Meneer Jannsen has declared that he can no longer operate his restaurant and is moving his business to another part of the city, outside of De Wallen. He hopes to find a place in the next week or so."

"That's not good news," Mathilde argued. "He's one of our supporters. Our clients know they can find us there."

"Exactly!" Punita responded. "He told us this evening that, as soon as he has moved out of the space, we should use it to entertain our customers. He owns the building, remember. We're to meet the others at his restaurant tomorrow morning before he opens for business. He wants us to discuss how we will divide the area and organize accommodations!"

"Oh! That's good news, indeed!" Mathilde said, clapping her hands in delight.

"And, even better," Punita said, "the German soldiers have been forbidden from seeking our services, and you know what that means —"

"We won't be seen as collaborators," Mathilde said, finishing the sentence. "What a relief!"

Punita sat at their small dining table where Mathilde was setting out a hot drink.

"I was beginning to worry that I might have to start reading tarot cards to support us," she said.

"My goodness, no!" Mathilde objected. "You could be exposed to another level of discrimination and scrutiny. Possibly collected with the Jews. Never would I have allowed it!"

⚜

Punita was surprised to realize how often she employed certain lessons Mathilde had taught her on that long-ago evening in Liegnitz, when everything in her world was happy and good. 'The art of communication, especially listening,' Mathilde had told her, 'is invaluable,' and, 'Always allow yourself a means of escape'. While Mathilde had shared that last advice to keep Punita safe from aggressive customers, Punita had employed it on a few occasions when she and her customer were forced to flee the kamer, albeit slightly dishevelled, in order to avoid an unexpected raid by a German patrol.

Since the beginning of the war, Punita had listened to many men tell their stories of loss and failure, and held them while they wept. Only once did a man try to vent his frustrations on her, but that violence ended quickly, when she threw a pot of hot water in his face. The culprit apologized and left abruptly. She had not needed to exercise her escape option.

✦

One Monday in late October, 1943, Punita and Mathilde sat at their small table, counting their earnings from the previous week.

"The work provides a good, steady income, and allows us flexibility," Mathilde said, validating the nature of their work. "And when the war ends, the income will be even better. Mark my words!"

423

"It provides a very good income, indeed," Punita agreed. "Much more than I would have earned working in a shop. But the work comes with risk, and we must always be aware of our surroundings."

"Of course! We'd be fools not to keep up our guard. We're dealing with all sorts of men, and who really knows what they're thinking when they visit us. Most of them have only one thing on their minds right now, however: how to survive this damned war!"

"And the raids by German patrols," Punita said with contempt.

"You're remembering to keep a means of escape?" Matilde asked.

"Absolutely!" Punita said, before taking a sip of her tepid water. "You know, I would never have ventured into this business had it not been for you. You taught me how to take care of myself, mind, body, and soul. Because of you, I have never worried or felt threatened. Annoyed with a client's behaviour, maybe, but nothing that was beyond manageable."

She ceased talking and grinned broadly at her friend with the white blonde hair.

"It's too bad that you couldn't write a book or a pamphlet, at least, on how to run a window business and stay safe."

"Who knows," Mathilde replied, grinning at the praise, "perhaps one day I will!"

As Mathilde counted the coins, bills, and produce paid by their clientele, Punita recorded the income in a ledger. Produce was set aside for their meals, and the cash was divided in half. In the centre of the table sat two identical cash boxes, one engraved with an *M* and the other with a *P*. Mathilde collected her share and deposited it in the cash box marked with the *M*. Punita closed the ledger, collected her share, and put it in her box. As she did so, the women heard light-footed thumps on the stairwell.

"That must be Mina," Punita said, looking at a clock on the dresser. "Hurry, we must put these away before she comes in." With efficient haste, the two women set the boxes and the ledger on a shelf hidden in the wall behind the dresser, replaced the wall panel, and slid the dresser into place. They giggled at their accomplishment as the door to the apartment burst open.

"Mina, my dear," Mathilde exclaimed. "Come in and take those wet things off before you catch a chill."

"I'll make us a hot drink," Punita said, jumping into action, "and you can tell us what your class learned at the Post Office today."

"I can't believe you're still wearing this old coat, Mina!" Mathilde said, sounding aghast. "Look at the sleeves, how short they are, and the thread is stretched close to breaking across your shoulders." She shook out the wet coat and hat and hung them on a peg inside the door.

"I've had it since I started school," Mina said matter-of-factly. She removed a clip from her hair and finger-combed it to collect loose strands, before fastening the clip again. "I can't button it any more either. Mama's moved the buttons over as far as

426

she can. There's no fabric to move them again."

"You've had it since you were six!" Mathilde exclaimed. "You're eight now, for heaven's sake! Punita, we really must find her a new coat."

"I'll look around tomorrow," Punita said, as she set cups and saucers on the table and poured hot water into a pot containing week-old tea leaves. "We're very lucky to have a girl as agreeable as you, Mina. You take everything in stride. Were the greedy Germans not here, you would have had so much more. For now, come quickly before the water starts to chill." The three gathered at the table and Punita poured each of them a cup of pale coloured hot water.

"How was school today?" Mathilde asked.

"We talked about the occupation a bit," Mina said, "and how it has affected our schooling. The class was even smaller today. Josef, Ana, and Abraham didn't come this morning. Someone said they were taken after dinner last night, with their parents and some neighbours. Where do they go, Mama?"

"I don't know, sweetheart," Punita replied. "We can only pray that they are safe and well and that we'll see them again soon."

"*Mevrouw* van Dijk says that we will have to move again. Our class is too small to take the space in the Post Office. Tomorrow, we are to go to the bakery. She said that the baker has only enough flour to bake on Saturdays, so we can study there. A bigger class is to move into the Post Office."

"You mean the bakery on the corner?" Mathilde asked.

"Uh-huh," Mina said, then slurped her tepid water and shuddered.

"Good," Mathilde said, rising from her chair. "We prefer that you stay close to home. Are you cold?"

"A little," Mina replied, suddenly adding, "I hate the Germans! They cause nothing but trouble."

Mathilde took a threadbare sweater from the hook by the door and helped Mina into it.

"Want the scarf too?"

"Yes, please, *Tante*."

Mathilde wrapped a brown woollen scarf around Mina's neck and kissed the top of her godchild's head.

"I'm glad you knitted these, Mama," Mina said as she pulled on her fingerless gloves and stuffed her hands under her armpits. "During the day, my hands are so c-cold!"

"They're indeed odd-looking," Mathilde agreed, admiring her own, "but at least we're able to use our fingers to complete our tasks, while most of our hand remains protected."

"It is almost dark," Mina said, blowing into her hands to warm them with her breath. "We can light the fire s-soon."

"Mina, I understand how frustrated and scared you must feel each time your class is forced to move to a smaller location,

429

especially when your classmates keep disappearing," Punita said, picking up the thread of the earlier topic, "but please take care never to share your feelings with anyone else, just me and Tante Mathilde and only in this room. It's too dangerous. You could be turned in by anyone overhearing your complaints." Punita rose from her chair and circled her arms around her daughter's shoulders. "Please, promise me that you will hold your tongue when you are out of this room, no matter what!"

"I will, Mama," Mina said. "Can we light the fire now?"

⚜

A month later, Mina returned home from the bakery and announced that Mevrouw van Dijk had been sent away to learn a new teaching system. Until she returned, the children were to stay home.

"I'm happy to hear that," Punita said quietly to Mathilde, looking at the thin wall between their apartment and the next. "I'm not convinced that the new style of teaching is appropriate for school children. I need to learn more about this Nazi ideology first. In the meantime, you and I can teach Mina instead."

As the months passed, Mathilde and Punita implemented a new routine that involved Mina's ongoing education.

"Punita! Mina!" Mathilde yelled, racing up the stairwell. "Come quick!" As she reached the top stair, the apartment door flew open.

"What is it, Mathilde?" Punita asked. "Are you ill?

"No!" Mathilde laughed. "The Canadian army has arrived in Amsterdam! The Germans are scurrying like rats." She grabbed their arms and danced in a circle. "Hurry, tanks and trucks are rolling right through the city. Everyone is shouting and singing!"

Punita and Mina grabbed their coats and tripped down the stairs behind Mathilde. On the streets, locals hastily exited De Wallen toward the main streets. The crowd thickened on both sides of the roadway as the first Canadian tanks and trucks rolled through the human corridor, followed by wagons and foot soldiers.

"Follow me," Mathilde said, leading Punita and Mina up a stairwell, through the back door of a nearby church. She scooted down a dark hallway that led to opened doors, and out onto a balcony occupied by clergy, nuns, and other citizens, all waving enthusiastically, as the vehicles trundled by, burdened with Dutch citizens.

"It's a wonder that the drivers can see where they're going!" Punita shouted to be heard over the din.

Nine-year-old Mina smiled at her mother and Mathilde, then squeezed between two nuns and hung over the balcony waving her scarf at the heroes.

"Look," she said, returning a few minutes later. "Chocolate!" In her hand, she held a partially opened bar, the foil rolled back to reveal the contents. "One of the soldiers threw it up to me!" She broke off pieces and shared. "Isn't it divine!"

❖

"Come, Mina," Punita called her daughter one morning in late May, 1945. "We have two errands to run today."

Punita stood at the door, setting her worn blue cloche hat over her dark hair. Mina scooted from her room and grabbed her green coat from the hook.

"What errands, Mama?"

"Shhh! Mathilde is sleeping," she said. "I've heard that a farmer from the north has brought produce to the old café. His sister works in De Wallen. He realized how difficult it is for us to go north to hunt for food, so he brought it to us. Bring your basket. I'll bring mine and Mathilde's. Hopefully, there will be enough to fill them."

She stepped through the door and into her street shoes.

"I also heard that old Mevrouw de Vries died two days ago. She had that dress shop two streets over. Her inventory isn't what it was before the war, but she was in a position to barter for used clothes. And you, my

433

dear, are desperately in need of a new dress!
If we had to collect wood today, I suspect
that dress you're wearing would split at the
seams!"

Punita considered her daughter from
head to toe and shook her head.

"Shoes!" she stated. "You need shoes
too!"

Mina looked at her feet. Both shoes
gaped near her small toes.

"You must be growing again," Punita
stated matter-of-factly.

"But, Mama," Mina said, "if Mevrouw
de Vries died, how will we shop?"

"Her daughter-in-law is selling everything. She and *Meneer* de Vries are leaving
Amsterdam. I think they plan to buy passage to Canada."

They descended the stairs to the street,
still chatting.

"Mama, will I be able to draw stocking
lines up the back of my legs when I have my
new dress?"

Punita stopped and looked back up the stairs at her daughter. Her hand reached to caress Mina's cheek.

"Not yet, my daughter. You are not even ten. You have a few years yet before you need to dress like a woman. Short stockings will do you fine. Besides, I only draw the lines when I'm working, and you're too young to think of that. Be patient. Your chance will come."

CHAPTER THIRTY-NINE

While many tenants were only too happy to flee the city when the occupation ended, Mathilde, Punita, and Mina continued to live in the De Wallen apartment. As Amsterdam recovered from the ravages of war, so too did the district of De Wallen. No longer restricted by curfews and German soldiers with guns, the prostitutes returned to their windows and took advantage of the brisk business. On the Saturday before they re-opened their window, Mathilde and Punita cleaned and tidied it.

"I sometimes wonder how much longer we will have to endure this unconventional line of work," Punita said to her friend. She raised her arms in the air and stretched her back.

"I for one have no intention of retiring," Mathilde replied, scrubbing a stubborn shoe scuff. "It will take a great event to stop me!"

"I keep thinking of Eamon's suggestion that we should train as birthing companions," Punita countered. "I think I'll need more information before I give up the income that comes from this window though." She stood with her hands on her hips and surveyed the readiness of their workshop.

When the public schools re-opened, and Mina returned to her studies, Punita realized that her daughter was capable of caring for herself and no longer required full-time supervision. She and Mathilde took advantage of the extra time and worked the window as often as they could.

⚜

On a sunny afternoon in 1948, Punita and Dr. Hendrik sat in a café not far from her apartment.

"How was the delivery?" Punita asked.

"Straightforward, I'd say," the doctor answered. "Marte has three children already, and her body is built for birthing. I expected to be with her until this evening, but she just dropped that child as easy as you please, soon after I arrived. I hardly had time to take off my coat and wash my hands!"

Punita noted the look of amazement disappear from the doctor's face, as he turned to the waitress who had brought their coffee. In answer to the server's question, they both declined sugar and cream.

"I'm so glad to have the rationing removed," the doctor said, before sipping his hot brew. "It has been a long time since we've been able to buy coffee."

"Mmm, this is delicious, and it smells wonderful!" Punita inhaled deeply, waving her cup under her nose, before she set it onto the saucer. "I'm glad that Marte was so efficient. We haven't seen much of you since before the liberation. It's nice to have a few minutes to visit."

Dr. Hendrik chuckled, eyeing the plate of biscuits that had been placed on the small table.

"I have been busy, haven't I?" He shook his head as if remembering the many events that had occurred in the past few years. "When the Canadian troops arrived, and the Dutch military returned, we thought recovering from the German occupation would be a simple process, but it certainly proved to the contrary. It seemed to take forever to discharge the German troops from the city. Why they would want to stay and hide while their comrades were being rousted and marched through the city is beyond understanding! And the jubilation that arrived with the Canadians! And the chaos!"

He dipped a biscuit into his coffee and popped the soggy mass into his mouth.

"Ah, bliss!" he moaned with delight.

"It was chaotic, wasn't it," Punita said. "Celebrating in the streets was one thing, but that has long passed. It's the other, troubling things that linger, tarnishing the good name of Amsterdam. Every time I see a new home built, I remember the looting that preceded it. I've heard that during the winter of 1944-45—the Hunger Winter, it's been labelled— four thousand six hundred houses were stripped of the wood used in their structures and twenty thousand trees were chopped down for fuel. And, of course, who didn't take at least one piece of wood from the out-of-service tram lines. I'm troubled by the aftermath though. I feel sorry for the poor Jewish folks who returned from POW camps after years of hardship, only to find their homes reduced to rubble because the wood was taken. And all of their worldly possessions stolen as well! How hopeless they must have felt."

Punita reached for a biscuit and followed the doctor's example, dipping it into her coffee.

"I'm still haunted by the sight of the women forced to sympathize with the Germans for whatever reason, being labelled *Kraut whores* and having their heads shaved in the square. If it hadn't been for the German commander forbidding his troops from entering De Wallen, that could have happened to Mathilde and me!" She shuttered involuntarily and hugged her arms across her chest.

"Between the celebrations, and the rebuilding of city and family, I have been worked to distraction," Eamon said. "The celebrations led to drunkenness, which resulted in any number of injuries, including broken bones and lacerations. Trips and falls, brawls, beatings—you name it. Then, of course, all sorts of construction injuries, some of which resulted in death. And, the burst in population some nine months later, and counting!"

He sipped his coffee and quirked a half grin for Punita.

"Yes, these past years have been very busy," he said, reaching for her hand. "But, the year just past hasn't been as horrid as the previous ones. We're busy, yes, but the shops are filling with meat, produce, and other goods. Thanks to the Marshall Plan, I'm sure. The city is looking less scarred every day because of the new construction, and you ... you look absolutely beautiful! Is that a new dress?"

"And hat," Punita added, unabashed, fingering the feathers of the small blue hat that covered her crown. Waves of her dark brown hair fell from beneath it to her shoulders.

"I had an opportunity to go into the town square yesterday. Mina needed new clothes. She's outgrown everything, again. So, I thought, if I'm going to buy her a new wardrobe, I may as well treat myself," Punita said. "The rebuilding of the port has helped, too. Shipments are arriving daily from other countries. New things are appearing on store shelves all the time, including a shipment of nylons from America. Look!" she said, raising her slender legs from under the table to give the doctor a glimpse of her ankles.

"May I?" the doctor asked, leaning forward with an outstretched hand.

"Eamon, no!" Punita gasped, slapping his hand away and tucking her legs under her chair. "Not here!"

❖

Over the next two years, residents of Amsterdam continued to restore and rebuild their city. Some areas were yet to be cleared of debris and damage, although the war had ended almost five years before. Elimination of vermin had been effective post-war, but more effort was required.

One afternoon in early January, 1950, Mathilde bent to retrieve a sack of flour from a lower shelf in the kitchen. An ominous shape scurried into the shadow of the cabinet, startling her. As she reached for the sack, she noticed that a hole had been gnawed into the far corner, and flour had seeped onto the floor. With one hand on the top of the sack, she reached the other to pinch the hole closed. *Waste not, want not!* the old adage rang in her mind. In that instant, a thin brown rat lunged forward and sank its teeth into her extended hand. Mathilde yelped, dropping the sack. The impact forced a plume of flour to shoot out the small hole, coating the rat. Before it could scoot through a crack in the wall at the base of the cabinet, however, she snatched a rolling pin from the counter and brought it down on the rat's head hard enough to split the tiny skull. Brain matter, blood, and other bits splattered on the floor and along the edge of the cupboard.

"Ugh! Not only have you stolen our flour," she muttered to the small corpse, "now I have to clean up after you!"

She bandaged her hand, rescued the flour, and cleaned up the rat's remains, then thought nothing more of the incident. *Rats,* she had reasoned as she swept up the last bit of flour from the floor, *usually stay outdoors, but they're hungry too, I suppose. Since the food shortages during the war, more and more are wandering indoors, but not all find success!*

"What happened to your hand," Punita asked when she returned from her shift in the window.

"Oh, look! I bought flour!" Mathilde answered, pleased with the remnants on the counter top. "I baked some rolls and small loaves of bread today." She pointed to the items cooling on the table.

"How wonderful!" Punita said, inhaling the aroma of fresh baked bread. "I noticed we were running low, but I didn't have a chance to buy more. It looks like you've made enough to feed the entire building!"

"That's my plan, sort of," Mathilde replied. "I thought we could share with the two elderly couples who live downstairs, and that young family on the main floor. They all have difficulty putting food on the table as it is. This might give them a little break."

"You're very generous," Punita agreed, standing with her hands on her hips. "but, you're avoiding the answer to my question: what happened to your hand?"

"Rat bite." Mathilde held up her hand. "It was him or us, and I didn't intend to share a perfectly good sack of flour with that vermin." She grinned mischievously. "I got him too, and he won't be stealing any more flour."

A week later, Mathilde complained that she felt unwell. Her symptoms changed from headache, fever and chills to a cough, nausea, and vomiting. The pharmacist gave her something for a cold and flu and she rallied for a time. While she rested, Punita worked longer hours in the window.

A month later, Punita returned from the window to find Matilde languishing on the settee.

"Mathilde!" she cried, switching a lamp on and kneeling beside her friend.

Mathilde raised her hand to shelter her eyes from the light and groaned.

"What's wrong?" Punita asked, gently resting the back of her hand on Mathilde's forehead, then her cheeks. "You're burning up! I'm calling the doctor!"

"I don't know what's wrong," Mathilde slurred. "I've had diarrhea all day, and I can't keep anything in my stomach. Turn off the light. It hurts my eyes."

Punita ran to the kitchen and dialled the number for Dr. Hendrik.

"How long has Mathilde had this cold?" the doctor asked shortly after he arrived.

"A month, maybe," Punita answered. "She's been suffering from occasional headaches, sometimes fevers and chills, even vomiting. The pharmacist gave her something for cold and flu symptoms, and they worked for a while. She's never been this bad though."

"Her cold is now pneumonia," the doctor announced. "Mathilde, you need to be in hospital where I can provide proper treatment."

Mathilde had never regained the weight she had lost due to the food shortages during the war. After several days of diarrhea and pneumonia, Punita worried that she looked skeletal. Her skin stretched tight and translucent. She had no body fat with which to fight her illness.

In the hospital, Dr. Hendrik ordered blood and urine tests, and eventually diagnosed Mathilde's illness as Weil's Disease. He asked her whether an animal had bitten her recently. She was too delirious to answer, but Punita told him about the rat that had bitten her friend the previous month.

"Then I'm sorry to say that my diagnosis is correct," he told Punita. He arranged for Mathilde to be quarantined and advised Punita that it was just a matter of time before the infection festering in her brain and kidneys claimed her life.

Mathilde's death left Punita and Mina heartbroken. Punita arranged for someone to cover the window for two weeks, while they took time to mourn their dear friend. The doctor visited as often as he could to console them through their loss.

❖

"Punita," Dr. Hendrik asked one evening not long after Matilde's funeral, "why don't you give up this business? Let me take care of you? I have declared my affection for you many times, and I love Mina like my own."

Punita held his eyes for several seconds, then reached to caress his cheek.

"You have always been a kind and generous patron, and a sincere and caring friend, but I cannot accept your offer, Eamon. As

I've told you every time you've asked … I need to take care of us."

"At least let me find you better accommodation," he pleaded.

She shook her head.

Following Mathilde's death and a thorough scrubbing of her friend's bedroom, Punita announced that Mina should have the second room for herself.

"The room may be small, but Mathilde was comfortable in it, and I think you will be too."

"Thank you, Mama," Mina said, "but I'd rather have Mathilde back. I miss her so much." Tears welled in Mina's eyes.

"Me too," Punita agreed, dabbing at her own eyes with a lacy handkerchief.

CHAPTER FORTY

As Mina prepared to graduate from school in the summer of 1951, Punita began to fuss about her daughter's future. She hoped that her daughter would find a husband as promising as her dear Stefan had been and realized that she did not have the connections necessary to find someone worthy of her daughter. She spoke privately of her concerns with Eamon Hendrik.

"Mina is still a few weeks short of her sixteenth birthday," he chided. "Why are you worrying about connections and marriage now?"

"I feel that I am letting her down," Punita lamented. "If she doesn't make a connection before she graduates, she'll have to find work. Perhaps I should train her to work the window with me. Then, at least, she will be self-employed and can control her own life, instead of working in a shop for a few guilders, at the beck and call of an oppressive shopkeeper."

"Punita, please wait," the doctor pleaded.

"I can't, Eamon." She thought for a moment, then a smile lit her face. "Eamon! Surely you must know some eligible young men."

"What are you looking for," he asked facetiously, "a husband or a patron?"

"Hmm, let me think a moment," Punita said, tapping her lip. "I suppose either would do. A patronage might be better for a few years at least. That way Mina can work and save money." Punita's eyes wandered toward the ceiling as she thought the matter through. "Yes, that's it! A patronage will do nicely."

"Mina is too young to be thinking of marriage and intercourse," the doctor argued, rolling his eyes to the ceiling in exasperation, "let alone working in a window and a patronage!"

"I must do something!" Punita declared, sighing deeply. "At times like this, I really miss my parents. They'd know what to do. They'd have connections." A tear of frustration slid past her nose and she swiped it away. She refused to hear any rebuttal from the doctor.

"You leave me no choice," he grumbled. "I'm being forced to help you find a patron, just so I can ensure Mina's safety!"

Several days later, he introduced Punita to a young man—Willem van Bosch—who had expressed an interest in becoming Mina's patron. Punita encouraged Mina to accept the offer, explaining that she would experience intercourse in a kind and respectful manner, and that her relationship with Meneer van Bosch would prepare her for window work after she completed her schooling.

"I will do it, Mama," Mina agreed at the conclusion of a tiring argument, "but I don't understand the hurry. I haven't even graduated."

"One day, I would like us to move out of De Wallen and find another way to earn an income," Punita said, sharing her dream with Mina. "The only way I see us doing that is if we both work the window until we're set. Meneer van Bosch is a nice young man, and I think you will find him to be an agreeable patron. By the time you finish school, you'll be ready for De Wallen. Just remember what I taught you. The last thing you want at this point is a pregnancy."

"Yes, Mama," Mina sulked. "I'll remember. Besides, I suppose your way of doing things is better than what I'm hearing at school. No one ever needs to know about Meneer van Bosch, and for that I am grateful. And, from the stories being told by the girls at school … well! Their experiences sound most unpleasant."

⚜

On the evening of the first encounter between Mina and Willem van Bosch, Punita closed the window and invited her own patron to spend the time with her.

They enjoyed a quiet meal in her tiny apartment and, while she cleared the last of the dishes, he meandered into her bedroom.

Moments later, Dr. Hendrick watched as Punita removed her apron, straightened her skirt, and sashayed toward him. He had already helped himself to a glass of the port that she kept on the dresser near her bed.

He sipped the liqueur, savouring a mouthful, and eyed Punita with singular appreciation. As he set his glass on the dresser, the port trickled down his throat and his imagination wandered to his prior experiences in her company. His cock stirred to life without instruction. *My God, despite all she's been through, and after all these years, the woman is magnificent!*

He watched Punita drop her hands to her hips and ever so slowly use her fingers to creep the hem of her skirt up her shapely legs, revealing the tops of her gartered stockings. He felt another stir of anticipation. Warmth spread from groin to tongue. He licked his lips, envisioning what would follow.

Eyes intent on his face, Punita faced the doctor and drew her tongue across her own lips. Despite the stiff rod tenting the front of his trousers, he stepped toward her, glancing at the bed.

"My desire for you," he moaned, tracing his hands gently down her arms, "will never cease. And since you won't marry me, I am driven to find reasons to be with you. Thank you for the delicious meal, by the way." He sighed in her hair as he sought a dainty ear on which to nibble. "Now it's time for dessert—"

In reflex, Punita tipped her head back, exposing the grace of her slender neck. He covered the length of it from ear to collar-bone with slow feather-light kisses. Raising his head, he lost himself in the chocolate brown pools that reflected the affection he felt for her. She snaked her arms around his neck and her breath quickened.

The doctor loosened the clip that held her hair and buried his face in handfuls of the auburn waves perfumed with lavender.

His hands slid sensuously, slowly down the curve of her back, halting where it narrowed into her waist. He took a deep breath and let it out slowly, enjoying the ease with which she aroused him. In one swift movement, he lifted her to the bed, pushing her skirt out of the way and baring her to the waist. A husky giggle percolated deep in her throat.

"How quick you are this evening! No time for intimacy?"

"Ha! Do you have any idea what it's like for me, being cooped up in that little kitchen with you so near?" he mumbled through kisses that travelled over her exposed belly. "That's not intimate enough for you? I've had the past two hours to imagine how I might enjoy your body. And I am ready to do so now!"

Punita closed her eyes, a soft smile playing on her lips. The doctor teased his fingers through the auburn mound of her womanhood, massaging her with his thumb. She gasped and reached for the zipper on his trousers, brushing her hand over the living creature throbbing within.

"Oh God!" he moaned, as she freed it, and he lowered himself for entry.

In response to the first thrust, Punita wrapped her legs around the doctor's hips, burying her heels into his bottom to encourage his rhythmic demand.

"Eamon!" she cried as her own urgency peaked with his. "Yes. Yes, I know!"

In Punita's line of business, engaging in such an intimate act was only for a few very worthy customers. For her, the doctor alone benefitted from her full service. She looked into the lustful, loving eyes of Dr. Eamon Hendrik, glad for his patronage.

⬧

A few months later, Punita sensed something was amiss when she arrived home to find Mina preparing the evening meal.

"Mina, what's going on? Aren't you supposed to be studying for an exam."

"Oh, Mama, we did what you said, but it didn't work, and ... and," Mina sank to the kitchen floor and covered her face with her apron to stifle a sob.

"Mina, child, what is it?" Punita asked, squatting to cradle her weeping daughter.

"W-Willem and I ... We did everything you told us to do, but ..."

Mina's eyes flooded with tears again. Punita used a free corner of the apron and dabbed at the drops that rolled down her daughter's cheeks.

"Mina, dear, take a deep breath and start again. You and Willem did everything I told you to but ... what?"

"Mama ... I'm pregnant!"

Punita lost her balance and sat on the floor with a thud.

"Pregnant? How can that be? If you did everything I told you—"

"The first condom broke! I rinsed and everything. We thought I'd be all right, but—"

"Shush, now," Punita reached for her daughter again, her mind racing. "Shush, everything will be fine. Does Willem know?"

"He knows the condom broke, but he doesn't know that I'm pregnant," Mina mumbled. "I just realized today that I've missed three months. I was so busy studying for exams that I didn't worry when I missed the first two, but I've never missed three before!"

Punita took her daughter's hands and held them firmly, forcing Mina to look at her.

"It's all right, Mina," she said. "Although condoms aren't always reliable, I never suspected that this would happen on your first encounter. You and I have survived much worse. We will survive this."

"Do I have to have an abortion?"

"Do you want one?"

"Yes! I can't have a baby now! The whole point of having a relationship with Willem was so no one would know I was sexually active. So I wouldn't end up with a child!" Mina grabbed her apron and covered her face again. "Now everyone will know!"

"Mina, stop. Let's think this through. If you are three months gone, that means

459

the child isn't due until January. You won't even show before you graduate."

"Mama!"

"Hush. Abortions are risky, and not legal. If you truly cannot bring yourself to bear this child, then an abortion can be arranged. I believe, however, that you should carry it to full term. An adoption can be arranged. Or, if you want to keep it, you can." Punita began to rise from the floor. "We can raise your child together." She extended her hand toward Mina. "Give this matter serious thought, Mina, before you make any decisions. You have time. Family is important. And Willem needs to be told."

"Tell Willem!" Mina shrieked. "How can I tell him?"

"He's the father. He has a right to know. But, we're getting ahead of ourselves. We'd better have Dr. Hendrik examine you first. There's no point raising an alarm for nothing."

The next morning, Punita escorted Mina to Dr. Hendrik's office. Following a routine examination and assessment, Dr. Hendrik determined that Mina had indeed completed her first trimester.

"What will you do now?" the doctor asked Punita. They were seated in his sparse office, waiting for Mina to dress.

"Mina suggested last evening that she'd like an abortion, but I'm not convinced that that's the best option."

"I don't like that idea one bit," the doctor agreed. "It is neither safe nor legal."

"That's what I said."

"If I hadn't agreed with your suggestion of a patronage, Mina wouldn't be in this predicament," the doctor continued, his voice full of regret. "I should have insisted against it."

"It's not your fault, Eamon. It was my idea, and I alone am responsible. If she decides to keep the child, Mina and I will raise it together."

CHAPTER FORTY-ONE

That evening Punita decided that her time would be better spent at home. For the second night in a row, she abandoned the window, and kept company with her daughter. Mina's pregnancy was foremost on her mind, as they cleared the remains of their evening meal. Punita made a pot of coffee and set out a plate of cinnamon cookies. As she did so, she kept a covert eye on her daughter, trying to determine her state of mind.

"How are you feeling this evening?" she asked.

Mina glared at her mother.

"As well as a girl who's just found out she's three months pregnant can feel!" she snapped.

"Mina—"

Mina slapped away the hand that reached to console her.

"Mama, I'm angry!" Mina hissed. "I'm angry at you. I'm angry at this pregnancy. I'm angry at Willem too. But, most of all, I'm angry because the damned condom broke!"

"Mina! Don't talk like that!"

Mina's fists balled as if she struggled to contain her rage. Once again, she collapsed to the floor heaving sobs of anguish.

"I can't live like this anymore, Mama. How many times did you and Mathilde talk about escaping this life? But, instead of leaving, you decide that I should be introduced to it! I love you, Mama, but sometimes your idea of what's right is beyond understanding!"

Punita lowered herself to the floor and embraced her daughter until the sobbing subsided, recalling her own experiences as a young woman. She alone had been responsible for the decisions she had made since her mother died in childbirth. She understood the fear of parenting alone and the anxiety that comes with being responsible for every decision she had to make. Unlike her, however, Mina was not alone. Tears welled at the corners of Punita's eyes. She gasped as long-suppressed memories bombarded her thoughts, demanding to be heard.

"Mina, my child, get up," she said, sighing heavily. "Sit here. I have something to tell you."

Punita guided her unresisting daughter to the sofa, then disappeared into her room. When she returned, she clutched her tarot cards in one hand. Setting them on the coffee table, she spoke softly.

"Since before you were born, each time I have spread my cards, I have been reminded of the prediction my aunt made long ago, about a wonderful future with your father. On the last day that I was ever to see him, my aunt told us that, if he survived his time in Hitler's Youth Military, we would have two beautiful children together. He did not survive, and now I have only you, the most precious person in my life." Punita reached to caress her daughter's face and forced a smile. "Shortly after my mother and I arrived in Amsterdam, we discovered that we both were pregnant. That should have been a happy time in my life—and it was for several months as our bellies grew and we anticipated the birth of our children—but then horrible things began to happen."

Punita hung her head, remembering the past around which she had built a wall to protect her broken heart. The room was silent until a second great gasp bubbled from deep within her.

"Mama?" Mina asked, breaking the silence. "Mama, what's wrong?"

"I stopped reading tarot cards then. I no longer wanted to know about a future so full of pain and loss. Had it not been for Mathilde arriving when she did, who knows what would have happened to us."

"Mama, you never speak of your past!"

"Perhaps it's time I did. It may be my past, but it's also your history. I won't ask you to excuse anything I've done. But, maybe if I tell you about my past, you might

465

better understand why I've made the decisions I have."

Mina straightened, a quizzical look on
her face.

"Mama, I would like that very much. I've
always felt as though something important
was missing from my life, but I was afraid
to press you about it. You seem to change
the subject whenever I try to ask."

Mina listened to her mother's story until
the coffee was ready, then poured them each
a cup. Punita placed the plate of cookies on
the table, next to her well-worn tarot cards.
For a few minutes, they sat quietly, sipping
their hot drinks and nibbling the cookies.

Punita allowed her thoughts to regroup,
then she related the story of her life in the
vista, where she had lived until she was nine
years old. She talked about the breeding of
horses, living in a vardo with her mother and
father, then living in a hotel with her beloved
Stefan Puchinski, and his father, Alexi. She
told Mina how she and her mother escaped
Hitler's 1934 round-up with the help of her

father's cousin, Konstantin Anker, of their arrival in Amsterdam, of Alexi's lovely lady, Mathilde Svensen, of the early days of raising Mina and of working in De Wallen.

"I tried to care for you, by myself, but along the way, I had the kindness of Konstantin and his family, of my dear friend Mathilde, and, of course, Dr. Hendrik. Each of them has in some way shaped my life, and, therefore, yours. And, of course, you have your own memories of the more recent events, of Konstantin, Mathilde, and the doctor, and of growing up through the war."

Punita talked until the early hours of the next morning, determined not to stop until she had answered all of Mina's questions.

"That's it," she said finally. "I have nothing more to tell."

Mina reached across and hugged her mother fiercely.

"Thank you, Mama, I understand many things so much better now."

"Can you forgive me for not telling you before?"

"I can. I heard the misery in your voice as you spoke of Stefan's—" Mina stumbled on her words, "of my father's death."

Punita heard wonder in her daughter's voice.

"And to lose your mother and her baby boy so tragically ..." Mina said sighing. "Mama, I am so sorry. I wish I could wipe the pain and loss from your memories."

Punita took Mina's hand in her own and peered into her daughter's chocolate brown eyes.

"Don't feel so, my sweet girl," she said. "It is in the past, and I no longer bear the burden."

Mina embraced her mother again, and the two women sat cuddled together on the sofa for some time, before Punita broke the silence and released herself from her daughter's embrace.

"We have lived a frugal life, but we are not poor," she said, setting Mina from her and watching her daughter's face for reaction. "We can move away from here if that is your desire. I have lived in De Wallen and worked as a prostitute far too long. Indeed, it's time for a change! Mina, would you like that? Would you like to move away?"

Mina nodded, tear tracks drying on her cheeks. Punita lowered her head again, this time in contemplation.

"I'm very tired, Mina. I need my bed," she said, glancing out the window. "The sun will rise soon."

The following morning, Punita slept late. When she finally arose mid-morning, Mina greeted her with love and calm.

"How are you, Mama? You slept a long time."

"Indeed, I did. I never thought that the telling of my tale could be so cathartic. I have carried my burden for more than fifteen years, and now it rests in peace. I am ready to move on."

Mina doubled the dishtowel and clasped the hot handle of the teapot. She poured for her mother and then herself, setting the pot on the warming plate and pushing one cup forward. Punita took a sip from the cup, winced, and set the cup on the table to allow the tea to cool. Instead, she picked up a slice of black bread and nibbled while she collected her thoughts.

"Eamon has been after me for years—and I mean years—to marry him. I have held him at bay, afraid to show any sign of affection. Everyone I have ever loved, except for you, has died. I was afraid that my love would kill him too." Punita brushed a tear from her eye. "I know my words sound melodramatic, but kept in the heart, they have a way of festering and making themselves sensible."

"Wait! Dr. Hendrik asked you to marry him?" Mina was stunned by her mother's remark. "When?"

"Two weeks after you were born, and every year on your birthday since. Many times," Punita said, chuckling. "I'm beginning to think his offer has merit."

"Mama, Dr. Hendrik is a good man! He has always been part of my life. He is not so old, and I think you could be happy with him." Her eyes pierced Punita with hope. "Hey! My birthday will be soon. You must say yes this time."

Mina was excited for her mother, and what happiness a marriage to the doctor might bring.

Punita smiled a quiet, content smile.

"Perhaps I will," she said, "but first we must share your news with Willem."

❖

Later that day, Punita telephoned each of Willem van Bosch and Doctor Hendrik and invited them for coffee the next evening. While Punita and Mina prepared for the arrival of their visitors, Mina made an announcement.

"Mama, I've given the pregnancy a lot of thought," she said. Her hands settled on her flat belly as she spoke in earnest. "I'm carrying a child. Another human being. I can't kill it. And I don't want to give it away. I want to love it the way you've always loved me." Her eyes flooded with tears. "Mama, can I keep it?"

471

Punita set the coffee urn on the table and embraced her daughter.

"Of course, you can keep your child," she said, gently pushing Mina from her. "I had every intention of convincing you to do just that!" She embraced Mina again, hoping to instill sincerity into her distraught daughter. "Now go splash some cold water on those tears. The men will be here shortly."

When Willem and Eamon knocked on the door ten minutes later, Punita opened it wide and welcomed them into the coffee-scented apartment.

"Good evening, gentlemen! Please come in," she greeted them. "Mina and I have some wonderful news to share!"

Punita invited each of the men to sit in one of the winged chairs that faced the settee, while Punita and Mina sat together on the settee. The coffee table, set with dishes and sweets, sat between them. Punita poured out the coffee, gesturing toward the cream and sugar. Quiet fell on the room, until Willem shifted his weight and leaned forward.

"Punita, I'd like to thank you for the invitation to coffee this evening," he said. "It was a pleasant surprise and ... well, now it gives me an opportunity to tell you about an uncomfortable predicament in which I find myself."

Three pairs of eyes, alight with curiosity, turned toward him. He fidgeted at the attention and roses seemed to bloom on his cheeks. He cleared his throat, appearing uncomfortable, when Punita indicated that he should continue.

"I regret ... that is to say ..." He cleared his throat again. "I ... uh ... I may have to change the timing of my visits with Mina."

Punita's hand perched lightly on her daughter's in response to Mina's gasp.

"I'm intrigued," Punita said. "Please continue."

Willem searched their faces before settling on the doctor's, as if he felt he would receive more support from another man.

"M-my father announced at breakfast this morning that I am to be married in the fall!" he blurted. "I have no say in the matter, you see. He and a long-time business colleague have determined that the marriage would be beneficial to their business."

"Do you love her?" Mina whispered, then lowered her head as if realizing the impertinence of her question.

"N-no! I don't even know her," Willem declared. "I mean ... I've met her at business functions a few times, but nothing has ever transpired that would suggest a relationship, let alone a marriage!" He sat back heavily into the chair, his hands clasped between his knees. "I am so sorry," he said to all of them. "I feel as if I've let you all down."

"You haven't let anyone down, Willem," Punita assured him. She looked from Mina to the doctor, before resting her gaze on the young man again. "Your relationship with Mina is a patronage, not a marriage. You are free to do as you please. Will you continue your patronage, or are you suggesting an end to it?"

"I definitely want to continue it, if I may." He sat taller in the chair. "I wasn't certain what you'd have to say about it though."

"Perhaps if we tell you why you were invited this evening," Punita said, "it might help settle your concern." Observing Willem begin to relax, she added, "Mina has some news of her own."

Mina sat forward, pink staining her cheeks.

"Willem, do you remember that first night? When the condom broke?" she asked. The pink stain spread.

Surprised by her statement, Willem's eyes jerked first to Punita, then to the doctor. His nod was imperceptible and abashed.

"It turns out that we ..."

"Mina is pregnant, Willem," the doctor interjected. Willem tried to speak, but words were lost to him.

"The condom broke, remember!" Mina asserted. Her blush deepened.

"Then I must tell father that his proposal is impossible," Willem said, jumping up from his chair and jabbing his fingers through his light brown hair. "Mina and I will be married at once!"

"No, Willem, that won't be necessary," Punita responded. "Please sit down."

The young man ceased his pacing and resumed his seat.

"Mina and I have no expectation of marriage, and we are quite prepared to raise the child ourselves. I have another proposal for you to consider."

Punita suggested that Mina and Willem continue their patronage relationship for the next several months.

"By the time your wedding rolls around, Mina's pregnancy will have advanced and she will need rest. Perhaps you could take a break until after the child is born and she has healed. In the meantime, you can get to know your wife. If you wish to resume the patronage in the spring, that will be arranged. Otherwise, we'll find another patron for Mina."

For the next half hour, they discussed the possibilities. The doctor objected to a continued patronage. Willem insisted that, at the least, he be financially responsible. Mina fussed about whether she and her child should be the object of the discussion at all. In the end, they agreed that the patronage would continue until Willem's marriage in the fall, and Mina would wait to hear from him as to whether their relationship would resume in the spring.

"I would recommend," Punita concluded, "that we never disclose to the child who the father is. I think all-round it is best."

"But I want to be involved in my child's life," Willem protested.

"And we'll find a way to ensure that happens," Punita assured him, "but I think your marriage could be complicated if you acknowledged that you had a child out of wedlock. Whereas, it matters not to folks who live in this district."

Willem simply nodded, appearing unable to find an argument otherwise.

Mina cleared the coffee table as Punita bid the men a good night.

"Well, that went better than I expected," Punita said, rubbing her hands together. "What do you think, Mina. How do you feel about it?"

Mina lowered herself into a wing chair and gazed at her mother.

"At first," she said, "I wanted to scream at him that he should be marrying me, but, as I listened to his predicament, I realized that marriage wasn't necessarily the answer. I could see my life playing out, married to him—which I believe could be a good thing—but ... he's told me of his father, how overbearing and demanding the man can be." Mina reached for her mother's hand. "I couldn't live like that. You've always guided me, but I've never felt controlled. I'd rather raise my child as you did, than live as Willem does."

"Very well," Punita said. "We'll find us a nice apartment outside De Wallen, and that will be that."

"Oh, no, Mama." Mina tugged the hand she still held. "Sit with me. I have something more to say."

Punita perched on the chair next to her daughter, curious.

"This morning, I took a walk through the red-light district, imagining for the first time what it would be like to actually work in a window. Eventually, I stopped at that little coffee shop around the corner from your spot. I was sipping my coffee, contemplating how it all might work, when a young woman came through the door. It was like it was meant to be!" Mina's face lit with excitement and she leaned toward her mother. "The young woman—her name is Astrid Hansen—looked hungry and frightened. I invited her to sit with me and I bought her coffee and something to eat. Mama, you won't believe how much she reminded me of Mathilde, and she's from Norway too. They could be sisters—same hair colour, same size. It's remarkable!"

"What was she doing there?"

"For reasons of her own, she left her home and decided to come to Amsterdam. She's in need of a job and I'm in need of a roommate."

"A roommate?"

"Mama, if you're going to marry Dr. Hendrik, then I'm going to need someone to help me pay the rent," Mina said, a mischievous grin spreading across her face. "And, if you are going to leave window work and become a birthing companion, Astrid will work the window with me!"

"Well, I never—I'm speechless!" Punita said. "You remind me of me! You seem to have found solutions to all of our concerns." Punita hugged her daughter, chuckling at the turn of events. "When am I to meet your friend Astrid?"

"I've invited her for lunch tomorrow. I think we'll all have lots to talk about," Mina said. "Oh! And I told Astrid that you would teach us everything we need to know to run the window well!"

CHAPTER FORTY-TWO

Within the week, they found a new apartment just outside of De Wallen, above a butcher shop. The butcher told them that his family had grown considerably and they needed more space.

"We will be moving to a new home at the end of the month," he said, climbing a staircase that led from the side of the shop to the floor above.

A row of shoes stood lined up outside the door in military precision. Inside, those children who were home played quietly, while the butcher's wife prepared the evening meal. The apartment was tidily littered with the debris of a family of six, including toys, school books, and clothing of all sizes sorted and piled neatly on any available flat surface.

The butcher introduced his wife, then showed Mina and Punita the other rooms.

When the tour concluded, and they stood outside the apartment's door, Mina looked to Punita and smiled.

"The apartment is suitable for our needs," Punita said. "We would be grateful if you would consider us as your new tenants."

"Just two of you, yes?" the butcher asked.

"Three to begin with," Punita said, smiling at her daughter, "another young woman—Astrid—will be living with us, and in the new year we will add one more. My daughter is with child."

The day after Mina graduated, the three women moved into the apartment above the butcher shop. The butcher and his wife were kind landlords, and even discounted the cost of the meat products they purchased.

Punita was as smitten by Astrid as Mina had been, agreeing that Astrid's resemblance to Mathilde was remarkable. The two young women proved to be apt students and by the end of July Punita determined them capable of working shifts in the window. The new living arrangement brought back old memories for Punita and Mina, happy memories of life with Mathilde.

On the day of Mina's birthday, the three women closed the window. Instead, they stayed home and prepared a birthday feast of Mina's favourite dishes. Their kindly landlord, having learned of the celebration, donated a whole rabbit, which Punita seasoned and roasted in the Aga Cooker. The butcher told them when they first met that he considered his Aga Cooker an item of pride and joy and lamented that he was unable to move it to his new home. His wife, he reported, was not concerned. She would have a new one. When he delivered the skinned rabbit, the butcher was pleased to see that the women were enjoying use of the Cooker he had left behind.

Following the tasty meal, Astrid cleared the dishes and Punita placed a spice cake in the centre of the table. Several white candles stood in the middle of the cake, waiting to be lit.

At precisely the moment that Punita set the cake on the table, a rap at the door interrupted their gaiety. Mina rushed to open the door before Punita could.

"Dr. Hendrik!" she said with enthusiasm. "Please come in. Let me help you with your coat."

She took his hat and coat and hung them on a peg behind the door, while he straightened his shoes in the hallway.

"Eamon, come in," Punita welcomed him with beckoning arms.

The doctor entered the apartment, embraced Punita warmly, then turned to Mina.

"Congratulations to the birthday girl," he said, removing a small packet from his pocket and handing it to Mina. "A little remembrance."

Mina smiled her thanks and set the packet on the table next to the wrapped gifts from her mother and Astrid.

"You remember Astrid, Doctor?" Mina said, extending a hand to her new friend.

"Of course!" the doctor said. "How are you finding the accommodations, Astrid?"

"The arrangement is very comfortable," Astrid replied with a lilting accent. "I consider myself most fortunate to have met such wonderful women."

"Am I the only one who thinks of Mathilde every time I meet Astrid?" he asked. "It must be the hair."

"The resemblance is uncanny," Punita agreed. "Sometimes it feels as though Mathilde simply went on a vacation and has now come home. If I close my eyes, I can hear her voice."

Mina reached for Astrid's hand and squeezed it with affection.

"How about some birthday cake," Punita said, swiping a tear from her eye.

Punita made a pot of tea while Astrid set plates and cups around the table. Together, Punita, Astrid, and the doctor sang the Dutch birthday song, clapping in time with the tune. At the end of the song, Mina made a great bow and blew out the candles.

Before the cake was cut, Mina opened her gifts. Her hands flew to her cheeks in surprise and delight when she unwrapped her gift from the doctor.

"Dr. Hendrik! This is too much!" she said tearing away the wrapper and holding up a box marked Chanel No. 5.

"I hope you like it," he said bashfully.

Mina expressed her gratitude by kissing him soundly on the cheek, giggling as a blush pinked his ears.

From Astrid, she received a bottle of red nail lacquer and a matching lipstick. "For work," the young woman clarified.

Punita fidgeted as Mina began to open the gift that she had wrapped. Her daughter tore the paper and stopped. She gazed at her mother, tears in her eyes. Gently, she tugged away the remainder of the paper, smoothing it as she did so.

"Mama," Mina said, laying each item from the packet on the table. "I can't accept the three things that are most dear to you."

Punita's smile was small, but her chocolate eyes expressed her love for her daughter.

"You can, Mina. I want you to have them. The emerald necklace is to be passed to the first daughter of each generation. My father made the bracelet of love knots himself and gave it to me for my eighth birthday. It belongs with the necklace. My mother made the shawl and gave it to me when I left to study in Liegnitz. Whenever I wrap it around me, I feel her love. It has brought me peace these many years."

Mina set the bracelet on top of the shawl and handed the two items to her mother. She kept the necklace and moved behind Punita, draping her arms forward, over her mother's head. Punita's hand clamped around the emerald, as she rose from her chair.

"Mina, if you truly don't want to accept the bracelet and the shawl, I'll take them back for now. They are things that my parents made for me. But, the emerald needs to pass. It's time." She reached around her daughter and allowed the emerald to fall, then fastened the clasp. Mina's hand wrapped around the stone. She felt the chakras of women before her pulsing warm in her palm and gasped at the sensation.

"Mama!" she exclaimed, turning in her mother's embrace. "I—"

A smile curved Punita's lips when she saw Mina's eyes widened with awe. Seeking to avoid further discussion, she drew her daughter into a tight embrace and whispered into her ear. "You feel its power, don't you?"

"Yes," Mina whispered in reply, "I do."

"Say nothing more. The others won't understand."

⚜

As Mina cut and served her birthday cake, Astrid poured the tea. When the last crumb was licked from the last plate, Mina pushed her plate toward the centre of the table and clasped her hands over her rounding belly. She looked directly at the doctor who sat at the opposite end of the table. With a quirk of her mouth and a look of mischief in her eyes, she caught the doctor's attention.

"Dr. Hendrik," she said. "I understand that you have extended a proposal to my mother every year, on my birthday."

"Mina!" Punita gasped.

A flush of colour crept up the doctor's neck and he cleared his throat. He held Mina's eyes without waver.

"Indeed, I have," he said. "And tonight, I will ask again ... as I do every year."

Turning to Punita, his flush deepened. He reached for a hand tucked in her lap and gazed deep into brown eyes that glistened like melted chocolate.

"Punita Kota, will you marry me?"

Mina and Astrid caught their breath in anticipation of the answer. Seconds passed before Punita finally spoke.

"Yes," she whispered.

A heavy silence followed. The doctor's expression shifted from incomprehension to surprise, and finally to wondrous understanding. Tears filled his eyes.

"Yes, Eamon," she repeated boldly, sitting taller in her chair and gazing into his eyes, "I most certainly will!"

CHAPTER FORTY-THREE

The following days were a scramble of arrangements and shopping. Mina insisted that Punita buy a wedding dress, and they spent a day wandering from shop to shop until they found a calf-length gown of pale pink trimmed with cream rosettes.

"It's lovely," Punita said, admiring her silhouette in front of a mirror.

The satin gown clung to her figure, accentuating her curves.

"But I can't justify the cost," she whispered, "It's such an extravagance."

"I agree, Mama. It is an extravagance. But, don't you think that Doctor Hendrik has earned the right to see you in something lovely on your wedding day?" Mina cajoled her. "After all, he's asked you often enough. And look!" She swiftly removed the emerald from where it hung around her neck and draped it over her mother's shoulders. "The emerald sits just so, as if it was meant to be worn with the dress." Mina noticed resistance on her face. "Surely, Mama, you can wear it for one day."

"All right," Punita said, "but only for the day. I will, however, buy these lovely pink shoes. They match the dress perfectly!"

On the morning of the wedding, Mina brushed out Punita's long chestnut hair and wove cream satin ribbons and tiny pink roses through it. When she was satisfied with her efforts, she helped her mother dress.

"What do you think, Astrid?" Mina asked stepping away from her mother to admire her handiwork.

"*Hun er en vakker brud*!" Astrid replied in her lilting accent, "a beautiful bride!"

When Mina excused herself to dress, Astrid stepped forward, carrying a small ceramic pot containing a pair of Norwegian Pine seedlings.

"In my country," she said, "this is a special wedding gift. It symbolizes fertility."

She blushed as she extended the pot to Punita.

"Thank you, my dear," Punita said, accepting the unusual gift. "It is a lovely thought. If you don't mind, however, I think I'll leave the child-bearing to Mina. The doctor and I have never discussed having children. I'm not certain that it's a priority." She smiled kindly on the young woman.

"I will find you another gift then," Astrid said, reaching for the pot, her pale skin turning crimson.

"Absolutely not!" Punita protested, setting the pot on the dresser top. "I think a symbol can have more than one meaning. Let's presume that, for the doctor and me, it means that we will deliver many healthy babies ... for others! We can plant one on either side of the door step, when they grow a little taller."

"As you say," the young woman said, ducking her head.

"You look absolutely lovely," Punita said, reaching to smooth the white blonde

cap of hair that framed Astrid's porcelain face. "Where did you find that dress?
The colour is the exact hue of the blue in
your eyes—so clear, they remind me of an
iceberg!"

"Mina helped me shop," the young
woman replied. "I have shoes the same,
which I should find quickly. Excuse me."

Finding herself alone, Punita stole
a few moments to ask her tarot cards
about the marriage and her future. The
cards assured her of a happy marriage
and suggested a career change, working
with infants. The cards also suggested a
renewed relationship with two men from
her past, two men who had the bearing of
soldiers. Punita shuddered, remembering
the German soldiers who had occupied
Amsterdam. When she asked the cards for
clarification, they reiterated that the men
had the bearing of soldiers. A shiver ran
down her spine as she reached into her past
and envisioned two tall men on the deck of
her cousin's ship. With that memory came

her mother's warning of the connection between the younger fellow, who Punita now knew to be Paul Lange, and eyes the colour of melted dark chocolate. The eyes of the women in her family.

"I wished you'd be more specific," she snapped. "It would make my life so much easier!" She rapped the cards sharply on the table and stuffed them into their box.

"Ready, Mama?" Mina called from the outer room.

"Coming!" As she bustled from her room, she checked her wristwatch.

❖

Two minutes later, Dr. Hendrik, wearing a black, fitted three-piece suit, a white Egyptian cotton shirt and black bow tie, knocked on the door. When Mina whipped open the door and welcomed him inside, he had eyes only for Punita. He walked toward her, wearing a grin that reached from ear to ear.

"I would never have thought that you could look more beautiful than you do every day," he said, his voice husky with awe. He reached inside his jacket and withdrew a small blue velvet box. "A small wedding gift, my dear. I hope you'll wear them." He grasped her hand gently and sat the box it.

"Eamon!" she exclaimed when she cracked the box open. "They're so beautiful! Of course, I will." From the box, she removed a pair of emerald earrings in a setting that matched the stone hanging from her neck, her features mirroring his loving countenance.

"You look particularly handsome today," she said, as she fastened the earrings in place.

Dr. Hendrik's ears pinked at her compliment. He took her hands in his and kissed them.

"Come," he said to the three women. "We have a wedding to attend and I for one have no intention of missing it!"

✤

The wedding was a small affair held on a sunny Monday afternoon in the middle of summer, 1951. The bride, her daughter and her daughter's new friend, one loyal doctor, a few of his associates, and the extended family of an old sea captain composed the wedding party.

Captain Zabar Anker ordered the *MV Silver Oyster II* into the Zuider Zee. His brother, Captain Konstantin, married the bride and groom on the stern deck, out of the wind and misty sea breeze. The smiles were constant and the tears many. The ship motored at a leisurely pace. Her cook oversaw service of a fine meal, and only the best Anker wine was served for toasting.

Toasts were made to the bride and groom and a divine wedding day, to Buduly and Walentyna Anker who had died during the war of age-related causes, to Nicolai and Rosalee Kota and their stillborn son Nicolai, to Stefan and Alexi Puchinski, and to Mathilde—all those who had paved the way

497

to the celebrated day, "... who are smiling down upon us and sharing this happiness," Punita concluded, clasping the large emerald that hung above her breast, while she raised a glass of champagne with the others and looked heavenward.

Those of the crew who were musical brought out their fiddles and guitars and sang to the bride and groom.

On more than one occasion that day, several topics distracted the guests, resulting in animated discussions about world politics, the hanging of Nazi war criminals, outstanding world sporting events, unusual natural disasters, and space rockets.

Regarding the execution of the Nazi war criminals, the consensus was of general concern and disgust.

"As a doctor," one of the guests was overheard to say, "I don't like to see a life taken."

"Surely, doctor," another replied, "you can't be suggesting that their lives be spared?"

"Let's just say that I'm glad I wasn't involved in the decision-making."

The discussion amongst the doctors and other guests became lively as they discussed the pros and cons of the hanging, until Captain Konstantin interjected.

"Talk of hangings is not an appropriate topic for a wedding, folks. Let's change the subject, shall we?"

"I find the space rockets fascinating," Doctor Hendrik said, niftily accommodating the captain. "I know exactly how the teams launching them must feel." He grinned at his guests and wrapped a possessive arm around Punita. "I am so happy to be married to this beautiful woman at long last. I feel as if I'm floating in outer space too!"

The conversation quieted when the wedding guests gathered near the forecastle to watch the ship dock. Punita excused herself and went in search of Captain Konstantin.

"He's midships, lee side," a steward told her.

"Have you a moment for a question?" she asked her father's cousin a few moments later.

"For the beautiful bride? Of course I do."

"It's a peculiar question, I'm sure," Punita said. "I'm wondering whether you know what became of the father and son Mama and I met years ago in Schinawa. Lange, I think their name was. I believe the elder was the retired major who helped us find Papa." Sadness flitted across her eyes, but her gaze upon Konstantin was unwavering.

"Gerhard Lange is the fellow of whom you speak, and his son Paul."

"Yes, of course," she said, noting an expression of affection on the captain's face. "I remember."

"They are very well. There was some trouble for them during the war—they were against it, you know—and they struggled for another year or two afterward, but they seem to have found their feet now." His

500

eyes wandered across the dock below, then he continued. "They lost their land in Silesia but managed to find a new location in Bavaria. I received word from them about a year ago suggesting that they would like to resume distribution of their sausage and some unique cheeses. We've been receiving shipments for several months now. Why do you ask?"

"No particular reason," Punita replied. "Just an old memory. Herr Lange was kind to us. And you are the only person I know who could have satisfied my curiosity."

"Well, you can take comfort in knowing that the Lange family is well and prospering." He gestured for her to walk with him as he headed toward the wedding party. "Say, would you like me to send over some of their famous Schmidt sausage? It truly is the best I've ever tasted."

"That would be wonderful!" Punita responded. "I remember tasting it at Alexi's hotel, but I don't know whether Eamon has tried it." Sadness began to tighten within her chest. *Stop! This is your wedding day. You will not go there*, she chided herself.

"Ah! And here is the happy groom," Konstantin said, shaking Eamon's hand. "I believe the crew is ready to see you ashore."

"Konstantin, thank you. I look forward to receiving the package," Punita said, taking her husband's extended hand.

By the time the *MV Silver Oyster II* was settled against the dock, the sun was beginning to set. The wedding party cheered as the bride and groom led them ashore. The groom encouraged them to gather around while the bride distributed small gift pouches, each containing five sugar coated almonds.

"For happiness, love, fidelity and prosperity," she announced. "and for those more adventurous, fertility!" She winked at Astrid, sharing a reminder of their earlier conversation.

Finally, Eamon led Punita to the silver Citroën that he had purchased in the spring. With special permission from the Harbour

Master, he had parked it alongside the ship's berth. They rolled down the windows and waved wildly as he turned the car away from the dock, homeward bound.

A short time later, Dr. Hendrik took Punita's hand and led her up the stairs and into his home, her new home, leaving Mina and Astrid to return to an apartment that echoed her absence.

NOTE TO READERS

Thank you for reading *The Emerald*, Book II of the Prophesy Saga. I hope you enjoyed the adventure as much as I did.

Other readers find reviews helpful for locating books they prefer to read. All reviews are appreciated.

Don't forget to visit my website: jerenatobiasen.ca, to read about my other works and inspirations.

✦

Turn the page for an exciting excerpt from
*The Destiny, Book III of the Prophesy
Saga* — coming soon!

✦

The Destiny

Hart and Miriam

As was often his escape, Hart took a skiing holiday in the Rocky Mountains. Each time he raced down a mountainside, with crystallized snow shushing under his skis, he felt free, light, strong. The weight of his oppressive marriage and divorce forgotten, he would reach the bottom of a ski hill, his head clear, creative juices and determination flowing again.

On one such occasion, after a morning of skiing under clear blue, cloudless skies and blinding sun, unexpected clouds had encumbered the mountaintop, strewing about a blinding blizzard that closed the ski hills. Hart decided to join a group of friends for some après ski conviviality in a ski-in ski-out pub at the foot of the mountain.

Hart's friends frequented the pub, but he had never been there, preferring a homey pub near to his lodgings. They stowed their skis in the racks outside and made the awkward march up to the door in their bulky boots.

Inside, the piercing collection of patrons' voices accosted his ears. The constant squeak of ski pants rubbing and ski boots clunking on the grated floor underlined the din of boisterous conversations as patrons came and went.

Hart spied vacant chairs in front of the smooth stone hearth.

"Let's sit near the fire," he said, as they mustered inside the door, slush dripping from their boots.

"The sign says we have to remove our boots and check them, if we want to sit by the hearth," one of his companions remarked.

"I'm okay with that," Hart said, already unbuckling his boots. "My feet are freezing."

The others grumbled similar responses, agreeing with Hart's suggestion. The promise of the fire was too inviting. They checked their boots and padded stocking-foot to the vacant chairs.

Most removed their ski jackets and gear and piled them near the hearth. Hart found an empty armchair, dragged it toward the fire, and put his feet up on the ledge to thaw them.

"I'm parched," one of the women said.

"Hey, honey! Over here!" one of the men hollered, flagging the waitress as she passed.

"With you in a minute," she waved as she headed toward the bar to place an order.

Moments later, the waitress returned.

"Sorry, folks. Busy, today," she said, slightly breathless. Smiling, she retrieved a pencil that had been lodged in her coiled hair, prepared to take their orders.

"It's always busy on weekends, Miriam!" one of the women said, laughing.

Hart noticed that the regular patrons seemed to know the staff by name, and the one called Miriam appeared to be a favourite. *Clearly, she's fast, efficient, organized, and pleasant. That must be the draw.*

Miriam took a headcount as she worked her way through the group, taking orders of hamburgers, fries, salads, cold beer, and hot chocolate. She stopped in front of the fire, next to Hart's chair.

"Can I get you something?"

Anticipating her question, Hart turned from his companion to order.

"I'll have a beer and the sausage plate, with fries." Then he looked at her, the sound of her voice taking time to permeate his frozen brain. "That's an interesting accent."

"Ja. Yours isn't so common, either."

They laughed together.

"Dutch," she offered.

"German," he answered.

"Hey! Come on, Hart. Small talk, later. We're tired, thirsty, and hungry. Miriam, can ya get a move on, honey?"

She winced.

She doesn't like being called honey, Hart noted, and found himself wondering what endearment might be pleasing to her. She smiled at his rude companion and excused herself to place the order. *Interesting eyes, like melted dark chocolate.*

❖

Hart bided his time, waiting for the crowd to lessen. When the bar quieted and his friends had peeled away for the evening, he stayed behind. Miriam exited the kitchen, empty-handed, and took a wet rag from behind the bar. Hart caught her eye and smiled. She changed directions and walked toward him.

"You're all alone—not joining your friends?" she asked, one hand on her hip.

"Ja. I will later."

"Coffee? Another drink?"

She pulled out her notepad to take his order.

"No thanks," he cocked his head to look at her more clearly. "I think I've had enough for now. I should pace myself. I've been invited to a party, after dinner."

510

"I'll bring your bill, then." She put the notepad back in her pocket and stuck her pencil in a knot of her hair. It reminded him of a Geisha, the way it penetrated the coil of hair on the crown of her head. "You're the last of my customers. I can sign out and go home."

"Thanks," he said, holding her gaze. "Say, I'm wondering whether you'd like to come to the party?" When she hesitated, Hart expected her to decline.

⚜

He's German. Mama and Oma would die, if they heard I went out with a German!

"I'm afraid I can't. I have to get home to my kids."

He kept her chatting long enough for her to disclose that she was a single mother with two young children, a boy and a girl, and that she worked during the week, while they were in school.

"I live in the town at the foot of the mountain," she said.

"Perhaps another time, then?"

"I don't know," she replied. "Juggling my schedule is challenging. Why don't you give me your number and I'll call if I happen to find I can meet up with you."

He seems intriguing. Maybe I shouldn't be so quick to bow to the prejudices of old women. What do I care anyway! Mama and Oma will never know I went out with a German.

ABOUT THE AUTHOR

"The thrum of city life runs through my veins, and I draw energy and inspiration from my west coast lifestyle. I've had stories swimming in my head my entire life, and when I returned to the west coast, those stories surfaced with a determination to be heard."

Jerena Tobiasen grew up on the Canadian prairies (Calgary, Alberta and Winnipeg, Manitoba). In the early '80s, she returned *home* to Vancouver, British Columbia, the city in which she was born.

Although Jerena has occasionally written short stories and poems since her return to Vancouver, it was not until 2016 dawned, that she began writing her first full-length manuscript, which was set primarily in Germany during World War I and World War II. When that draft was complete, she travelled to Europe and traced the steps taken by the story's primary characters. Then, she rewrote that manuscript, embellishing it with experiences and observations. The manuscript evolved into three volumes, the first of which tracks a family of German soldiers through two world wars (*The Crest*). The second volume tracks a family of Roma who are forced to flee Germany during the early years of Adolf Hitler's round-up of undesirables (*The Emerald*). The third volume reveals what can happen when the paths of two very different families collide (*The Destiny*). Together, these volumes became the saga *The Prophecy*.

Printed in April 2023
by Rotomail Italia S.p.A., Vignate (MI) - Italy